# *his temporary wife*

## BRIDES OF SUNFLOWER FALLS
### BOOK 2

## KATIE LILLIG

*also by katie lillig*

## BRIDES OF SUNFLOWER FALLS

Not So Runaway Bride

# summary

**A secret summer fling wasn't supposed to lead to a surprise pregnancy.**

When Melody Keller's secret summer fling turns into an unexpected marriage to a man she hardly knows, some growing pains are to be expected. Finding out he's lying about his true identity, though, brings up family trauma she can't get over. Which is the worst possible time to also find out she's pregnant.

Tony Caputo never imagined that he'd meet the woman of his dreams while in his own version of witness protection in the small town of Sunflower Falls. The false relationships of growing up in Hollywood have him craving reality in his 30s, and no one's more real than prickly Melody. But now he has to convince Melody that while his name was false, his feelings for her never were. But the clock is ticking down before the long arm of the court system calls him back to Los Angeles.

# *content notes*

I always want for my readers to have the best reading experience possible. To that end, these are the story elements which I know some readers may have issues with. Obviously, I can't know everyone's individual trigger points, but if you encounter something, please do stop reading and choose another book from your to be read pile 😊

- Pregnancy
- Discussion of options regarding unexpected pregnancy
- On-page instance of vomiting
- Reference to historic psychological manipulation of younger school-aged child by parent
- Reference to historic physical altercation parent and older teen child
- On-page physical altercation between parent and adult child

# *texts*

BACK IN JUNE, AFTER THE SUNFLOWER
FALLS START OF SUMMER FEST


TONY

Hey Melody. It's Tony.

MELODY

As my phone indicates since you were the
one who put your number in.

Are you sure you're not stalking me?

TONY

You were the one who handed me your
phone.

MELODY

I was drunk.

TONY

I hung out with you for over four hours
before then and all I saw you drinking was
water.

MELODY

Could have been vodka.

TONY

If that was vodka, your liver needs to be gifted to science for its magical anti-drunk properties.

MELODY

...

Did you have a reason for texting other than to annoy me?

TONY

Yes. I decided on a property. I want you to do a final walk through with me.

MELODY

You realize I'm in bed, right?

This could have waited until the morning.

TONY

Let's go back to you being in bed.

MELODY

TONY

I'm currently wearing boxers with SpongeBob on them. How about you?

MELODY

We are not having this conversation. I'm going to sleep. Email the office in the morning. I might reply. Or I might sic my puppy and her siblings on you. Who knows?

TONY

 I'm going to marry you.

MELODY

:changes contact name to Mr. Delulu:

# *one*

SNEAKING AROUND WAS NOT in Tony Caputo's wheelhouse. Even with the restrictions currently placed around him, he couldn't help but find ways to make connections and be in the spotlight.

At least a little bit.

The one thing about spending his time in a small town like Sunflower Falls meant he was frequently in the spotlight. Especially as he had been here for months now, and everyone knew he wasn't planning on becoming a permanent resident.

Being here with his friend Zach Troy, the hometown bad boy who'd made good by going off to the Marines, meant there was even more attention. The second week they were here, he'd had at least five people come up to him and ask what was going on because Zach hadn't spent more than a weekend in Sunflower Falls since he'd left for the Marines a week before high school graduation.

The answer they'd agreed on—after the second time he'd been cornered and asked—was that he'd had enough of the Hollywood life for now and wanted to see what life in a small town was like while he figured out his next moves. And since his good friend Zach had grown up in a small town, here they were.

But as he approached Melody Keller's door for a night of adult fun, he felt like he should be looking around for paparazzi. Sunflower Falls was barely big enough to have a weekly newspaper—forget paparazzi.

Hell, he knew production companies back in Hollywood with HR departments that might as well employ former paps for some of the stuff they got on your back about.

Rarely the right stuff—

Before he could complete the thought, Melody opened her door. Her dark hair was pulled up into a messy bun and earrings marched up the shells of both ears. She must have changed after coming home from work as she wore a worn tank shirt featuring a band he'd done some promotional work with back in the day and leggings instead of her usual work uniform of heavy duty pants and shirts branded with the logo of the construction company she ran with her brother Eric.

Her puppy Button was wriggling in her arms, a ball of fluffy energy.

He grinned. "Hey, lady."

Melody grinned back at him. "Get in here before any of the neighbors see you."

And there it was. He'd been fully prepared to ask her to keep things quiet when they hooked up, but she'd been the one to insist no one find out about them.

*"I've got a reputation in this town to maintain."*

*"What? Ball buster?"*

*"Always. No. It's no one's business what I do or who I do it with. I don't intend to be gossip item number one."*

*"I'm going to marry you."*

*"Why would I want to marry someone who's delusional?"*

When he'd tried to dig around, she'd closed up and changed topics. Which was fair since he still hadn't told her why he was hanging out in Sunflower Falls. Couldn't tell her.

But, he hoped, maybe soon. The last call he'd had with the district attorney seemed promising. Robert's attorney was making noises that he wanted to cut a deal, but that depended on Robert actually having something of worth and Robert not being a complete and total dick.

As Robert being a complete and total dick was the main reason Tony had his ass planted in this town that could maybe staff an independent production, that wasn't much to count on.

Tony shook off the morbid thoughts and bent down to kiss Melody as she closed the door behind him.

"Hello. Marry me."

She laughed a little against his lips. "As always, no. Give me a couple minutes. I need to take her out back."

"I can."

"No. Mr. Higgins is out back working on his tomatoes."

"What is it with the people around here and gardening? Zach's dad's into roses. Mr. Higgins has his tomatoes and whatever other green stuff he eats."

"County fair's coming up. Generations of Higginses and Troys have won the blue ribbons at the fair. Zach's lucky the Marines picked him up. Otherwise he'd be right there making sure they've got the best American Beauty in bloom in time."

Tony laughed. "Good to know. Want to show me what a county fair's like?"

Her step hitched as she walked to the back door. "Think you'll still be around in October?"

He crossed his arms as he studied her back. She didn't even really give him a chance to answer before she was out the back door.

Some people might wonder why he'd gone and fallen in love with probably the most emotionally closed off woman he'd ever met, but it was the moments where she let herself be free that had reeled him in.

The first time he'd gone to the Sunflower Falls Diner with Zach, they'd ended up with platters of food coating them thanks to one of the servers, Melody's best friend Ana, getting distracted and tripping over her own feet while carrying an order-filled tray. Thankfully, no one had been hurt and the diner owner had everything sorted within minutes.

Melody had been at the next table, and the absurdity of the moment had her laughing. It had been so bright and sparkly, like the earrings she wore.

As he and Zach had explored Sunflower Falls since their arrival, he'd spotted her helping around town. From small things like repairing a broken birdhouse for some little kids to coming over to the house next to where he and Zach were staying and spending some time with the elderly man who lived there while she ostensibly was there to check on a report of fallen roof shingles from another neighbor.

He knew for a fact that was a lie as she hadn't ended up on the roof any of the five times she'd pulled that excuse despite being with the older man for at least an hour each visit.

Melody claimed to be a ball buster, but he knew that she'd planted her heart here in Sunflower Falls and did her best to care for its residents.

Even Mrs. Smith who, if this was a screenplay, Tony would cast her as a retired spy with the amount of gossip she had on the residents of Sunflower Falls—despite being a relatively new transplant herself—as well as the world at large. He'd caught Melody hanging out with Mrs. Smith more than a handful of mornings at the counter service seats of the diner.

At first, the fact Melody wanted nothing from him had been refreshing. He'd spent his entire life being used for access. As a kid, it had been people wanting to be close to his parents. So much so that "play date" meant "my mom wants to be cast in your dad's next movie." In his early 20s, he'd gotten it from all sides with people wanting access to fame and clubs and power players wanting that fame to bump up their own. These days, he was mostly out of the spotlight, but in Hollywood, almost every relationship was transactional.

People wanting to take advantage of his access to celebrities was how he'd ended up in the mess with Robert. Extortion and organized crime went hand-in-hand, but Robert decided to be enterprising and expand the scheme into getting access to celebrities and their dirt from the production side of the business.

Tony had been duped into partnering with Robert for his first test of the scheme thanks to a request from Robert's godmother who'd been a long-time friend of his father's. Kind of hard not to feel salty about everything when his choices to do the right thing after finding out what was going on had landed him in his own, unofficial, version of witness protection.

He rubbed his chest. There was that twinge again. Doing the right thing was to tell Melody who he really was. He'd come close to telling her several times. But every time, he remembered the murder-board connections map he'd been shown with Robert off in his own little hub of the spiderweb. Melody didn't deserve to be brought into that mess, so it was on him to fix what he could before telling her.

For now, he'd focus on learning everything he needed to know to be allowed into the walls that surrounded her heart. Even if that meant hiding their relationship in plain sight.

She didn't want the neighbors to know about him, but they met at her house. The house he was staying at was a non-starter with Zach being there. So was the town's motel as her mom was the manager. According to town gossip the Sunflower Falls Motel was the host for numerous town indiscretions that everyone knew about, but pretended they didn't.

Secrets were hard to keep in Sunflower Falls.

The only reason he'd been able to keep his was wholly because of Zach and his closed mouth nature.

His friend—and bodyguard—knew the value of when to keep things under wraps and when to put it on blast.

The fact Tony had been hooking up with Melody for over a month now—since just after the town's street party back in June—was something Zach had not been happy about. But he hadn't breathed a word to anyone.

That first time had almost been accidental. Zach had left them at the house Tony had just bought and planned to rip down to run some errands. Tony was sure Zach thought there wasn't anything that could happen while discussing lakefront views and load-bearing walls.

But throw in some good-natured bickering, a woman who was hot as hell when explaining town ordinances and building materials, him proposing and getting turned down yet again, and next thing he knew they were going at it in the kitchen. Mainly because it was the only place not covered in the ugliest carpet known to the planet—including the bathroom.

He shuddered at the memory. That bathroom still haunted his nightmares.

The island counter probably hadn't been the most sanitary either, but since neither of them had been carrying a condom with them, they'd only gotten undressed enough to get each other off.

Zach had sensed something when he came back to pick Tony up, but he had said nothing until Tony had gotten a text inviting him out to look at flooring options. By himself.

At that point, Zach had talked to him about safety while going out in more public spaces without him.

Tony'd gestured to his face. "I've got the beard now. No one has recognized me. Besides, everyone around here just accepts that I'm a friend of yours from Hollywood visiting for the summer. Not that I'm here because you're my bodyguard and I'm in hiding."

Back in the present, his thoughts were interrupted as Melody yanked open her back door. "Sorry about that, Mr. Higgins."

Tony wondered what had happened as Button was wriggling around in Melody's arms and yipping.

"Everything okay?"

She didn't reply right away, just closed and locked the door before she set Button down on the floor. Button yipped at the door a couple times before turning around and puppy running over to Tony.

She stopped a couple times as her paws and legs seemed to lose connection with each other. But after a moment, she got right back up and continued running to him. She went up on her hind legs, pawing at his leg. He bent down and picked her up. "How are you settling in, little lady?"

Melody snorted. "That little lady just attacked one of Mr. Higgins's squashes he's growing for the county fair. She's lucky she's so damn cute as he only laughed."

Tony cradled her like the baby she was and scratched her soft belly. "You are a cute one, aren't you? Take it from me, looks can only get you so far. You need to work on developing your smarts while you can."

"Looks can only get you so far? I'm amazed. Deep philosophy from you."

He held his arm up so that Button's face was next to his, and batted his lashes. "Am I not book boyfriend material?" He winked. "I know your tricks, Melody Keller. When you sound like you're trying to insult me, you only want me in your bed."

She walked over, wrapped her hand around his neck, and pulled his head down. "What do you think you're doing over here?" She kissed him, and like every other time, she took his breath away.

He'd never been so fixated on how one woman tasted before her. Every time felt like a new experience and he had to keep uncovering the secrets she kept.

They only stopped because Button began wriggling and nipped his biceps. "Ouch."

Melody took Button from him. "Okay, that's enough biting from you tonight. We'll need to work on that."

Tony followed them upstairs, but headed to Melody's bedroom while she went into the spare bedroom where she kept Button's crate.

A few minutes and two closed doors later, he and Melody picked up where they'd left off. He was kissing his way back up her legs after stripping off her leggings when her doorbell rang.

He looked up at her. "Do you need to get that?"

With glazed eyes, she shook her head. "What? No."

He was about to place a kiss at the juncture of her thighs when the doorbell rang again.

"Damn it. Whoever's there, I'm going to kill them."

Tony sat back on his haunches, watching as Melody grabbed a robe from her closet. She threw it around her body before heading downstairs.

He was tempted to follow her down and scare off whoever had interrupted their time together, but it would be him she killed if he did that.

When Melody didn't come back right away, Tony opened her bedroom door and stuck his head out. He heard voices. Melody's of course and... He listened to the deeper tones. Eric. What the hell was Eric doing here?

Melody's brother had been moping around town while his girlfriend Libby had gone back to New York to deal with her dad who had done some very fucked up legal shit. Even the weekly Sunflower Falls *Gazetteer* had covered the story.

Tony stepped out into the hall so he could better hear what was going on. Only minutes later, Melody came back up the stairs. She looked at him and started undoing the belt of her robe. "Where were we?"

He moved to her and stayed her hand. "Was that Eric?"

"Talking about my brother won't get me back into the mood."

He bent his head and kissed her jaw below her ear. "If you need to go do something with him, it's fine. I can stay here with Button. Or I can go?"

Melody pulled back. "What's going on?"

"Nothing. But it's not every night that your brother comes over here, right? So something's up."

"He wanted to let me know that he's headed down to the city to be with Libby. I'll take lead on the Sullivan project until he gets back."

"That's it?"

She wove her fingers through his hair and pulled him down. "That is it. Can we forget my brother now?"

Their lips met, and he let himself get lost in the kiss. The nagging thought that she never wanted him to focus on anything outside of their sex life or work life together was buried in the heat that was never far away when they were together. They moved back into the bedroom.

He bent down, wrapping his arms around the back of her ass, and lifted her up. She wrapped her legs around his hips, and he walked them to the bed.

When they were together like this, all he could think of was how best to worship her. Tony had lived his life as far from monkhood as possible. But for the last five years, he'd felt restless, not as engaged with the women he met.

It felt like all the fascinating-for-more-than-a-couple-dates ones were already in relationships. But Melody?

Every one of his senses had woken up in her presence. He needed to be firing on all cylinders to keep up with her.

In some ways, he felt like he'd met his soul mate. But he doubted because wouldn't his soul mate want to be with him? Openly.

Before his thoughts could spiral out further, Melody yanked him to her. "What's going through your head?"

Falling back on habit, he grinned at her. "Just figuring out the best way to make you come. At least twice."

Melody settled back onto the bed, her arms raised above her so that her breasts were on delicious display. "I bet you can't make me come three times before you need attention."

He won the bet.

After they'd both caught their breath, he settled down next to her. "Want me to get Button?"

"Why? She needs to learn to sleep in her crate. I'll spoil her in other ways." She was quiet for a few minutes. "You should go."

He heard the reluctance in her tone, but also the resolution. "I'm beginning to feel you only want me for my body."

She pushed up on her elbows. He couldn't help but admire the view of her breasts as she didn't have any false modesty. The woman was fit as fuck.

"Eyes up here, buddy."

Dragging his gaze upward, he cocked an eyebrow. "Want to deny it?"

She cocked an eyebrow right back at him. "No. I told you I have a reputation in town to maintain. No overnights. We've both had our fun, so it's time for you to go."

He let the hurt wash through him, but tried one more time. "What if I promise some more fun later? I'm not an eighteen-year-old, but I've still got moves."

She wrinkled her nose. "Ew. Eighteen-year-olds are babies. Time for you to go."

He let out a sigh. "Fine. But one of these days, I'm going to wear you out until neither of us are coherent until morning so I can sleep over by default."

"You can try. Get going."

He climbed out of bed. As he didn't have any false modesty either, he didn't rush to cover himself up. "Give me a kiss goodbye?"

This time he could tell that her put-upon groan was her

sarcastic side showing through. "Fine, since you're being so needy."

She climbed out of bed and wrapped her arms around his neck. Their kiss went from teasing to hot in moments. He was trying to figure out how to best get her back into bed when she broke the kiss by shoving at his shoulders. "Get going."

He groaned, but rested his forehead against hers. "Just so you know, I consider this cruel and unusual punishment."

"But you keep coming back."

He heard a note of wonder in her tone, and he pulled back so he could see her eyes. But in the dim light of the room, all he found was a screen hiding whatever emotions she'd let seep through.

Melody was a hedgehog. Prickly on the outside, but a soft underbelly that she protected at every opportunity. Not that he'd ever tell her that because she might decide for punishment to bring back the carpet he'd been assured had been trucked to a landfill.

The only time he felt she let that soft underbelly show was with Button, and he'd bet Melody would say that was because no one could resist cute puppies. He vowed to himself again that he'd find a way to make her feel safe enough that she could reveal it to him.

He brushed a lock of hair behind her ear. "Always. Whenever. Wherever."

She blew out a breath. "Stop being so sappy. Get out of here. With Eric gone, I've got to get up early tomorrow, anyway."

Tony got himself together and headed out after one more kiss.

Melody didn't watch him leave. The front door closed

right behind him, and he would have sworn he'd have felt her gaze on him if she had watched.

Fighting off the frustration in favor of the enjoyment of the evening together, he walked back to the house he shared with Zach. Luckily, he didn't run across anyone during the trip.

Zach was still waiting up, watching some cooking show, when he got back. Tony leaned against the doorway between the kitchen and the living room. "I thought you'd have gone to bed."

"Since I'm not going to sit in Melody's living room or outside like a pervert while the two of you are having sex, this is the best I can do. You in for the night?"

"Yeah."

Nodding, Zach turned off the TV and headed toward his bedroom. "Good. See you in the morning."

Once he was in his bed, Tony worked to shut off his mind so he could fall asleep. But he couldn't help but think again about the tone he'd heard in Melody's voice when she noted him coming back. For her? He'd come back until the end of his days.

# *texts*

**TONY**

Congratulations!

**MELODY**

Why?

**TONY**

You finished the Sullivan project, right?

**MELODY**

Yeah. So?

**TONY**

We should celebrate.

**MELODY**

I am celebrating.

With my crew.

Who did the work.

**TONY**

And you led them.

**MELODY**

With Eric. He did most of it.

TONY

Are you always this resistant to being celebrated?

MELODY

I celebrate when warranted. In this case I am doing the appropriate amount of celebrating.

TONY

Let me treat you.

MELODY

Again, why?

TONY

Because. You. Deserve. To. Be. Celebrated.

MELODY

TONY

…

How about this: can I treat you to a weekend in Niagara Falls where we can go out and enjoy ourselves as two people who enjoy spending romantic time together out in public?

MELODY

:raised eyebrow emoji:

Public?

TONY

Since you don't want us to be seen together in Sunflower Falls, let's go to Niagara.

MELODY

…

…

...

TONY

Melody?

MELODY

Sure. Fine. Sure. When?

TONY

😎

Next weekend. Room is booked. My treat.

MELODY

How do you talk me into these things?

TONY

I'm a very charming individual.

MELODY

:snort:

TONY

Marry me?

MELODY

You're not that charming.

*two*

MELODY'S ARMS ITCHED. She would have blamed it on the sweater she was wearing, but it was made of the fanciest merino wool and cashmere. Plus, she'd worn it many times since her mother had given it to her as a Christmas gift five years ago and had never had a reaction to it. No, she was missing her puppy.

It wasn't like she'd never spent a night away from Button, but this was the first time since Button had come to live with her full-time. And she was spending two nights away from her. She looked over at the man relaxing in the passenger seat.

For him. Glanced down at his lap. Well, parts of him.

She shook her head and returned her attention to the road. If she couldn't be honest with herself, then she was no better than her dad. She didn't want to be honest with herself in this case, though, which made it all that much worse.

Because she didn't want to be a liar—and worse—like her dad, she forced herself to list the things she liked about Tony and not include the amazing sex.

19

One, he made her laugh. It always gave her a shock because she didn't want to admit that someone as attractive as him could also have a perfect-for-her sense of humor.

Two, he gave her space when she requested it. He'd sometimes try to charm his way into staying, but he was never a dick about it.

Three, he was good for her ego. Every time he asked her to marry him, it gave her a thrill. Even though she didn't believe he was being serious about it.

Four, he was great with Button and Button liked him back. Dogs, even puppies, knew when someone wasn't a good person, and she trusted dog instincts a hell of a lot more than her own when it came to men.

Five, it was like she'd known him in a previous life. From the day they'd first met, she felt a connection to him she couldn't explain as she definitely had never met him before he'd come to Sunflower Falls.

All of it had germinated a little bloom of hope in her that she might be a person who could be in a supportive relationship that was about more than the banging. That bloom was so fragile she wanted to hide it away, keep it under lock and key. If she gave in and let it fully grow, she didn't think she'd survive its destruction.

"You want me to drive for a bit?"

She glanced over at him. "Why would I want you to drive?"

"Because you keep looking over at me. I thought that was you being subtle."

She snorted. "When have I ever been subtle around you?"

Out of the corner of her eye, she saw Tony reach over. Moments later, his fingertips trailed down from her ear to the collar of her sweater. She did her best not to shiver, but knew she hadn't been successful when he grinned. "I do appreciate your lack of subtlety in certain areas of our relationship."

"You're not exactly subtle yourself."

He shrugged. "Subtlety has its place and time."

She thought he was going to say something else, but he stayed quiet and looked out the front window. They'd taken the more scenic route after passing through Rochester, and there wasn't much to see but farmland and some trees.

"Thanks for agreeing to this."

She frowned and glanced over at him. "What do you mean?"

He reached over again, this time resting his hand on her thigh and giving it a squeeze. "I want to celebrate you. You don't let me do that."

"Why? I can celebrate myself."

He squeezed again. "You don't always have to. I'm sure other people want the opportunity to celebrate you."

Her frown deepened. "That's what birthdays are for."

She felt his fingers begin stroking her inner thigh. "Since your birthday's in March, I haven't been around for one of those. But I bet that you've never once let Ana plan one of your birthdays, have you?"

Squeezing her thighs together, and trapping his wandering fingers between them, she looked over at him and licked her lips. Of course he would play the best friend card. Ana probably knew her best out of anyone in the world, but Melody also felt more comfortable ensuring she had the experiences that she wanted rather than relying on anyone else to set them up. "I know what I want. Is that a crime?"

Tony grinned at her. "Not in my book. But I also know what it is you want that you're not willing to tell yourself."

He might think he did, but there was no way he knew her that well so she brazened it out. "Is it kinky?"

His laughter filled the car and a small part of her heart she worked hard to keep hidden. "No. But we can explore that any time you'd like."

She waved her hand. "If it's not kinky, then I don't need to know about it this weekend, do I?"

He pulled his hand from her thighs, grabbing her hand. Brought it to his mouth, and kissed her knuckles. "How about a bet?"

"What is it with you and bets? You're always betting on things." And if he wasn't betting, he was negotiating. She wondered if he'd been a lawyer in his life before coming to Sunflower Falls.

He kissed her knuckles again, this time added in some light licks. Which put her in mind of other places she'd prefer him to be licking.

She realized she'd started letting the truck drift toward the shoulder and corrected course. This was why the idea of road head had always seemed like a bad idea to her. She pulled her hand away from him. "No licking while I'm driving."

"Right. Safety first. I'd rather spend my time with you this weekend in bed and not on the side of the road waiting for a tow truck."

She tried to remember what they'd been talking about and then decided that it wasn't worth the effort. Whatever it was would come up again or it wouldn't.

"It's about another hour until we get there. We haven't talked about what to do while we're there."

He winked at her. "I'm fine with staying in bed."

She snorted. "You would be. I haven't been there in years, but the boat tours can be fun."

"No one special to come with?"

"I told you, I can celebrate myself. That also means I can take trips and do a lot of things on my own."

He twisted in his seat and leaned back against the passenger door. The weight of his gaze felt like a heavy blanket she wasn't sure felt comforting. "What?"

"To go back to that earlier conversation point, why do you feel like you always have to do things on your own or be the one to plan everything?"

Scowling, she tried not to shift in her seat like she had back in second grade and her teacher was asking where her homework assignment was. Not like she could say that her dad had gotten drunk and used it to light a fire in the fireplace.

"Does there have to be a reason?"

"Little tip for you, Melody. One thing I've learned in my many years..."

She snorted. "Many years? What are you? The elderly man on the mountain? You're not even thirty-five."

"My skin care routine thanks you. No, I'm thirty-six."

She looked him dead in the eye and then rolled hers. "Like that's a huge difference."

He pointed at her. "That. That right there."

"What?"

"You deflect, evade, and distract. At least you try anytime someone gets too close to something deeper."

She slowed for the reduced speed limit as they entered the next town. "I thought this weekend was supposed to be just about fun and sex. And not necessarily in that order. Not an interrogation."

"It can be about fun and sex. But, Melody, I can always

tell when you're hiding something. When anyone's hiding something. They always answer a question with a question. If you don't want to tell me something, be honest about it. That's all I ask."

Silence filled the car, and Melody tried to find a better grip on the steering wheel as her palms had become sweaty. "Look. I just..." She licked her lips as words failed. Danger signs with skulls and bones and do not enter signs flared up in her mind. "Fun. Can we just focus on some fun?"

He leaned over and brushed his lips against her cheek. "Absolutely."

She closed her eyes for a moment and nodded. One more hour.

---

TWO HOURS LATER, they were being led into a corner suite that had a fucking jacuzzi just sitting in the corner of the windows overlooking the Niagara River and the Falls. The concierge—because of course Tony had somehow gotten the concierge to guide them—pointed out the various features of the room, and then quietly slipped out.

She tossed her purse on the bed. Waved at the jacuzzi and the entire room. "I didn't bring my swimsuit."

He walked over and settled his hands on her hips. She hated how good, how calming, it felt to be in his embrace. Feeling this good from his touch could lead her down the road to relying on him, and she never wanted to feel reliant on a man to make her feel this way.

"There's nothing saying you can't go in without a suit."

She leaned back so she could see if he was being serious. "I'm sure their cleaning staff is excellent, but I have no idea what previous residents of this room got up to in there."

He waggled his brows at her like he was one of those smarmy cartoon pick up artists. "Probably the same thing we can get up to in there."

She pushed hard enough against his chest that he took a step back. Thanks to working in construction and taking regular self-defense classes because both Eric and Uncle Stef wanted to make sure she could handle herself alone on a site, she knew what move to use and could put power behind it. But Tony wasn't a lightweight. He was easily a half-foot taller than her, and his clothes disguised a body that was ripped in all the most delicious places.

"Let's make it a bet."

"Ew. No."

He moved back against her and crowded her up against the bed. It was either wrap her arms around his waist or sit down.

She wrapped her arms around his waist.

He cradled her head in his hands and began working his magic fingers in the best head massage she'd ever had. A moan slipped from between her lips. Shaking her head, she managed to get words out. "No. No bet."

"Fine. The jacuzzi is off the table. But how about another bet?"

She leaned back enough to look at him. There was something in his gaze that had yellow flags waving in her brain. "What?"

"We have fun together, right?"

"Yeah."

"What if we could have fun together forever?"

He leaned in and began kissing his way down her neck.

The feeling of his lips pressing against and then lightly sucking at her skin, had her brain shorting out. "What... what do you mean?"

"How about we go, now, and get a marriage license? And if I can't convince you in twenty-four hours to use it, we just toss it away. But if I can show you the best time of your life, we get married?"

When he bit down on the spot where her shoulder and neck joined, she almost melted into a puddle of need. Grasping for words, she latched onto the one thing that had tickled her mind. "Why twenty-four hours?"

He nibbled on her skin before answering. "That's the waiting period for New York."

"You researched marriage licenses?"

He pulled back enough so that his eyes met hers and the seriousness in them had her shivering. "I am never joking when I ask you to marry me."

"But..."

His diabolical fingers slipped down the front of the leggings she'd worn for the drive. He could have gone in for the kill, but instead he tortured her. He stroked the skin where her lower abs met her pubic area. Just brushing back and forth. Back and forth. Until she reached the point where she tried to grab his hand and push his fingers into her.

Guiding his hand through the fabric of her leggings was impossible, and her own fingers got tangled when she tried to stuff her hand inside them.

"What do you say? Is it a bet?" He began inching his fingers down. Closer to where she craved their touch.

"Just fuck me."

He laughed, and his breath puffed against her neck, triggering another wave of shivering desire.

"Not until you agree to the bet."

"That's coercive."

He scraped his teeth against her neck, and she swore she had a mini-orgasm from the move.

"Hmmmm. You're right. I'll fuck you no matter what. Mini bet. If I can get you to agree that I've just given you the best orgasm ever, you'll agree to the marriage bet?"

His fingers were millimeters from where she desperately needed them. She tilted her hips forward, but he flowed with the movement, keeping her on edge.

She grabbed his face and pulled him down for a kiss. "No bet. But if you give me the best time of my life, I might consider doing a test run of the concept with you. I'm not marriage material, Tony. You may not want me as a wife once you've got me. Now give me what I want."

He growled. "I may not always give you what you want, Melody, but I'll always give you what you need. And you are marriage material. You're mine."

Ignoring the treacherous emotions those words conjured up, she pressed her lips against his. If there was anyone who could convince her to try marriage, it might actually be Tony. And she was scared he might actually convince her. Giving her heart fully over to him and having something happen would break her.

He nipped at her lips. "Lie back down, baby."

"Make me."

"You are the most contrary person."

"But you love that, don't you?"

She felt a sudden pressure from his fingertips, but it eased as he began petting her once again. "I do. God help me, but I do."

The deeper tone of his words confused her. She pulled back a bit, but he followed, and kissed her, taking command of her mouth as he slipped his fingers lower. He began a slow, relentless circling of her clitoris, and she moaned.

The steady pressure never wavered even as her nerves began to shimmer with sensation.

"Tony."

He didn't answer with words, but moved to kneel before her. Stripped her leggings down along with her panties. She reached for his shoulders, but he brushed her hands away before she could grab hold.

Hooking his hand under one thigh, he brought it up and over his shoulder. Leaving her fully exposed to him. He didn't let her dwell on the unusual position. The first press of his lips against her sex wasn't a gentle kiss. No, it was a cupping of her clit and a strong, steady suck.

"Unf." She grabbed for whatever she could clutch, which ended up being hanks of his hair.

He curved one of his palms around her ass and stroked the strip of skin where her other cheek met her thigh with his fingers.

His touches felt both forbidden and lightly teasing at the same time. "Tony..."

The pressure from his fingers increased, and he moved them closer to her core. He continued the strong, steady suck of her clit, only briefly pausing to draw in air.

When his fingers finally entered her, the angle had her awkwardly hunching over him to ease the pressure, but not so far away to disconnect from his mouth.

She wanted to wrap her body around him and never leave this pleasure zone.

Without warning, he pulled her hips forward, sending her off-balance. She landed on the bed, her hips and legs in the air, with his mouth still attached to her clit and his fingers buried in her pussy.

"Tony..." She tried to figure out where to put her one leg, but before she completely lost control of things he pulled his fingers from where they were working magic and guided her free leg to his shoulder.

With both legs now anchored, she could use the leverage to press harder against his mouth. But the moment she tried, the slick material of the bedspread had her slipping back on her shoulders.

Tony hummed against her clit. Probably in warning, but it only made her eyes roll back as hot pleasure radiated out through her entire body. He hummed again, and Melody realized how much deeper and weightier the orgasm that was building was. Her lack of ability to control the situation, the unfamiliar environment, Tony's dedicated attention to her clit all combined to send her mentally to a place she'd never contemplated.

Moments later, a dark rainbow exploded in her mind and her body bowed up from the intense pleasure as the orgasm hit.

She heard Tony's voice, and only then realized that his mouth was no longer attached to her clit. Shudders began wracking her body as it overloaded with sensations.

The slick comforter against her back contrasted with the slightly rough skin of Tony's palms rubbing up and down her body. Unable to concentrate on anything, she drifted off with the waves still buffeting her nervous system.

When she became aware of Tony's hard body—naked body—pressed against her, and his breath washing against her ear as he murmured nonsense that sounded suspiciously like the word "mine", she had no idea how much time had passed. The view outside the window showed there was still daylight out, which meant it couldn't have been too much time.

Enjoying the feeling of Tony's skin against hers, she shifted and wrapped her legs around his hips, aligning his cock against her core. The feeling was delicious, especially as they'd never been bare skin-to-bare skin like this before. Not that he'd get inside her bare. She knew better.

"Mmmmm." Tony moved his head and bit down again on the base of her neck.

Arching her head back, she threaded her fingers through her hair. "More. Not inside. But I want to feel you on me."

He paused, then groaned and began grinding against her. After only a few strokes that had her reconsidering her "no entrance without a condom" policy, she orgasmed again.

Even as another, harder wave from that one hit her, she felt Tony stiffen against her and the splash of hot release just above her pussy.

This time she clearly heard the one word he uttered, "mine", before she drifted off again. Because, damn it. He'd been right. This had definitely been one of the best times of her life.

Melody wondered if she needed a dress to go get a marriage license.

ANA

:photos of Button being goofy:

Your mom had to deal with some issue at the motel. Something about multiple overflowing toilets, so I've got Button for the rest of the weekend.

MELODY

Does she need help? I can be back in a couple hours.

ANA

NO!

She said your Uncle Stef was on the job and everything would be fine.

She just needed to not worry about Button while they sorted it out.

MELODY

Weren't you working this weekend?

ANA

I was, but Nancy decided business was slow enough to let me go early.

MELODY

I thought you were saving up for a place of your own? Don't you need the hours?

ANA

I'm fine. Distract me with photos. You didn't tell me where you were going.

Or who you were going with.

:gif of Abed waggling his eyebrows:

MELODY

Not for you to worry about.

:photo of the Niagara River with the Falls in the distance:

ANA

GASP! Are you getting secretly married without me?!?!

:gif of Judge Judy shaking her finger:

MELODY

Like I'd ACTUALLY get married without you, let alone my Mom or Eric.

ANA

That was not a denial.

MELODY

Gotta go. Love you. Kisses to Button.

ANA

Melody.

MELODY!

We are talking when you get back since you're not even taking my calls. Hmfph.

Button's going to be so spoiled when I give
her back.

*three*

TONY ROLLED over in bed and curled around Melody. Even in sleep, she kept trying to push him away. But he'd reel her in.

His thumb found the slick metal band newly seated at the base of his left ring finger. They were married now, so she had to give him a chance. Super officially once they actually filed the license.

Which he'd need to find a way to amend with his real name.

After he told her.

Which he'd totally do before they filed the license.

Once he figured out how to tell her.

But he'd totally do that, too. He just needed some inspiration.

He'd figured out how to get her to agree to marry him in the first place, so he'd totally figure out how to tell her he had another name. That was actually his real name. That he hadn't told her yet.

And hoped to hell he didn't fuck things up.

He nuzzled her neck, drawing in the scent of her skin to soothe the nerves that were making themselves known.

A faint buzzing came from around where he'd dropped his pants when they'd stumbled in from celebrating their marriage. He'd paid the hotel's concierge handsomely to arrange it, and it had been perfect.

Just the two of them, the officiant, and a couple witnesses recruited for the moment. Thankfully, no one had recognized him.

They'd kept their vows simple, telling each other what they liked best about each other. She'd told him how she liked how he made her laugh, that he was the missing puzzle piece that made her believe in the possibility of happy relationships for herself, and how much she loved watching him play tug with Button because his ass looked great when he was down on the floor.

He'd told her how he loved watching her talk about load-bearing walls and town ordinances because competence was sexy as fuck, how seeing her be a great friend to Ana made him want to be a better friend himself, and that what he loved most was the dimple that would pop out in her cheek when she thought she was being especially devious about something.

Like the one she'd gotten when she got him to agree that this was just a tester thing and that they'd burn the license if they decided being married wasn't right for them.

The buzzing started up again, and he realized it was his phone. He slipped out of bed, trying not to wake Melody. When she began murmuring, he thought she was about to wake up, but she only rolled over again and buried her face in the pillow.

By the time he dug his phone out of his pants, the call had flipped over to voicemail. Damien. His lawyer. "Shit."

Damien calling this early, and on a Sunday, was not a good sign.

Before he could unlock his phone, it began buzzing again. Damien. Again. He glanced over his shoulder and saw Melody was still facedown in her pillow. He sent the call to voicemail and quickly opened his messaging app.

After shooting Damien a text promising to call in the next ten minutes, he scrambled to get dressed. Melody didn't stir, but he wasn't about to sneak out of the room without telling her. Even if she was still ninety percent asleep and unlikely to remember him making the effort.

Tony stroked her ring finger where a simple gold band that matched his sat. He'd have to get her a silicone band to wear for work, but the visceral punch of pleasure at seeing his ring on her finger had him wanting to crawl back into bed. Melody mumbled something into the pillow and burrowed deeper into it.

He bent down so his mouth was close to her ear. "I need to make a call, so I'm going down to the lobby. I'll bring you back a coffee."

She only mumbled again and shifted so her face wasn't as buried. He pressed a quick kiss to her cheek and headed out the door before he was tempted to crawl back into bed and wake her up in a more pleasurable way.

Once he was down in the lobby, and in a secluded corner, he called Damien.

His attorney answered before the first ring had finished. "Where are you?"

Frowning, Tony watched a little drama unfold in the elevator lobby. "I'm in New York."

"You're not in Sunflower Falls where you promised me you'd keep your ass planted."

A woman, maybe around his age, was stalking through

the hotel lobby with a guy who appeared to be maybe five to ten years younger chasing after her. He couldn't hear what the guy was saying, but the woman's face got harder and she flipped him the bird without even looking back. "How do you know I'm not in Sunflower Falls? Did you bug my phone or something?"

"No. Though I wish I had. I called Zach first. All he said was that you were out of town, but he knew where you were and had assessed the situation as not dangerous."

"Why are you so worried then? You were the one who agreed that Zach could handle anything."

"Providing he was there watching you every moment. Where. The. Fuck. Are. You?"

"Zach didn't tell you?"

"No." Damien sounded like he was going to find a way to bend reality and reach through the phone to strangle him.

"Don't worry about it then. I'll be back there tonight. Now tell me Robert's flipped and I can come home." With Melody in tow so he could show her the life he could help provide her. First thing he planned on doing when they got back to Hollywood was introduce her to the various heads of production companies who specialized in the home renovation market.

Maybe they'd look at houses near him that could use updating and she could do a show about doing that.

Damien growled. And since the man had been a pro football player before an injury had forced an unexpected career change, he could growl with the best of them. "No. He hasn't flipped. And to make matters worse, he's gone off the grid."

Tony blinked. Off the grid? Robert who couldn't live without all the finest luxuries? Robert who needed to have his manicurist on set in case he cracked a nail? When he barely did anything in the first place? Besides trying to dig up or manufacture blackmail material for all the talent on set.

Partnering with the man to produce the film they'd worked on had been one of the worst decisions of his life. He still regretted not going with his instincts and requesting a deeper background check when his dad's friend had asked the favor of helping Robert get a foot in the industry. Robert had done too good of a job of hiding his ties to certain beyond shady people and organizations at least for basic checks. If they'd dug even the tiniest bit deeper, they would have found the dirt.

During pre-production, Robert's questions hadn't seemed out of line for someone newer to the industry and looking to learn more. Once filming started, however, little red flags had popped here and there.

Tony had first noticed it with some of the female crew. Anytime Robert was on set after the first couple weeks, their crew leads stationed them on other duties away from him. Any time a female crew member absolutely had to interact with Robert, there was another, male, crew member right by her.

When he'd questioned the crew leads, all of them said there were no specific issues they could point to, but all of them had a bad feeling. He'd kept a closer eye on Robert after that and had commissioned a deeper background check which revealed a history of gambling debts and bankruptcies.

It was the day that he'd gotten the report when their lead actress had stormed into his office threatening to quit if Robert wasn't banned from the set.

Apparently, he'd delivered his initial extortion demand

which included sleeping with him. Tony had completely believed her, but as she'd been having issues with an ex, she'd set up her own hidden cameras in her trailer and had recorded the exchange.

Tony had assured her that Robert would be dealt with. The only problem was that when Tony went to confront Robert, it was to find the man meeting with a guy Tony certainly had recognized thanks to his father once pointing him out as a man to avoid. Neither Robert nor the known crime boss had spotted him, so he'd recorded the transaction and slipped away.

After consulting with Damien, they'd turned everything over to the authorities. They'd quickly found out that Robert was in deep with the crime organization. Had been since college, so he knew many of their secrets after fifteen years.

Damien had told Tony the prosecutor was salivating at the thought of finally cracking the group.

Which was why he was in Sunflower Falls. Thanks to Robert getting arrested for the extortion attempt, and other decidedly illegal things found in his residence, the production had shut down. The prosecutor's office had managed to keep his identity under wraps, so with his parents' help, they'd put it out that he was taking a break due to the "unfortunate incident".

Tony was pretty sure everyone believed he was in some rehab facility despite him not having a reputation for any kind of substance abuse.

Robert turning up missing did not fill Tony with confidence.

"Anthony? You still there?"

Before Tony could answer, he could hear arguing on Damien's side. Then Damien's wife, Aspen, was on the line.

"Do you need me to kill someone? I learned how to do it when I played that medical examiner."

More fumbling, with Damien's muffled voice coming through. "How many times do I have to tell you to stop saying that? Just because you played one on television does not mean you can actually do that. And this is not a secure line. The bail fund does not cover conspiracy for murder." A few moments later, Damien's voice came through clearly. "Sorry about that."

Tony grinned. Spending time with Aspen, even over the phone, was always a good stress reliever. "She really wants to off someone. Good thing she's never played a mob princess."

"That's only because she has the on-screen reputation as the good girl, and everyone in this town is a little afraid of the things she'd do for character research at this point. Getting back to me calling this early."

"Can I say for just a moment, that I appreciate that you as a couple have a bail fund? It shows commitment to each other."

Damien snorted. "You know damn well that's primarily for Aspen. Stop trying to derail me. I need you to come back to Los Angeles as soon as possible."

"No." Tony's reaction was immediate. He wanted to go back to California. It was his home. But, he and Melody had just gotten married, and he needed more time to figure out how to tell her about his real life. Ease her into it. Make her secure that while he'd omitted his real name, he'd been telling her the truth about his emotions for her. That she was the missing part of his soul. When she'd talked about him being a missing puzzle piece for her, he'd known exactly what she meant and hoped that she would one day realize that he was her soulmate the way she was his.

"What do you mean no? The DA needs you here. They've warned me they'll compel you to appear."

"They agreed to this plan."

"That was before Robert went missing. With him missing, they don't want you mysteriously falling off the radar either."

"Can you stall them?"

"Stall them? You want me to stall the DA's office when they're threatening to compel you to appear?" There was silence at the other end of the line. And then more sounds of scuffling.

Aspen's voice filled his ear. "Hey, do you need me to come out? I can have the jet ready by this afternoon. Is it a woman? Did you finally find a girlfriend?"

More scuffling sounds. Damien's voice was muffled, but Tony still clearly heard him. "Did you leave Hannah and Kieran alone in the kitchen?"

He couldn't hear what Aspen said, but he did clearly hear Damien. "Then go check on them and make sure they're not blowing up the kitchen like they did the back shed. We can't afford another citation from the fire department."

Aspen must have said something else as Damien's next words had a growling tone to them. "I promise I'll find out. Please go make sure our entire house is still catastrophe-free."

Damien let out a long sigh on his end.

"The kids blew up the back shed?"

"Last month. Hannah had found some experiments online and raided the lawn care supplies in the garage."

Tony thought of nine-year-old Hannah. She was the spitting image of her mother. And eight-year-old Kieran followed his sister around, doing whatever she needed him to do. "Experiments?"

"As I reminded Aspen, this is an unsecured line, and as Hannah's parent, I'm invoking her fifth amendment rights."

Tony chuckled. "Good to know who I should call if I need evidence destroyed."

Damien was silent for a few moments. "Don't think you're distracting me."

"Who? Me?"

"You. Besides the facts that my wife would find new ways to torture me if I don't ask you and then would fly out immediately if she didn't like my answer, you would have assured me immediately if there wasn't a woman in the picture. Who are you hiding?"

"No one you need to worry about at the moment."

"Which means, yes, I do." A heavy sigh came over the line and Tony imagined Damien rubbing his face. He hated to cause his friend worry, but Tony could handle himself. And Melody. It would all work out. "Does she know who you are?"

Tony winced. "Kind of?"

"That's it. You need to come back here, and never go back to Sunflower Falls. Wait. Have you been sneaking out of Sunflower Falls, and she's not a local?"

"Ummm... She's local. And I can't leave."

"You know, with every word you say, I'm tempted to send Aspen out there. Well, if she doesn't know exactly who you are, at least that means you're not married."

This time all Tony could do was fidget in his seat.

"Anthony..."

Before he could say anything, he spotted Melody getting out of an elevator on the other side of the lobby. "Gotta go."

"Anthony…"

He hung up before Damien could finish what he was about to say. Before Damien could call him back, he turned on the do not disturb setting.

Melody was halfway across the lobby, but she must not have spotted him as her attention had locked on the coffee shop. He hurried over and got himself positioned in front of her. She really wasn't paying attention to anything but the coffee shop as she literally bounced off him when they made contact.

"Sorry." She didn't even look up. Just waved her left hand with her ring finger extended in his face and tried to skirt around him.

He laughed even as he tried to get a grip on her shoulders.

"Hey."

The outrage in her tone put him on alert. "Hey back." He waved his own left hand in front of her face.

She blinked and looked up. It was like watching the sunrise come up over the mountains when visiting Damien and Aspen's hideaway in the Sierras. "Tony. Why are you here?"

He frowned, but pulled her in and wrapped his arms around her shoulders. She eventually relaxed against him, slipping her hands under his shirt and tracing patterns on his skin. He blew out a breath. "Did you hear me say that I needed to head out?"

"Kind of? I felt you kiss me, and then just drifted for a bit. I think I'm still drifting."

He leaned back to look down at her. She kept her cheek against his chest, not looking up at him. "Are you okay?"

"Probably. I'm not exactly at my best in the morning. I need some coffee."

"I thought you were a morning person. That's what you've been telling me when you kick me out at night."

This time she looked up, her brows scrunched down. "No. What I said is that I had to get up early and go to work. Being a responsible business co-owner does not mean I'm a morning person."

"How do you cope?"

"Lots of coffee. Which I need right now."

"You woke up just fine yesterday."

"Because we had sex first thing. Like you're going to notice how coherent I am when I've got my mouth wrapped around your cock."

He thought that over for a moment as he turned them to walk toward the coffee shop. "Fair. What do you want?"

"A large drip coffee with a double shot of espresso."

He bit his tongue and pointed to an empty pair of seats around a small table. "Go grab that, and I'll get your coffee. Want something to eat with that?"

"Just the coffee."

He placed their order, the IV of caffeine for her and a pumpkin spiced latte joined by a decadent slice of chocolate and hazelnut cake for him. Melody was staring out the window when he joined her with the drinks and cake.

Without taking her gaze off the window, she broke off a piece of the cake.

"I thought you didn't want any food?"

"You brought it over. Communal property now."

He snorted. "Does that mean that you're excited about being married to me?"

"We'll see." She stared at her coffee for a long moment before she brought it to her mouth to drink.

She seemed to be thinking something over. As he needed to figure out a way to broach the subject of his real identity before either Damien, Aspen, or, worse, LA County sheriff's officers showed up to drag him back to California, he let the silence grow between them.

"Tony?"

"Mm-hmm?"

"Can I ask you a favor?" He watched as she rubbed the metal of her wedding ring with her right hand.

"Always."

"Do you mind if we don't tell anyone for a while?"

He jerked his gaze up to meet hers. "Are you regretting it?"

She shifted in her seat before shaking her head. "I don't know? I just..." She bit down on her lips and then blew out a long breath. "Look. I never expected to get married. It wasn't my thing. Ana was the one who always wanted to play wedding day. I just wanted to run a construction site. I..." She fell silent, still playing with the ring.

Seeing her agitation over the situation stabbed him in the gut. He reached out and wrapped both his hands around hers. "I just want to take care of you."

The confusion on her face broke his heart. "But why? I don't need taking care of."

He pulled her forward so he could kiss her knuckles. "Melody, everyone needs taking care of. Some more than others, and everyone in their own way. I want to be a support for you when you need one, and your cheerleader when you're conquering the world of home renovation. And, when you absolutely need it, the shoulder you can cry on."

She was shaking her head again. He leaned in. "Give me time. I wouldn't have proposed any of the times I asked if I didn't want to marry you. The first time I laid eyes on you, that day in the diner when Libby hit town and Ana dumped her entire tray onto Zach and me, I knew I had to get to know you. You shined so brightly."

"I think I was on my fourth cup of coffee at that point."

He grinned. "Whatever. I couldn't take my eyes off you, and I couldn't stop trying to find out more about you. Every time I spotted you in town, I didn't pay attention to anything else. You're my North Star. Give us a chance."

She blew out another long breath, but didn't take her eyes off him. He held the contact because he knew this was do or die. "Fine. But no telling anyone. If we can't make it work, I don't want anyone to know. It's bad enough everyone knows about what a shithead my dad is. I can't be the person who's so unreliable she gets married to what should have been a summer fling and divorces the guy within months."

When he felt the muscles of his chest relaxing, he realized how tense he'd gotten over what her answer might be. "Fine. Lips are sealed. No one in Sunflower Falls will know."

Her breath was a bit choppy as she drew one in and then let it out. "Okay. Fine. We're married, and we'll see if we can make it work. In secret. Let's head back to the room. Check out's in a couple hours."

He winked at her. "Just enough time for another round of celebration."

Her laughter was rocky, but she was laughing. They'd figure it out. He'd figure it out. What could go wrong now that he'd bought himself some time?

# *texts*

DAMIEN

You let him off-leash?!

ZACH

Not completely. I have him bugged.

DAMIEN

Do you know who he's with? Can she be
trusted to keep quiet?

ZACH

I know who he's with. Between the two of
them, Tony's absolutely the one most likely
to talk.

About anything.

DAMIEN

WHO IS SHE?!? I NEED TO
KNOOOOOOWWWWWW!

ZACH

Aspen, please give Damien his phone back.

DAMIEN

No. Spill. I need all the details. Now. Who's
my new best friend?

ZACH

DAMIEN

Sorry about that. I have my phone back.
Just give me a head's up if there's anything
I need to handle.

Please.

ZACH

Will do.

DAMIEN

Also, we need to talk. I'll call you when
Aspen's putting the kids to bed.

ZACH

Noted. Tony's due back in a few hours.

DAMIEN

Give me ten to get Aspen and the kids
outside.

ZACH

*four*

THE MORNING of the annual fundraiser for the volunteer fire department, Melody woke to a queasy stomach. She had made dinner for Tony last night, and was sure she'd cooked everything properly. After the brief wave of nausea subsided, she climbed out of bed.

Button was whimpering in her cage, so Melody got her outside as quickly as possible. After ensuring that Button did her business and didn't start snacking on what she could reach in Mr. Higgins's yard through the fence, she headed back in to make her morning coffee.

Tony had left a bit after midnight as usual, but had told her he'd probably see her today. Despite the promise, she could tell something was up with him. They'd been married for nearly a month, and she'd seen him less than she had before they'd said "I do."

The only times she really spent time with him were when they were discussing the build for his new house or when he came over at night. And when he was over at night, they usually spent more time making out or having sex rather than engaging in deep discussion. Any time she brought up the possibility of doing something outside of work or intimate time together, he said he had to work on some things with Zach.

Since she still wasn't sure what she wanted to do about the marriage, she couldn't exactly be mad that he was fine with not being seen with her in public beyond the fact they seemed to have become part of the same friend group. But she also was questioning how she ended up married to a man she was realizing she didn't know well outside the bedroom.

Yeah, he probably should be given a gold medal for his bedroom skills, but being good in bed didn't qualify someone for gold medal marriage material.

The only answer she could come up with that made any kind of sense was that he made her feel like a million bucks whenever they were together. He always listened to her when they did talk, whether she'd had a not great day at work with a supplier sending the wrong custom flooring order or when things had gone great with securing another contract.

She felt so seen when she was with him. In ways she didn't with anyone else. Even Ana. He paid attention to the shows she liked, the food she enjoyed, the music that made her dance. And then brought little gifts or found things they could watch together that brought her joy. But when they were separated, doubts crept in.

Someone like Tony who radiated pleasure and fun couldn't possibly want to spend the rest of his life with her. Melody was a realist. She could, and did, dream big with Eric, but she was the one who was always looking for the details that needed to be taken care of for those dreams to actually happen.

Relying on someone else for any portion of her happiness made her itchy.

But when they were together? Him holding her as they talked about the possible future, his breath blowing against her ear. Tony telling her about the places he'd been to in Hollywood, and one day taking her there one day to show them all to her. He got her excited about the possibilities of what life together could be like. Going back to Hollywood to visit where he'd spent his life there. Building something together here in Sunflower Falls.

She felt so safe and hopeful when he held her in his arms.

But whenever she tried to dig into the details of his past, he'd either divert her attention to something else or would gloss over anything that might give a richer depth to his story that it might as well have been a generic tale from anyone spending any time in Hollywood.

All he said was that he'd had a good childhood with parents that loved him.

He wouldn't even name any celebrities who he'd crossed paths with. She knew from Greer, her and Eric's media agent and Libby's business partner, that running into celebrities in Hollywood was like encountering a caffeine junkie in Starbucks.

The signal on her coffee maker pulled her out of the funk she was spiraling into. Pouring the coffee into her favorite mug, she inhaled a deep breath of her favorite smell. And wrinkled her nose.

Something was off.

She took a tentative sip and spit it back out into the sink. The coffee tasted like a mouthful of quarters. Grabbing the bag, she checked the expiration date. There were months left, and she always put the bag back into the freezer after she was done with it in the morning.

Another sip confirmed there was something off. She poured the coffee into the sink and mourned it as she watched it swirl into the drain.

She'd just pick something up later at the Sunflower Diner.

The fundraiser didn't start until noon, so she had a few hours to get showered and then work on interior designs proposals for Tony's house on the lake. He still hadn't told her what he intended to do with it beyond being some kind of investment property. If she decided to keep him, she figured he'd just move into her house. Somehow.

Three hours later, when her alarm went off, she pulled herself out of the deep dive she'd fallen into on forecasted trends for paint and upholstery in the coming year. Button had come into her office and fallen asleep on the bed Melody had set up for her on one side of the desk. Grinning at her puppy, lying spread eagle on her back with a penguin-shaped squeaker toy hanging out of her mouth, Melody grabbed her phone and took a quick photo. Then sent it to the group text with Libby and Ana.

Neither of them responded, so Melody assumed both were busy with something. She deliberately stopped the thought of what or who Libby might be busy with there. There were things siblings absolutely did not need to know about each other.

Instead, she called her mom.

"Sunflower Motel, how can I help you?"

"Hi, Mom. Okay if I still bring Button over?" Hearing Melody say her name, even in sleep, had Button stirring.

"Absolutely. Everyone scheduled to check out already

has, and we only have a couple reservations starting today, so it's a fairly quiet day."

"Thanks. I need to stop at the diner and pick up a cup of coffee. There's something wrong with the batch I've got."

"Wrong, how?"

"It tasted like metal." Button came over and began chewing on the squeaker, so Melody missed what her mom said, but she thought it was something about ladies. "What was that?"

"Never mind. It's probably nothing. I'll see you when you get here."

"See you soon." Melody hung up the call and stuffed her phone into her back pocket. And then got into a ten-minute tug of war with Button. By the time she'd worn Button out again, Melody had to rush around to get ready.

She was rushing when she picked up her takeout order of coffee at the diner, intent on getting over to the motel, so she forgot to ask if Ana was working this morning.

Back in her truck, she poured the coffee from the takeout cup into her insulated one so she could save it for later, then headed over to the motel. Her mom wasn't at the reception desk when she walked in.

"Mom?"

No answer, so she went over to the door that led to her mom's private quarters. She and Eric had grown up in a small house not far from Melody's current home. Things had been tight, even when their dad was around. She knew Uncle Stef had helped out where he could. But ten years ago, after both Eric and Melody had moved out, her mom had taken the job as manager of the motel which came with on-site lodging.

Some out-of-town business had bought it with Zach's mom acting as the local real estate agent, and everyone thought they'd demolish the old motel in favor of some-thing not right for Sunflower Falls. But whoever bought it had decided to renovate instead of tearing it down. The renovation had been Melody's mom's first job after taking over as the general manager. That move had led to the revi-talization of the downtown area.

Everyone was grateful, but to this day, no one knew who was behind the business.

Melody knocked, and she heard a muffled noise. A minute later, her mom answered the door, smoothing back her hair. "Melody. You're here."

Frowning, Melody nodded. "Should I get Button's stuff from the car?" Button was sniffing around the door, trying to get inside. She knew Grandma Keller's apartment well, and treats were always waiting inside for her.

"That would be great. Give me a moment, and I'll be out to help you."

"No problem. If you can take Button?" Melody held out Button's leash.

"Oh. Yes. Sure." Her mom took the handle and scooted Button back so she could close the door behind her.

"Everything okay?"

"Yes. Everything's fine. Go get her stuff so you can head over to the fundraiser."

Not sure why her mom was acting so squirrelly, Melody shrugged it off and went for Button's travel crate and bag of supplies.

When she came back inside, Mayzie, Libby's dog and Button's mom, was in the office area, fending off Button's puppy playfulness.

Melody paused in the doorway. "Where did she come from?"

"My apartment. Where else do you think she was?"

Recognizing that calling her mom out for weird behavior would do her no good, Melody just shrugged and handed over the bag where she kept the puppy sitting supplies. "I'm not sure when I'll be back. Since Mayzie's here, I'm assuming Eric and Libby are already there?"

"Yes. Eric got a call to help with some last-minute setup, so they dropped Mayzie off an hour ago."

"I'll keep an eye out for them. Thanks again. I'll call you when I'm headed back."

Her mom bent down and picked Button up from where she was play growling at Mayzie. "Enjoy yourself. You've been working a lot, and I'm sure you could use a little break. Have you noticed anything else besides the coffee tasting off?"

She shook her head. "No. I must have gotten a bad batch. Just didn't notice it until this morning."

Her mom hummed. "Are you planning on meeting anyone there?"

"Where?"

"The fundraiser. Where else would I be asking about today?"

There was something about her mom's questions that had Melody's mental stud finder pinging. She couldn't see what was behind the questions, but something was there. "Only Libby and Eric. Maybe Ana if she's not at one of her jobs today."

"What about Zach? Or that friend of his? Tony?"

The little hairs on the back of Melody's neck stood on end. Did her mom suspect something? "Nope. Not planning on seeing either of them today." That didn't mean she didn't hope to run into Tony, but they hadn't made specific plans on where and when to meet up.

"Anyone else special?"

Now Melody narrowed her eyes. Her mom was most definitely on a fishing expedition. She was acting like she had back when she was trying to find out if Melody planned to go to her senior prom. "No one special either. What's with all the questions?"

Her mom shook her head. "Nothing. You go have fun. Parking is going to be rough as it is. I don't want you to have to drive all the way back here to park."

Melody reached out and petted Button's head. "Thanks again for watching her." She kissed her mom's cheek. "Love you."

"Love you, too."

To clear the weirdness of her mom's questions from her head, she blasted her favorite radio station on the drive over to Geraghty's, the dive bar where the fundraiser was being held. Parking was indeed rough, and she ended up having to turn around and drive back a half mile past it before finding a spot on the side of the road.

A long line had formed at the parking lot entrance that was open as the gate area, and Melody found herself standing behind Mrs. Smith. The owner of Secrets and Whimsies, a shop a few doors down from her own business's storefront, was carrying a cardboard box with her purse hooked onto her arm. Her snow white hair was styled into an elegant helmet that wouldn't dare wilt in the humidity that was lingering even in late September.

Mrs. Smith turned around. "Hello, Melody dear. I've got something at my booth for you, so be sure to stop by."

Rubbing her hands together, Melody grinned. "Excellent. Want to give me a clue?"

Mrs. Smith grinned back at her. "You do know how I love a good secret. You'll find out when you come over."

They moved closer to the front of the line, and Melody

saw Andy Kavanaugh, one of her classmates from grade school through high school, manning the ticket table. "Come on, Mrs. S. You keep secrets closer than the CIA."

She sniffed as if offended. "I would hope so." She was silent for a moment as she shifted the box and began rooting around in her purse. "When I was setting up the booth this morning, that nice Tony Caputo was helping out with Zach Troy."

Melody pursed her lips and hummed. Mrs. S must not have heard it as she kept her focus on her purse. Tony hadn't mentioned that he was going to be here, let alone helping with Zach. A searing in her gut reminded her of the time the popular kids in high school had made a point to talk about a party they were going to in front of her and then turn and say she wasn't invited. She took a deep breath as she realized her emotions were way out of proportion for the situation.

Maybe she should have downed the coffee from the diner immediately. Or maybe she was coming down with something. Either way, she'd spend some money for the fundraiser and then head back home. No one needed her cranky ass around at what was supposed to be a fun event. "Oh, really?"

"Yes. So nice. And so nicely muscled. You should consider going out with him. Get some fresh blood here in Sunflower Falls."

Shocked, Melody looked down at the older woman. "Are you trying to matchmake, Mrs. S?" Or did the woman know something no one else in Sunflower Falls, not even her own mother, knew? Mrs. S herself had moved to Sunflower Falls only recently, so the fresh blood comment was kind of funny.

"There it is." Mrs. S held up an old-fashioned leather

wallet. There were gorgeous embroidered flowers still visible in the patinated leather.

They'd reached Andy. "I've got you, Mrs. S."

"Hello, ladies." He took the twenty Melody held out for the entrance fee and began making change. "Melody, I already told Eric, but Alex is going to be in town next week. We're going to try to get everyone together for a night out."

"Great. Keep me updated." Back in high school, she'd had a crush on Alex Kavanaugh, Andy's older brother, but as he'd been a senior with Zach when she'd been a freshman, he'd never taken any notice of her. Plus, he'd been playing some sport all the time before getting drafted to a farm team for one of the pro hockey teams a month before graduation around the same time Zach had left for the Marines. He'd stopped back in town every few years and they would periodically end up in the same place at the same time because Sunflower Falls was that small, but nothing had ever happened.

And now there was Tony. Who, now that she thought about it, had a vague resemblance to Alex.

Something she would think about later as she still needed to decide what to do with him. For now, she followed Mrs. S over to her booth, set up on the far side of Geraghty's parking lot.

After getting herself settled, Mrs. S pulled out a small, wooden box from a tub underneath one of her display tables. It was gorgeous. The top of the box was an intricate design of a woman holding a pomegranate and reclining on the bank of a river made of marquetry. She'd have to ask Uncle Stef what the woods were.

"Where did you find it?"

"At an estate sale in Montreal."

Melody stroked the cover. It was as smooth as it must

have been on the day the craftsman finished it. There were no dips indicating any missing pieces. "It's gorgeous. How much?"

At that moment, a shiver took over her body, and the hairs on the back of her neck rose. Heated breath licked across her skin. Without even turning around, she knew who was behind her.

"One hundred dollars."

Caught up in the moment, she didn't get a chance to begin the haggling process she had been looking forward to engaging in with Mrs. S.

"She'll take it."

She was about to turn on him when he crowded up against her back, and a hundred dollar bill filled her vision as he handed it over to Mrs. S. Lips brushed the top of her hair, and were gone in a moment.

Mrs. S grinned and shoved the bill into her till before Melody could say anything. By the time she spun around to confront Tony for stepping in where he shouldn't have, he had almost disappeared into the crowd that had formed in Geraghty's parking lot.

She turned back to Mrs. S. "Can you hold on to this for me? I'll be back for it."

"Absolutely, my dear. He's such a nice boy. Be sure to hold on to him."

Biting her tongue as it wasn't Mrs. S who was the source of her ire, Melody tracked after Tony. Ire that, again, was way out of proportion for what happened. When she finished chewing out Tony for interfering with her play time with Mrs. S, she definitely was leaving after dropping some bills into the tip jar at the bar and the donation bucket at the exit. She'd only wound her way through about half the crowd when she spotted him heading into the bar itself.

By the time she made it in, the bar was just as packed as outside. Tables were filled with families, and both pool tables were barely visible thanks to the tournament that was running. Libby and Eric were seated at the counter service bar.

Libby saw her and waved. Melody made her way over to them. "Have either of you seen Tony?"

"Caputo? Why?" Eric took a sip of beer.

"Nothing. I just need to talk with him. Have you seen him?"

Libby pointed over to the pool tables. "I thought I saw him head that way."

"Thanks." Not waiting for either of them to say anything more, she began tacking her way through the crowd. It wasn't easy, and by the time she got near the pool tables, she saw him on the other side of the room, heading back to the kitchen area. "Damn it."

The tables were tightly packed with people wanting to get their lunch on, plus part of the deal was that Harry, current owner of Geraghty's, donated all profits from food and drink sales to the fire department so people came in intending to eat. Melody had to make her way back to the bar area before she could make her way over to the kitchen entrance. By the time she got back there, the only people in the kitchen were Harry's two cooks for the day.

"Did Tony Caputo come through here?" He, Zach, and Eric hung out here often enough that she hoped the cooks would recognize him. The one at the fryer pointed to the back door. She hurried back there, but when she tried to push through, she was stopped in her tracks as the door refused to move.

She spotted rust on the hinges and a can of WD-40 sitting on a shelf next to them. She'd have to talk with Harry to see if he wanted the door updated. Hinges on an exit door shouldn't be this rusted. She quickly sprayed the hinges, and, this time, the door opened with only a small amount of resistance and scraping of metal.

It sounded to her like an eagle screeching, but Tony must have been so involved in his conversation that he didn't hear it. In fact, she stood on the steps leading down to the back lot area while he paced, phone held to his ear.

"I don't care what you need me out there for. I'm staying here."

Confused as it didn't sound like he was talking with Zach, she stepped closer.

"Until I get this marriage sorted and registered under my real name, I'm not going to California."

The words slammed into her worse than the sledgehammer Eric had once hit her with when they were teens as he hadn't been paying attention to his backswing. Back then, she'd had to avoid wearing a bikini all summer because the bruising had taken months to fade. Now? There was a gaping hole in her chest where her heart had once resided. The hope that had been slowly growing there withered and died.

Before she could slip back through the bar and head the fuck out of town so she didn't have to face him, her worst mistake turned around and spotted her.

He froze. Mouth open for what felt like forever before he grimaced. "I'll call you back." He tapped on his screen and shoved his phone into his back pocket.

Before he could say anything, she pointed at him. "No. I want a divorce." Unable to think beyond that and needing to hide, she whirled around and opened the door.

Thankfully, the WD-40 was still working, and she ran inside.

As she passed Libby and Eric she caught sight of their shocked faces, but ignored them. All she wanted was to get back to her den and take cover.

She craved the comfort of having Button love all over her, but she couldn't face her mother. Her mom would immediately know something was wrong. To tell her that Melody hadn't learned from her mistakes and married a liar herself? Never.

She was halfway down the road to her car when Libby finally caught up to her.

"Where are you going?"

"Home."

"What happened?"

"Nothing."

Libby ran ahead and stopped in front of Melody. But as she tried to walk around Libby, Libby just matched her move for move. If it weren't for the steady stream of cars, she would have run into the road just to get away.

It was when Libby bear hugged her that Melody finally stopped and dropped her head. "Can you please let me go wallow in peace?"

"Not until you tell me why you're wallowing? What did Tony do?"

"Nope."

"Melody. What the hell is going on? You're never like this."

Realizing she wouldn't be able to shake Libby, she gave in. "Can we please just go back to my place? I can't deal with this."

"Fine, but I'm driving."

"I can drive."

"But should you?"

Melody opened her mouth to push back, but all that came out was a choked cry. She'd already been feeling off and on edge all day, but discovering Tony had been lying to her the entire time they'd been together was too much. On the verge of breaking down, and not wanting to do it in public, she pulled her keys out of her pocket and tossed them at Libby.

They got back to her truck, and Melody climbed up into the passenger seat. She spotted the mug of coffee. If she was drinking, then Libby would hopefully be less inclined to interrogate her.

She grabbed the cup and took a deep swig. As soon as the coffee hit her stomach, it came right back up again. Only by the grace of the truck gods was she able to open her door in time to avoid messing up her interior.

When she was done, Libby was staring at her.

"What?"

"Even when I've seen you drunk off your ass, you've never thrown up."

She turned around and began hunting for a clean one of the rags she kept in her truck for cleaning up after being on work sites. "I don't throw up. Except on carnival rides."

"Um-hmmm."

Melody looked at Libby. "Why the humming?"

"You're not pregnant, are you?"

LIBBY

When do you get off work? I need help.

ANA

What's going on? I thought you were at the fire department fundraiser.

LIBBY

We were. I'm at Melody's now. She's sick in the bathroom right now.

ANA

Oh, no. Does she need Gatorade? Pepto?

Is it the flu? Food poisoning?

LIBBY

I think she needs a pregnancy test. She seemed fine, physically, when we got in her truck, but then she took a drink of coffee and immediately threw it back up.

ANA

PREGNANCY TEST?!?!?!?!

LIBBY

Does she ever get sick to the point where she throws up?

Besides on carnival rides?

Because I've never seen her sick like that. And she seemed really fine before we got into the truck.

Pissed at Tony about something, but being pissed won't make someone throw up.

At least, not Melody.

ANA

No. She's never been sick like that unless she's SUPER sick.

Like with food poisoning.

I get off in fifteen minutes.

…

Are you sure she needs a pregnancy test?

LIBBY

Better to be sure she's not, right?

ANA

Right.

LIBBY

Also, you might want to get over here ASAP when you get off work.

ANA

# five

TONY SWORE as Melody ran from him. How the hell hadn't he heard the door open? When he'd come through it, it sounded like someone running a block of metal across an industrial grater. His Foley guy would have had a field day with all the sounds in the bar's kitchen.

For Melody, the door opened like magic.

He chased after her, but he skidded to a halt when Harry walked through the kitchen door. Second generation dive bar owner, a few inches taller than Tony, many more inches around, and a pale white face framed by a deep red beard, the man was not someone anyone with any thought in their head messed with in a physical confrontation.

"Move, Harry."

"No."

"I've got to talk to Melody."

Harry shook his head. "Doesn't look like she wants to talk with you." With his size, people mistakenly assumed he moved slowly. One night, when the crowd was particularly ornery thanks to a bachelor party of mostly out-of-towners, he'd witnessed Harry clear the disturbance in under a minute. Not one of those guys had wanted to go up against him to come back in.

Tony held up his hands. "Look, I don't have a beef with you, but I've got to make things right with her."

The kitchen door bumped up against Harry's solid back. He didn't move.

"You can do that when she's not ready to board you up in a basement."

Knowing Harry probably wasn't wrong about Melody's reaction, Tony rethought his plan. And shook his head. "I've got to talk with her now."

The door bumped up against Harry again.

"Can we come in?"

Harry kept staring at him, but shifted to let the door swing open. Eric and Zach stood on the other side. Eric looked between Harry and Tony. "Okay if we talk with Tony, Harry?"

"Is Melody out there?"

Eric shook his head. "She left. Libby's going with her."

Harry gave a curt nod. "Fine." He pointed a finger at Tony before leaving. "I have never seen that girl run with tears in her eyes. Whatever you did, you fucked up bad. That is going to require an epic grovel from you if you want her back."

Without explaining further what he meant, Harry headed back out to the bar area. The kitchen wasn't exactly private with both cooks still working away at orders. Also, the pass-through window let all the noise from the front in.

Tony scrubbed his face and looked at Zach. "Can we go back to the beach house?"

"For you to explain what the hell's going on?"

"Yeah."

Zach nodded and gestured to Eric for him to come with

them. Once they were outside, Mrs. Smith ambushed them. And it was an ambush. One moment, they were moving toward the parking lot's exit, and the next, the elderly woman was standing in front of them, lips pursed and disapproval written all over her face.

"I saw Melody leave." She lifted one hand, and Tony saw a plastic bag with something in it hanging from her fingers. It was like she was magic, conjuring things out of thin air. "She didn't stop by my booth for this, and as you were the one who paid for it, it is now your duty to deliver it to her."

Tony felt Zach's and Eric's stares, but ignored them for the moment. "I'll be sure to get it to her." He hooked his fingers into the bag's loops, but Mrs. Smith didn't release it.

Her gaze felt like it was drilling into the depths of the secrets he kept hidden away. "Truth is never simple or easy, but it is what opens doors to forever."

With that cryptic statement, she released her grip on the bag and walked away. Eric elbowed him. Hard enough that Tony almost took a step forward. "What was that about?"

Tony glanced at Zach. The man's sunglasses blocked Tony's view of his eyes, but he had the feeling his friend was staring at Mrs. Smith's retreating back. "I'll tell you later. Let's go."

Libby had driven Melody home, so Eric agreed to meet them at the beach house. He pulled in right behind Zach, and Tony had to fight the feeling of being trapped. If he truly needed to get away, Zach would have no issues getting him out, but it still had him rolling his shoulders.

Once inside, Eric lifted his sunglasses to the top of his head and looked around the small home Tony and Zach had been sharing since they'd hit town back in May.

"This needs updating."

Zach nodded. "I know, but that's on my parents. Want a beer?"

Eric looked at Tony. "I don't know. Do I need a beer?"

He set the bag containing the box he'd bought for Melody from Mrs. Smith down on one of the small tables by the front door. "Sure." Maybe it would loosen Eric up, and he wouldn't feel the immediate need to punch Tony's lights out when he heard the full story.

At least Zach had the reason that he wasn't supposed to beat up his own clients holding him back.

Zach came back in with three bottles of beer in hand. He held one out to Eric and the third to Tony.

Once they'd all taken a swig, Zach pinned him with the gaze that Tony had first seen back in that dive bar in Hollywood and some asshole had tried to make trouble with the new guy. "What happened back there?"

Tony grimaced. "Just so you know, Damien only found out for sure today."

Zach's brows rose, but it was Eric who asked a question. "Damien? Who's Damien? And what does he have to do with why Melody was so pissed off?"

Tony went over to the recliner he'd claimed as his own and sat down. Stared down into the bottle as if it held the answers he needed.

"Tony?"

He let out a long breath. "Remember about a month ago? Melody was gone for the weekend?"

"Yeah, she said she was going off for a weekend in the city. So?"

Eric sat down on the couch, and Tony met his questioning gaze. "It wasn't New York she went to. We went off to Niagara Falls together."

"Niagara Falls? What were you doing in Niagara Falls?"

Zach paused with the bottle at his lips. "Fuck. Did you get married?"

Eric's eyes widened and swiveled between Tony and Zach. "Married? Melody got married? Without telling me? Telling our mom?"

Zach glared at him. "Did you use your real name?"

"Real…? What the fuck?" Eric slammed down his beer. "What the fuck is going on?"

Tony winced as the beer bubbled out of the bottle, but it was probably better than having Eric punch his lights out. From the look on Eric's face, though, the possibility wasn't off the table.

He looked over to Zach, but his friend wasn't exactly the most friendly person at the moment either.

Tony scrubbed his face and leaned forward. "Look…" He was at a loss for words, when he was never at a loss for words. No matter what he said, he was just digging his grave deeper and deeper. He hated the churning in his gut. He closed his eyes and let out a long breath. "Zach?"

"What?"

"Can we tell him?"

Eric stood up, his fists clenched hard enough that Tony heard his friend's knuckles crack. "You'd better tell me. Whatever it is. My sister's been fucked over enough in her life."

"Stand down, Eric. Go ahead and tell him. You're going to get your ass kicked one way or another by the end of the day, anyway."

"Thanks." Eric didn't sit down, but as uncomfortable as it was to have the other man looming over him, Tony stayed seated. He met Eric's gaze. "There is a good reason why I'm here, and why I'm using the name I am."

Eric's jaw moved as if he was grinding his teeth. "Oh, yeah? That's what my dad always said when the cops would show up at our door looking for him because he'd stolen someone's identity."

"I did not steal anyone's identity. My full legal first name is Anthony. Not even my parents call me Tony. Caputo is my nonna's maiden name. My legal last name is Dewitt."

Eric frowned. "Anthony Dewitt? Why does that sound familiar?"

Tony glanced at Zach, but he only shrugged. After he'd left the show, he'd dropped off most of the celebrity gossip sites, and the regular news outlets rarely had any reason to cover him. He'd pop up occasionally, but those were almost all red carpet appearances for projects he'd produced. "I work as a producer in Hollywood with my dad."

"Dewitt? Producer? Leo Dewitt? Married to Vittoria Schreiber? The actress?"

"Yeah. How did you know?"

"Mom loves your mom's work and would always talk about how great it was to meet your parents."

Tony swallowed. When the words couldn't get past the ball in his throat, he cleared it again. "Your mom knows my parents?"

"I wouldn't say that she knows your parents. More that Uncle Stef had my mom out for a taping of his show when your parents were guests on it for some reason. Probably some celebrity gives back through home renovation thing. Mom still talks about it."

Tony let out a breath. The last thing he needed was his parents finding out what was going on with Melody and deciding to come meddle. "Okay. Good."

"Getting back to why you're using a name that isn't your legal name. Why are you here?"

"I took on a partner for my last film project. It was supposed to be as a favor to an old friend of my dad's, but the partner had other ties we weren't aware of. The criminal kind."

Eric crossed his arms against his chest. "And did you also partner with those other ties?"

Tony bit back his instinctual response because he recognized it as a reasonable question. "No. I caught my partner doing things he wasn't supposed to be doing and meeting with people he wasn't supposed to be meeting with. Those people weren't happy when my partner got arrested for the things he'd been doing on the set of our project. To the best of my knowledge, my part in the arrest wasn't leaked, but everyone decided it would be best if I left town and went somewhere to lie low until my partner flipped or went on trial. I honestly can't be any more detailed than that."

Eric looked over at Zach. "And, what? You're his bodyguard or something?"

"Yep." Zach took a sip of beer and relaxed back into his chair.

Eric waited a few beats. "That's all you're going to say? You brought him to Sunflower Falls knowing danger might follow him, and now he somehow married my sister?"

Zach took another sip of beer while staring at Tony. It was the deliberate movement more than anything that told Tony how pissed he was. "Sunflower Falls was a reasonable choice. He has no ties to the area, and someone would have had to do some serious digging to both discover our connection and my hometown. My group is very good at what we do."

Eric frowned. Opened his mouth, but then shook his head. "We'll talk about that later. What do we do about... Wait a minute. Anthony Dewitt. Undercover Immortal." His eyes were wide as he stared at Tony.

Tony winced. "Yeah. Were you a fan?"

The look of shock on Eric's face slowly transformed into one of glee. "No. But I watched it. With Melody. Who was a huge fan. She had a poster with your face up on her wall. She is going to murder you."

Tony blinked. She'd been a fan? And she hadn't recognized him? He didn't think he'd changed that much in the last twelve years. Even with growing the beard. Had she been lying to him the entire time?

Did she really want something from him?

Eric sat back down on the couch and picked up his beer. Pointed it at Tony. "You had better hope she gives you the time of day to explain and doesn't flat out kill you. Make sure she doesn't have any tools in hand or close when you approach. And let me know when you plan to tell her. I want to watch."

Tony scowled at him. "What? So you can make popcorn ahead of time?"

"Finding this out? And not being invited to the wedding? You bet your ass I want to watch when you tell my sister." He drank deeply from the bottle. "And who was this Damien you mentioned?"

"My attorney." Tony winced when he realized what he needed to say next. "He wants me back in California."

Zach frowned. "We've been in touch, but he hasn't said it was definite."

"Because I've been stalling him."

Eric snorted. "Are you sure you want him as your attorney if you can put him off so easily?"

Tony scowled. "Believe me, it hasn't been easy. Damien's one of the top attorneys in the state. He has to be to keep his wife out of lockup."

"What, is she a mob princess or something?"

This time it was Zach who let out a low chuckle. "No, but she'd like to play one." When Eric frowned, he continued on. "His wife is Lily Whitting, known to friends as Aspen."

Eric's brows rose. "The actress? Wait. Damien? Damien Brandon, the quarterback?"

Zach nodded.

"Damn. If he has to come here to haul your ass back to California, I want to meet him. I idolized him in high school."

Tony flipped him the bird. "I'll let him know."

Zach cleared his throat. "What aren't you telling us?"

Tony leaned forward. "Look, I know I've fucked up. Melody asked me not to tell anyone that we got married." Eric opened his mouth, but Tony held up a hand. "I was trying to respect her wishes. I want to be with her. Fully. In public. Forever. I get that she's not the most trusting person. I was doing what I thought I had to do. And I realized that by not giving her my real name, I've fucked up even more. But I need time to make it up to her. If she still decides to divorce me, fine. I'm going to fight for her though. And I'll fight both of you if I have to."

Eric looked over at Zach and then back to Tony. "The only reason I'm not beating you into the ground right now is not because of your bodyguard here. It's because I know my sister. And she will do everything in her power to end you because not only have you lied to her, but you've humiliated her. Like Harry said, you're going to have to epically grovel."

Zach stood. "Just so you know, if she needs help hiding your body, I'm helping."

"Thank you for the warning."

Eric grinned. "If you do manage to convince her to stay married to her, or marry you again because I don't understand how that was even legal in the first place, the wedding reception is going to be one hell of a party."

*six*

MELODY STARED at the bag of coffee she'd used this morning. Which felt like a lifetime ago. She opened it and smelled the grounds. They smelled fine.

She scooped out enough to make a pot and turned on the coffeemaker. Libby sat at the little dining table in her kitchen, but didn't say anything. Since her bombshell of a question, she hadn't said anything more.

At least to Melody.

The first thing Melody had done when she'd come into the house was head to her bedroom to clean up. She'd heard Libby on the phone with someone then.

But the emotional curtain that had fallen the moment she'd realized the words Tony had been saying was still in place. When she'd returned downstairs, Libby had opened her mouth to say something, but Melody had just shaken her head and went into the kitchen.

By the time the coffee had finished brewing, Ana walked in the front door carrying a plastic bag.

Melody grabbed a mug from the cabinet and poured a half-cup.

"You had better appreciate the grilling I'm going to get from my mother about this." Ana tossed the bag onto the counter.

Melody ignored her and focused on the dark liquid. Out of the corner of her eye, she saw Ana look over at Libby who shook her head.

Drawing in a deep breath, Melody lifted the mug to her lips and inhaled the deep roasted scent of the coffee. Smiling, she drank.

And immediately spat it back out into the sink. The wretched metallic taste hadn't changed since this morning.

She rinsed out her mouth, but the taste sat on the back of her tongue. If coffee was ruined for her for the next nine months, she was going to be pissed.

Ana had crossed her arms over her chest and was tapping a foot on the floor when she finally met her best friend's eyes. "Hey."

"Hey? What the hell is going on, Melody? Libby texted me and told me to get over here as quickly as possible with a pregnancy test. I would have raided Bethie's stash, but Libby said ASAP and the store was closer."

Melody closed her eyes. Of course Ana would first think to raid her sister Bethie's stash. Bethie at least would keep her mouth shut about someone needing a pregnancy test. She wanted to be mad at both of them for making more of this than was necessary, but even she knew something was off. They'd used condoms every single time, and she was on the pill, but nothing was foolproof.

"I'll explain everything later. I'll be back."

She grabbed the bag and headed up to her bathroom. She wouldn't put it past Ana to follow her, but as she headed up the stairs, she heard Libby say something and Ana reply.

Grateful to Libby for giving her the space she needed, Melody closed the bathroom door behind her. And locked it.

She read the directions first because she didn't want to fuck this up and have to take a second one. This was a one and done deal. Yes or no. And if it was yes, no way in hell was she telling Tony.

Fifteen minutes later, thanks to Ana buying the Rolls Royce of tests, the word "Pregnant" was clear as fucking day.

Her knees went weak, and she had to grab hold of her vanity to stay upright. Of course, that sent the test flying into the gods damned toilet. "Mother…"

Someone started banging on the bathroom door, making Melody jump.

"Open up. What happened? Am I going to be an auntie?"

Melody reached over and opened the door. "Grab it out of the toilet if you want the answer."

She tried to push past her best friend in the world, but despite Ana barely reaching Melody's chin, her friend could —and had—held her own. Melody blamed it on Ana being the youngest of four, but Ana always said that the mightiest came in the smallest packages.

Ana pushed her back into the bathroom. "It's your test. You get it."

"Ugh. Fine." She tried not to hork when she reached into the toilet even though she'd flushed and had cleaned the toilet only yesterday. She held it out to Ana.

"Ew, Melody. No. Just hold it up."

Melody caught sight of Libby standing outside the door. "Want to see my humiliation, too?"

Ana started screeching, causing Melody to nearly drop the test again.

Libby's eyes crinkled. "I'm good. I can guess the result."

Melody pursed her lips. "No telling Eric."

Ana clapped her hands. "That's so romantic. Tony should totally be the first to know."

"Excuse me? Why would I tell Tony I'm pregnant?" Melody hadn't told a soul that she'd been seeing him. Anger punched through the curtain of muffled emotions. Let alone fucking married him.

Ana rolled her eyes. "Come on, Melody. We've known each other since we were in diapers. I know when you're getting some. Since you've given up on dating anyone from here, the only new person who's been around long enough for you to give them a shot is Tony."

Melody placed the test on the vanity counter and washed her hands again. "It could have been Zach. He's been away long enough."

"Nope. I've seen Zach at Geraghty's some of the same nights you've come in later, glowing like you just had sex."

"It could have been a quickie. He could have come over after eating."

Ana shook her head with the smuggest grin on her face. "The fact you're trying so hard to convince me of the possibility means it's totally not Zach."

"Plus the face you make whenever you catch Tony's eye."

Melody looked over at Libby. "What are you talking about?"

"The face you make. You'll glance over at him, he's already looking at you, and you get...I don't know. Soft, I guess? Not hard. Like you are when you catch other guys around town giving you the eye."

Melody ground her teeth together. How in the hell had she become so transparent that even Libby picked up on something she thought she'd been hiding?

Ana squealed again and damn near tackled Melody to the ground with her body hug. "I'm going to be an auntie. I'm going to be an auntie!"

Melody turned her head to look down at her only to see Ana doing a happy dance even while hugging her. "You're already an auntie. All of Bethie's kids and Hank's."

"But you're my sister from another mother, and I'm never going to have to hear my mother's criticisms about how I'm interacting with your kid."

Melody met Libby's gaze and rolled her eyes. Libby had her hand over her mouth trying, and failing, to contain her giggles. She looked back down at Ana. "Who says I'm keeping it?"

Ana paused in her dancing, and Libby straightened. Libby reached out and pulled them into the hall. "Okay, this discussion should happen with our drinks of choice in the living room, not the bathroom."

They filed back down the stairs, and all opted for ice water. Once they were settled onto the couches, Melody took a deep drink of her water. "I mean, this wasn't planned. It's... Not... Gods, I don't know."

Ana reached out and squeezed Melody's hand. "Whatever you want to do, you know we'll support you, right?"

Melody squeezed her hand back. "Yeah. I know. Thanks. This is not what I was expecting today. None of this was what I was expecting today."

Libby shifted in her seat. "Speaking of that. What happened? One minute you were looking for Tony, and the next, you were storming through the bar with tears streaming down your face."

Ana straightened up. "What? What happened? Damn it. I wish I hadn't had to work at the library today."

Melody stared into her glass, wishing it had the answers waiting for her like one of those crystal balls fake fortune tellers liked to use. She drained what remained and then got up to refill it. She needed the space to process everything that had happened. Once in the kitchen, she checked the clock. Jesus. The last hour. All of this had happened in a little over an hour.

How could one's life change so drastically in that span of time?

She filled her glass and went back into the living room. Both Ana and Libby were staring at her. Melody took a deep breath. "When I left town last month, it wasn't to celebrate finishing the Sullivan project. Well, it was, but it wasn't down to the city like I said. I went to Niagara Falls. With Tony."

"You never answered my question about marriage after you sent me that photo. Since it was Niagara Falls and all. You would have told me when you got back if you had. Plus, I knew it was Tony because Zach thought he was being all smart and staying out of sight in town, but I spotted him at Target. He didn't see me. If he had, I think he would have hid from me." Ana had the smuggest look on her face before it morphed to shock. "Oh. My. God. Tell me you didn't get married! You got married, didn't you? And you didn't tell me!"

Melody winced. This was not how she'd seen the conversation going down. If it ever went down. She didn't enjoy having her hand forced like this.

Libby's head whipped around. "What? You got married? Did you tell your mom? Did you tell Eric, and he didn't tell me?"

Melody pinched the bridge of her nose. "I didn't tell anyone. And I told him not to tell anyone. Turns out for good reason. Tony Caputo apparently isn't his real name. That's what happened. I overheard him telling someone that he needed to have the marriage filed under his legal name. So I'm probably not married. Especially as I'm pretty sure he didn't file the license. I told him I just wanted to try out the idea of it before we made it official official."

Ana's mouth opened and closed a few times before she paused. Drew in a deep breath. "But you're still pregnant."

Melody plopped down onto the couch. "Yeah. Pregnant."

"Okay. We can handle this. When are you going to tell Tony?"

Melody stared at her friend. Ana was so optimistic and positive about life. An outlook Melody had never mastered. "Nothing. I'm telling him nothing. This is a man who somehow tracked down a DVD copy of one of my favorite movies ever after I mentioned it once, but then tried to marry me under a fake name. Even if I decide to have the baby, he doesn't deserve to know after lying to me like that. I'm not subjecting my kid to a father who wouldn't be able to tell the truth from a swift kick in the ass. I had enough of that growing up, and no kid of mine deserves that."

Ana's mouth gaped open a couple times and then a look of pure fury came over her face. She pointed at Melody, her finger damn near inches from Melody's nose. "This is not a romance novel. There will be no secret babies."

Melody blinked. "The hell, Ana?"

"I had enough teasing from Hank when he tried to convince me while we were growing up that I wasn't Mom and Dad's kid, even if I sometimes wished that was the case with Mom. All because Bethie and I are so close in age. This kid deserves to know who both of their parents are."

"Hank's an ass. Always has been. And you know my dad. How could I knowingly subject my kid to a father who's just as bad?"

Libby raised her hand like she was back in school. "Can I say something?"

Melody slumped back into the couch cushions. "Sure. I mean Ana's got all the thoughts."

"Only on being honest with the father of your child. Not on anything else."

Melody shot her a glare, but Libby cleared her throat. "I still haven't met your dad, but I know the stories Eric's shared with me. And you both know that my father is the epitome of shitty."

Melody nodded because Libby's dad had actually made national news over what a shitty father he was. He'd not only stolen much of the money that Libby's grandparents had left in trust for her, but he'd also tried to have Libby put into a conservatorship so she couldn't legally make any decisions on her own behalf. He'd also screwed over countless of his law firm's clients, and the authorities were still trying to untangle everything.

"I've also hung out with Tony over the last few months, and being a through and through liar is not the vibe I get from him. Did he explain why he said what he said?"

Melody's whole body flinched at the question. "Are you questioning me over what I heard?"

"Not at all. I saw your face when you came out of the kitchen. I'm just saying that if he lied about his name, there might be a reason. Whether that reason is understandable is still questionable, but if you don't know the reason, then you can't do the evaluation."

Melody shook her head. "You are such a lawyer."

Libby beamed. "Thank you."

"That wasn't a compliment."

"But I choose to take it as such. For now, the first thing you have to do is finish your water. Then maybe take a nap. Ana and I can get Button from your mom's, come back, and make you dinner. How does that sound?"

"Fine. I guess. I had planned on eating at Geraghty's, so I don't know what I have to eat."

"That's fine. We'll go to the store first and pick some things up." Ana leaned over from where she was sitting and gave Melody one of her patented bear hugs. "We've got your back no matter what. I still think you need to tell Tony. Give him a chance to explain. You don't need to take him back or anything. But I agree with Libby. He's never struck me as someone like your dad. And I do know your dad and all the shit he pulled that you told me about."

"I'll think about it. That's the best I can do."

Ana grinned at her. "You know I love your grumpy ass, right?"

Melody blew her a raspberry like she'd done when they were kids. "I'll get the kitchen cleaned up while you get Button." The urge to cry smacked her, and she swallowed down the emotion. She could do that after they left. "Thank you. Both of you."

They stood up, and Libby gave her a hug, too, before they headed out.

Melody began cleaning the kitchen. The coffee pot sat on the counter, and she mournfully poured what remained down the sink. After rinsing out the pot and placing it in the dishwasher, she patted her stomach.

"You weren't in the plans, Peanut." This time she let the tears flow. "And I don't know what the deal is with your dad, but I'm glad you're here." She drew in a deep breath. "It may just be you and me, but I'll find a way to make it. If nothing else, we've got your Uncle Eric, Aunt Libby, and Aunt Ana. Plus Grandma Nina and Great-Uncle Stef. We'll always have your back. Even if your dad doesn't."

Melody slid down the cabinets to the floor and bawled. She thought of all the times he'd made her laugh. How he'd been so kind to Button and the other puppies when he'd been around them. The ways he'd done small things for her like massaging her shoulders after a long day when she'd let him. She'd felt like she was becoming a better version of herself by letting him into her life. But now? How could she trust him? Not only with her heart again, but her kid's? Liars never changed their stripes. Her dad never had. Tony, or whatever his real name was, likely never would either.

# *texts*

**MELODY**

I need you to do me a favor.

**ERIC**

Whatever you need.

**MELODY**

Bury a body?

**ERIC**

Do I need to call Uncle Stef?

**MELODY**

No.

Just wanted to make sure whatever was
truly whatever.

**ERIC**

:gif of old Saturday Night Live noogie
sketch:

**MELODY**

…

I need you to call Tony for me.

ERIC

Okay. About what?

MELODY

I want to set up a meeting with him.

ERIC

Who am I?

Tom Hagen?

MELODY

Who?

ERIC

Robert Duvall? The Godfather?

MELODY

I'm not going to make him an offer he can't refuse.

ERIC

As long as I don't have to put horse heads in anyone's bed. Sam would beat the crap out of me.

MELODY

I'll ask him if he has any at Button's next vet visit.

ERIC

Getting back to Tony.

What do you want me to tell him?

MELODY

Monday morning. At the house.

ERIC

Your house? My house?

MELODY

His house.

The one we're building.

ERIC

Done.

Love you.

You know I'll beat him up if you want.

No horse heads, though.

MELODY

I can beat him up myself if I want.

ERIC

Yeah. Take Libby with you to your next class, please?

MELODY

Sure.

Love you, too.

*seven*

TONY FIDDLED with the top of the coffee he'd bought for Melody. He and Zach had gotten up early to make a detour to the fancy coffee shop in the next town over. The one here in town wasn't open this early as they didn't want to compete directly with the diner and therefore Nancy. Everyone loved the diner's owner even though she was crotchety as hell.

Late Saturday night, he'd gotten a call from Eric saying that Melody wanted to meet with him. Thanks to intervention from Ana and Libby.

As far as he could tell, she'd blocked his number as he hadn't been able to get through to even her voicemail.

However, the meeting place was the home that Keller Construction was building for him. Eric had assured him that while the crew would be reassigned for the day to give them privacy, it wouldn't affect the build progress.

To a degree, it was neutral ground.

His property, but Melody's territory for the time being.

Once Zach parked his SUV behind Melody's, Tony climbed out, trying to be careful with the tray of drinks. He couldn't remember being so nervous over anything. Even when he'd been up for Emmys and other awards, he took them with a grain of salt. If he won, he won. If he didn't, that didn't affect his worth.

Not being able to make things right with Melody, though?

He'd be fucked.

He walked around Eric's truck, just in time to hear some power tool firing up from inside the house. From what he could remember from hanging around the trades on set, it was a saw of some kind.

He and Zach walked through the temporary door in the front to find Melody and Libby standing where the kitchen would eventually be. Melody had a water bottle in hand.

She caught sight of them and shot him a dark look. He wasn't sure if it was anger or something else that made her glow from within, but she was even more gorgeous than when he'd last seen her. Without saying anything to him, she headed to the back of the house.

Libby scowled after her, but waved at him.

He held up the tray of drinks. "I bring a peace offering."

Out of the corner of his eye, he saw Melody's shoulders stiffened, but she didn't turn around. He plucked one drink from the tray and held it out to Libby. "I texted Eric to find out what you drank, and he said just a hot tea with lemon."

She grinned at him. "Thank you. I've already had my morning coffee."

He held up the next drink. "Where's Eric?"

"Upstairs. He said that he wanted to get started on putting up drywall in one of the rooms."

Zach reached out and grabbed the cup. "I'll take this up. Can't do much, but I can help hold up drywall."

Libby nodded. "I'm sure he'll appreciate it."

Tony frowned. "I thought you were going to stay down here to help."

"Already told you. If she wants to kill you, I'll help hide your body."

Tony flipped him the finger, but Zach ignored him and headed up the temporary stairs to the second floor.

There was nowhere to set the container down but the floor, so he carried it over to where Melody stood by what was going to be the floor-to-ceiling windows with a view of Lake Ontario. She ignored him standing there, even though there was little to look at beyond the plastic sheeting.

He cleared his throat.

She took a deep breath, closed her eyes, and then turned to face him. "What?"

He held out the tray with the remaining two cups of coffee. "Peace offering? I got it exactly how you like it."

She stared down at the cup. He watched her throat move as she swallowed before she looked up at him. It was like watching the curtain go down at the close of a show. "I don't drink coffee anymore. Not good for my health." With that, she turned again on her heel and walked back over to Libby.

She didn't drink coffee anymore? Only a few days ago, she'd let him stay over until she had to leave ass-early in the morning to meet a supplier over in Buffalo. She'd mainlined two mugs of the stuff while he watched.

Recognizing that pushing back on her statement wouldn't win him any points, he walked back over to the kitchen area and set the tray down on the floor in a corner. Melody leaned back against the exterior wall, her arms crossed against her chest. She obviously wasn't about to begin the conversation, so he opened his mouth to apologize.

Before he could, Libby held up a hand. "I'm going to lay down some ground rules, first."

Recognizing the tone from Damien, Tony nodded. "Sure."

"Whatever."

Libby shot Melody a look. "We are here to gather answers. There will be no threats, all parties will be heard out, and, if necessary, we will agree to reconvene at another time in the future to continue discussions if the first two conditions are not met."

"I agree."

Melody glared at him. "Fine. Him first."

Even he could see Libby's jaw tighten, but she just shook her head. "Tony, I'd like to ask you some questions as I believe that would speed up the process. Are you amenable?"

He smiled at Libby. "I had trouble seeing you as an attorney. Please accept my apologies as you're obviously a well-trained one."

"Ugh. Stop it with the ass kissing."

He looked over at Melody to see her dramatically rolling her eyes. He had to bite back a laugh. Even with her angry at him, she still could hit his amusement button without even trying.

"Tony, Melody stated she overheard you telling an unknown third party that you needed to have your marriage license amended to be filed under your legal name. Is that correct?"

Libby's specialty might have been contracts, but she knew where and when to verbally slice you open. He kept his gaze on Melody who looked everywhere but at him. "She did."

"Who was this third party?"

Keeping his gaze on Melody, he let out a slow breath. "My attorney and an assistant district attorney for the County of Los Angeles."

Melody's gaze snapped to him, and he saw Libby's head swing in Melody's direction out of the corner of his eye. Neither of them said anything for a few moments, but then Libby continued her line of question.

"Why would a district attorney need to know about this?"

When he'd talked to Damien to explain what happened, Damien had told him to share within reason and to be honest about not being allowed to talk when he couldn't discuss something. Since Damien and Aspen had been together for over ten years, he had a clue on how to make relationships work.

"I'm a potential witness to a major case they're building. A former business partner of mine was arrested, and appears to have ties to certain parties wanted by law enforcement."

Melody finally spoke up. "What does that have to do with being in Sunflower Falls and lying about your name?"

"I don't qualify for witness protection, but everyone involved agreed that it would be better if I disappeared for a while. We had shut down the production I'd been working on, and I didn't have any other pending projects."

Her mouth turning down into a sneer, Melody threw up your hands. "And you're unemployed, too. Just great. My dad's going to love the fact that I got knocked up by a guy who's both someone who can't hold down a job and is a liar."

"I'm not..." And then the rest of her words gut punched him. He reached out and took a step toward her, but she stepped back. "Pregnant? You're pregnant?"

She winced. "Damn it. Damn it. Damn it." Rather than standing there, she stormed out the front.

"Shit. Melody. You promised you'd stay." Libby threw him a worried glare. "What are you standing there for? Go after her."

"She's pregnant?"

"I'm not the one you need to be talking to about this."

The shock finally loosened its hold on his brain, and he ran out the front hoping to catch Melody before she drove away. Her truck remained where it was, nicely pinned in by Zach's vehicle.

But Melody wasn't sitting in the driver's seat cursing them out for blocking her in. He tried to figure out where she'd gone, but the wind had kicked up waves on the lake and the sound of them and the saw Eric was running drowned out pretty much every other sound that would give him a clue of where she may have gone.

He ran to the end of the drive, but didn't see Melody storming back to town on foot. The only place left was his yard leading down to the lake. Backtracking and doing his best to avoid running into construction equipment and supplies, he made his way back there. His worry wasn't that Melody would do anything to harm herself, but he also felt like he could no longer predict what she'd do.

Once he cleared the side wall and the last pile of lumber, he spotted her down by the small beach. Even from this distance, he could see she was vibrating. Whether in anger or something else, he had no clue.

Melody on a good day was someone to approach with caution. A pregnant, distressed Melody? He should probably be wearing a hazmat suit inside of nuclear protective gear.

In all his time of having Zach on staff as his bodyguard,

he'd never felt more in need of his friend's services. Letting his hands hang loose by his legs, he approached where she was pacing.

He got within ten feet of her, and she still hadn't noticed him thanks to the waves and the grassy landscaping. Tears streamed down her face, and he ached to pull her into his arms. She'd never let him comfort her. Never let him see her vulnerabilities.

But he knew they were there. She was protective of her soft core, but he could see how the softness, the caring she had for others gave her the strength she projected to the outside world.

He doubted even Eric saw how wounded Melody was. Some might accuse him of wanting her because she was wounded. He knew Melody absolutely would at this point. But all he saw was a queen who deserved to have a knight at her back. He wondered what she'd say if he commissioned an illustration of a porcupine wearing a crown.

And now she was pregnant.

"Melody."

She jumped and whirled around, her one foot sliding on the sand. He reached out and wrapped an arm around her middle. His palm came to rest on her lower stomach. Where their baby was.

Both of them froze.

"Do you mind?"

Her tone was cutting, but he could hear the tremor. Even over the waves.

Resisting the urge to press a kiss against her temple, he blew out a breath. "Are you steady?"

"Why wouldn't I be?"

"Wet sand. I'm sorry for startling you. That wasn't my intention."

She snorted, and he could hear the disbelief and distrust in the sound. "Intentions mean nothing. Actions and results are what matter."

He felt her hips shift under his hands and he knew she was steady enough. Forcing himself to release her was one of the hardest things he'd done, but giving her the space she needed to feel safe around him was what was most important. "I'm sorry I didn't tell you about who I really am. What's going on in Los Angeles. I couldn't."

"We fucking got married. What the fuck do you mean you couldn't tell me?"

He raked his fingers through his hair. "I'm not supposed to tell anyone. If it gets out that I'm here, then the DA's going to pull me into actual witness protection. It was keep quiet and stay here, or sit in some safe house in Los Angeles for gods know how long."

Even as he said the words, he could see her rebuilding her emotional armor. "I'm not leaving." He scrubbed his hands over his face. "I'm trying not to leave."

She tilted her head. "Guilt finally eating at you for being a lying liar?"

"No. I did what I had to do."

Anger lit her up like a spotlight. "You didn't have to fucking lie to me to get in my pants. You didn't have to do things like play with Button. You didn't have to make me think you cared about how I was feeling. You didn't have to manipulate me into marrying you. And you certainly didn't have to fucking continue lying to me since we did that fucking marriage ceremony in fucking Niagara Falls."

He could feel her slipping away from him. If he lost her completely, there was no way she'd let him near her ever again. He'd have no chance to win her back. "Melody, hear me out. Please. For the baby's sake if nothing else."

She took a giant step back and cradled her stomach with both hands. "Don't you ever use this baby to get your way. Never."

Remembering the bits he'd heard about her and Eric's father over the last couple months, he could kick himself. He still didn't know the entire story, but he knew the guy had been arrested a few times for various con jobs. He held up his hands. "I'm only trying to explain. Please let me explain."

He could see the war inside her of wanting to do some serious damage to him and listening to someone else, probably Ana, and hear him out. He would bet anything Ana had made her promise to find out the full story.

"We can get a divorce, whatever to undo it, but I need you to know the full story. Please, Melody. Please, just hear me out."

"Liars who lie on their marriage licenses don't need divorces." Her reply was automatic, but he could tell she was wavering.

If he was going to do it, he had to throw out the lure now. "You're probably right. But one more bet. I'm willing to bet that once I explain everything I can, tell you everything about who I am, you'll give me a chance to make things right."

He watched as her eyes shifted, her shoulders square off. Hooked. He'd been hoping he'd be able to get through this without betting her, but he knew this was his last chance. He'd bare his soul to her if it meant she'd give him the space and time to make this right.

"What? What would you have to bet with to get me to give you another chance?"

Fear had him taking a deep breath, but he never broke eye contact with her. "If I explain everything, and I mean absolutely everything I can tell you bar the legal shit I can't share because the attorneys have told me not to, and you still refuse to give me another shot, I'll leave town and won't contest custody."

Melody sucked in air. Her hands continued to cradle her stomach. "You'll sign over all rights?"

"Yes. I won't fight you. But if the kid comes and finds me in the future, I will be there. I won't abandon them if they need me."

"They'll never need you."

He could see the tears in her eyes as she said it and he knew she was trying to convince herself of her own lack of need for her father. Without thinking, he reached out to enfold her in his arms, but she stepped out of reach again. The stab in the gut was what he deserved, but he wished she would let herself receive some comfort.

"Start talking."

Remembering what Eric had mentioned after the fundraiser, he started at the beginning. "I grew up in Hollywood. My dad's a producer, and my mom's an actress. When I was in high school, it felt natural to go into the business since I'd spent so much time on sets. I eventually got cast on a show. Undercover Immortal." Melody froze. "My real, legal name is Anthony Dewitt."

"Mother. Fucker."

## A COUPLE MONTHS AGO...

NINA

I hope this is still Vicky Dewitt's phone number. This is Nina Keller.

VICKY

Nina! Darling! So good to hear from you.

NINA

Oh, good. I was so worried I'd be texting a wrong number.

VICKY

I keep telling Leo I can't be bothered to learn any new numbers. God help all of us if I have to.

NINA

I feel the same way.

I was thinking of you because I saw someone who reminded me of your son.

VICKY

Anthony? Too funny.

NINA

Right? Why would your son be spending the summer in Sunflower Falls?

It took me this long to figure out who the man reminded me of.

Anyway, it was nice talking to you. I hope we'll get the chance to see each other again.

VICKY

You're in Sunflower Falls?

NINA

Oh, that's right. I don't think we ever got around to me telling you where in New York I lived.

I'm the manager of the Sunflower Falls motel. I doubt you'll ever find yourself in the area, but I'd love to show you around if you do.

VICKY

You're such a darling. I'll talk to Leo to see what our schedule's like. In the meantime, I'm going to be in New York for a short run show in December. Please come visit. My treat!

NINA

I'll have to see about arranging coverage, but I'll let you know.

MELODY STARED AT HIM. How? How could she have missed it? As soon as he said the name, it was like having the plastic sheeting serving as a window ripped away.

The beard. The matured, heavier features. She finally could see beyond all of them to the young man she'd had a crush on back when she'd been in high school.

She'd spent hours staring at posters of him on her walls dreaming of what life with him would be like. Going to fun parties. Living a bigger life than the one she had in Sunflower Falls where everyone knew everything about her and her family. Living a life where no one knew who her dad was and what he did.

She should have known better.

He was an actor which meant he lied for a living. Just like her dad. Except Tony had found a way to do it legally.

She cringed. Ana. Ana couldn't ever find out. Her best friend had been witness to way too many embarrassing incidents in her quest to meet Tony back then. Including getting her mom to let them take the bus into the city and then they ended up on the wrong bus.

"Melody. Babe?"

The endearment stabbed her in the heart. She'd loved it when he dropped little things like that because she'd honestly thought he'd cared about her. But he was a manipulator. Just like her dad.

Shoring up her defenses, she drew in a deep breath. "What else? You said you'd tell me everything." And she was determined to hear him out and then tell him it wasn't enough. What little credit she could give him was that he'd yet to fail on adhering to the terms of a bet.

He raked his hands through his hair, and she tried not to be attracted to the windblown look. As a young man, he'd been beyond hot in the pretty sort of way men in their early 20s could be. As a full-grown adult, he radiated wicked knowledge to go with his attractiveness. He'd absolutely known how to use that knowledge with her.

Even now, with everything that had happened in the last few days, all she wanted to do was bury her hands in that hair, kiss him senseless, and have him fuck her to oblivion. And beyond the orgasms? The best part about being with him had been lying in his arms afterward.

Talking about their days. Him asking about designs she had in mind for new projects. Tracing whorls in his chest hair. Breathing in the scent of his skin and absorbing the warmth radiating out from him. Feeling as if insulation foam had surrounded all her jagged edges. Protected from the world that wanted to poke at them.

The security she'd felt in those moments had to be an illusion, but she craved them even now.

When they'd first started having sex, she'd always kicked him out of bed before the night was over so she didn't get used to it. She'd been spoiled by their time in Niagara Falls and waking up in his arms almost every morning.

That one day when she'd woken and he'd already been downstairs had gotten her way up into her feels. Since they'd come back, she'd let him stay later and later into the night every time he came over until she was kicking him out as the sky began to lighten with the first hints of morning.

Pushing the chance of someone discovering them as a couple.

Now she was all up in her feels again.

She'd never really contemplated getting pregnant, so she hadn't realized how much the changing hormones could fuck with emotions and the brain. Tony had started talking again, and she did her best to focus on what he was saying.

"...then I caught Robert meeting with someone who I knew he shouldn't be talking to, let alone joking around with."

She held up a hand. "Start over again. I couldn't hear you over the sound of the waves." As soon as she said that, she realized she'd made a tactical error as he moved closer. There wasn't any way she could reasonably backtrack, so she had to endure the sensation of his body within reach. Even over the smell of the lake water, she could smell his cologne. Woodsy and citrusy. Her hands itched to reach out and anchor herself with the feel of his body.

Thankfully, he didn't do anything like push her hair behind her ear like he frequently did because she wasn't sure if she could resist wrapping herself around him. "I said that we caught my business partner Robert on tape trying to extort one of the leads of the film we were producing, and when I followed him to confront him, I saw him meeting with people he shouldn't have been."

That's what she had missed. "I thought you were an actor." Even though she hadn't seen him in anything in years. In fact, when he'd famously quit Undercover Immortal, it was right after what turned out to be the final season had been announced. There had been rumors of drama with the actor who'd been brought on as co-lead and that Anthony, Tony, had quit because he was a diva. She'd assumed he'd done indie movies or the like.

"You're right. I had been an actor. I've been working with my dad for the last ten years."

"Your dad?" And then she remembered. The award-winning producer, Leo Dewitt. And his mom was the even more decorated actress Vittoria Schreiber. This man came from money. She cradled her stomach. If he decided he wanted custody, he could crush her.

Since she'd gotten the positive result on the pregnancy test, she'd given a lot of thought to what she wanted for her future. Becoming a mom hadn't ever really been on her radar, so she'd given serious thought about getting an abortion. Maybe at some other point in her life, it would have been the right decision.

Now? It felt like if she was going to have a kid, this was going to be her one chance. The moment she envisioned her baby opening presents at Christmas, she'd been hooked.

But here was a man who could easily tear those moments away from her. With minimal effort.

Libby.

Libby's specialty was contracts. She'd get Libby to write an airtight contract that he was giving up all parental rights.

Libby would help her protect her baby.

All she had to do was stay strong and tell him she refused to give him another shot.

Which meant she really had to pay attention to what he was saying.

"...they're in Europe right now. Dad's filming, and Mom's shopping and visiting relatives."

"You won't tell them, will you?"

His face was the most serious she'd ever seen. "I will. If you decide to kick me out, that's your decision. I'll make sure they understand and agree to not bother you, but I'm not hiding the fact they have a grandchild out in the world from them."

She rubbed her arms. She could have used another layer, but she hadn't planned on spending much time outside today. "You're close to them?"

"Very." One corner of his mouth kicked up. "Probably didn't help that I was an only child. Mom wanted more, but there were fertility issues. She's been hounding me for grandchildren for the last few years."

A shiver racked her body. She tried to hide it, but she knew he'd seen it when he frowned.

"Can we go inside? Please? You're cold."

Her instinct was to deny and fight, but it was the perfect excuse to hide that it wasn't the cold chilling her from the inside out, but fear.

The thing that even she knew about lawsuits was that the people with the most money usually won because they could drag things out until you went bankrupt from legal fees. And a powerful celebrity family had to have a lot of money.

Yeah, Uncle Stef had some fame and would have a comfortable retirement thanks to his show. But being a grumpy-ass favorite on a decades-old home improvement show was nothing to people who had won multiple gold statuettes.

Being the focus of local gossip the many times her dad had been arrested for some fraud scheme had been bad enough growing up. But a custody battle with Tony and his parents would be plastered all over the national tabloid sites.

As soon as they walked into the house, Libby caught sight of her and rushed over. "Are you okay?"

"Fine." Even she heard the clack of her teeth thanks to the shivering that refused to stop.

Libby looked over at Tony. Who shrugged. "I'm not sure what's going on. I thought she was just a little cold from the wind. We were standing out by the beach."

Melody wasn't sure why Tony's voice sounded like it was echoing through a tunnel, but when a blanket was thrown over her head blocking the light, she embraced the darkness.

---

MURMURS FILLED the air above her. The pillowcase under her cheek was scratchy instead of the silky cover she had on her own at home, but she wanted to go back to sleep. Even if her dreams were on the unhinged side with Tony telling her he'd been her high school TV crush.

Her eyes flew open.

Not a dream.

Reality.

"There you are, honey."

A warm hand brushed her hair off her face. Soft lips pressed a kiss against her forehead.

Mom.

Her mom was here.

Tears leaked from her eyes. Maybe if she kept them closed, she wouldn't have to face reality.

"I'll be back later."

The voice was familiar, but she couldn't place it. She waited until she heard a door close before opening her eyes again. This time, she made out the light beige walls and bland art hanging on it.

Her mom's smile at her was watery, but she patted Melody's hand. "How are you feeling, baby?"

It took her a moment to realize she was in the local urgent care clinic, not in some room at the motel. "Okay. I think? What happened?"

"You fainted. Tony caught you, so you didn't hit your head or anything."

Melody untangled her hand from her mom's and pushed up on the bed. Her brain swam, along with what was in view, but her stomach felt rock solid. "Fainted? I don't faint."

"You did this time. What happened?"

The tone of voice was exactly the same as it had been when her mom had caught her sneaking back into the house hours after curfew when she'd been in high school. It sucked to realize that even when you were a full-grown adult and pregnant, your mom pulling out her patented Mom Voice had you feeling like shit. "Nothing?"

Her mom sat back in her chair, crossed her arms, and tilted her head. "Would you like to try a different answer?"

Melody winced and tried to play it off as a sore hip. But she could tell her mom wasn't buying it.

She shook her head at Melody. "Do I need to bring Tony in here?"

"Why should he be here at all?"

"Because that boy is frantic with worry. He's been pacing in the lobby since the staff brought you back here. I know you like your independence, but you could have told me you were seeing him."

Gods, she really was in trouble because when her mom was truly mad, her enunciation got more precise the longer she talked.

A knock on the door saved her from answering. It was Maeve Geraghty, one of Harry's nieces and the doctor on staff at the clinic. "Can I come in?" It had been Maeve's voice she'd heard earlier.

"Yes. Sure."

Maeve smiled and closed the door behind her. "You've got a worried crew waiting out there."

Melody looked at her mom who cocked an eyebrow at her. "That's what Mom tells me."

Maeve looked down at her tablet. "Now that you're awake, I'd like to do an ultrasound to verify everything's okay with the baby. There wasn't any blood present, and your vitals were normal when you were brought in, but it never hurts to do a quick check."

"Baby?"

Maeve looked up at that question from Melody's mom. "Um..." She tapped the screen. "Sorry, I just got a message from my admin. I'll...uh...I'll be back in a few." With that very confident doctor speak, she fled the room.

Melody wondered if she could pretend to faint again.

"Melody Nikki Keller. What. Baby?"

She flopped back down on the clinic bed and pulled the sheet over her head. Yes, she was hiding from her mom like a little kid. "You're going to be a grandma in about nine months."

"And Tony's the father?"

How? How had her life spiraled so out of control. Her grand plan of getting him to leave town, and then announcing her pregnancy a few months down the road so people would forget who could have been the dad was dead in the water.

Her mom ripped the sheet off her face. "I asked you a question, Melody Nikki Keller."

She rubbed her hands over her face. "Okay, fine. Yes, Tony's the father. Except Tony isn't his real name, and he lied on our marriage license." As soon as the words tumbled from her lips, she realized what she'd revealed. "Shit."

Slowly lowering her hands from her face, she saw her mom looking more furious than she'd ever seen her. Her mom's chest expanded as she drew in a deep breath. When she finally spoke, her words were incredibly precise. "I see. When were you going to tell me this? Any of this?"

The answer she wanted to give—never—was not the correct answer at the moment. Even that penetrated her addled senses. "When I sorted it out. I only just found out on Saturday."

"About the baby?"

"Yes. And Tony."

"I knew I should have pushed when you told me about the coffee tasting off."

It took her a moment, but she finally realized what her mom was referring to. Probably not the best idea to mention that she hadn't been paying attention to what her mom had said.

"Look. He's agreed to sign away all custody rights. Let me get that sorted, and we can move on."

Her mom pinched the bridge of her nose. "Melody. You are an adult. I love you. I will let you make the decisions that are right for you."

She tried for a joke. "Positive affirmations to get you through the day?"

The Mom Glare in addition to Mom Voice. "You are not helping. You may be thirty-one-years-old, but I will not support rash decisions which will affect your child's future." She paused and then reached out for Melody's hand. "That is...are you going forward with the pregnancy? I will support you whatever your decision."

Even when she pissed her mom completely off, the woman still loved her. She entwined her fingers with her mom's and moved their hands to lie on her stomach. "Yeah. I'm going to keep the baby."

Her mom's breathing grew shuddery, but she nodded. "Okay. We'll figure it out. First thing, I need to get Tony."

"Mom. I told you. He lied to me. He's giving up parental rights." Hopefully. She wasn't sure exactly where they stood on that since she'd fainted before she could confirm that was happening.

"We will get to that. But that man is worried about you. He deserves to know that you're awake and okay."

"He's just like Dad."

"Oh, honey." Her mom sat down in the chair next to the bed. "That man is nothing like your father."

"He lied. He manipulated me into marrying him, and then it wasn't even under his legal name."

"I'm not saying that isn't an issue, but I can guarantee you that why he did it didn't come from a place of meanness like your father." She blew out a breath. "I'm thankful to your father because I got you and Eric. I'm only sorry I didn't do a better job of protecting you from his worst tendencies. They were always there, but I always hoped he'd see his own potential. He had you two to be better for, and he had Stef as a role model. But your father always wanted the easy-for-him route."

"I wouldn't have known Tony was lying to me if I hadn't overheard him telling someone about it. He didn't admit it to me directly."

Her mom brushed Melody's hair back from her face again. "The man didn't run. He's stuck around and is facing the consequences. That is something your father has never voluntarily chosen to do. That alone tells me he's a much better man than your father."

Melody turned her head away. Yes, her mom loved her. But her mom had also given her father a stupid amount of chances to fuck them over. It wasn't until he'd gotten into a physical fight with Eric when Melody was fourteen that she'd finally kicked him out of their lives.

But the moment Melody had turned eighteen, he'd come crawling back asking for help.

Her mom sighed. "There's a lot going on. All I ask you is to not make any rash decisions. If Tony truly is a rat, we'll do what we need to so the baby's protected."

Melody bit her lip, not wanting to let the rest of the news slip. Her mom had once met Tony's parents. It would come out eventually, but she couldn't deal with any more arguments on why she should let a known liar into her kid's life.

Her mom pressed a kiss to her temple and then left the room.

A few minutes later, Tony came in. After closing the door, he leaned back against it. His face was haggard, and his hair was a mess.

"The doctor and your mom said you're okay?"

She shrugged. "Mom said I didn't hit my head thanks to you."

"You scared the shit out of me."

"It's not like I planned it."

He scrubbed his face with his hands. "That's not what I said, Melody."

She massaged her chest with her hand. She wasn't supposed to feel bad for him when she was the one who'd been lied to and fainted. How had she been so wrong about him?

"Can I sit down?"

"Sure."

When he did, he rubbed his hands on his knees. "Look. I know what I said earlier about explaining everything and leaving if you heard me out and still didn't want to give me a chance."

She narrowed her eyes at him. "Reneging on the terms of the bet?"

He let out a slow breath. "No. I'm asking for an amendment. Give me one month? I will be completely honest with you. Tell you absolutely everything. Do whatever you need from me to rebuild what trust with you I can. I know I broke what we had been building, but the thought of losing you terrifies me. Losing you means losing half my heart. Please, Melody."

His voice cracked on the last bit. She swallowed. "What about the baby?"

He swallowed. "I don't want to lose the baby either, but the thought of living the rest of my life without you? I'd be a shell of a person."

This was something her father had never done. Whenever he'd come back around after fucking them over, it was always for more money. Or an alibi. All Tony was asking for was time. She rubbed her palm on the sheet. "One month."

He slumped in the seat. "Thank you."

Something else her father had never done. "I'll give you one month. If I'm still not satisfied, you leave and never contact us again."

He held up his hand, pinky finger extended. "Pinky swear?"

Even with the strain she could see in his face, he gave hot puppy dog face. She snorted, but hooked her own pinky in his. "Pinky swear."

THE NEXT DAY...

MELODY

Next Tuesday. 10 AM.

TONY

Is...?

MELODY

First doctor's appointment.

TONY

Okay.

MELODY

Be here by 8 if you want to come with.

TONY

I do. I always want to be there for you.

MELODY

...

See you Tuesday.

TONY

...

You're going to be great, Melody. See you Tuesday.

nine

TONY KNOCKED on Melody's door.

"Just a moment."

Her voice was faint, so she wasn't likely standing on the other side of the door hoping he'd go away. Even though she had been the one to extend the invitation for him to be here. A few moments later, he heard scratching on the other side of the door along with whining. "Button, get back here."

Button yipped in response.

"No, you're not coming with us." Melody's voice grew louder with every word.

Button yipped again. Melody pulled the door open, wet hair hanging down on her shoulders, a wriggling Button in one arm, and a frazzled look on her face. "It's you."

"Expecting someone else?"

She sighed. "No." She held Button out to him. "You got her riled up, so you can calm her down. We need to leave in five minutes."

Once he had Button in his arms, Melody let go and raced back upstairs. She didn't give him a chance to hand her the box he'd bought for her, so he set the bag down on the low table she had in front of her couch.

A minute later, he heard a blow dryer turn on. He held Button up so he could look her in the eye. "It's you and me, dollface."

Button licked his nose.

He grinned and set her down on the floor. "What do you want to do?"

Button raced for a pile of toys over in a corner, rooted through them, and brought back a thick length of rope with frayed edges. She sat and dropped it at his feet.

"Tug. Excellent choice."

He squatted down and grabbed one knotted end of the rope. Once he had a good grip on it, he grinned at Button and gave the command. "Play."

She viciously attacked her end. Within seconds, he realized that Button had gained strength since he'd last played with her. He braced his free hand on the floor and tried to shift his feet, but Button took advantage of his moment of imbalance and yanked on the rope with a twist of her head.

Tony laughed as he toppled to the ground and lost his grip on the rope. Button shook the rope some more in victory, but then dropped it in favor of pouncing on him and licking his face.

That was how Melody found them when she came back down. "You were supposed to calm her down. How am I going to get her in the crate without a fight?"

"Not fight with her? We can bring her with us."

She rolled her eyes at him. "This isn't California. The only doctor offices which allow regular pets are vet offices. You can put her in her crate. Libby will be by in a couple hours to pick her up."

Tony stroked the soft fur between Button's shoulder

blades. If dogs could have blissed out expressions, Button had it. "What about your mom? Don't you usually leave Button with her for the day?"

"Yes, but Mom's got her own appointments today. Eric's on site today, and Libby's got some video meetings this morning which means she can't have Button getting Mayzie all hyped up. Button will be fine in her crate until Libby comes by." She held out her wrist and tapped her watch face. "We're going to be late."

"Fine." He pushed off the floor and carried Button upstairs. The growing puppy huffed her displeasure into his neck, but didn't squirm out of his arms. Probably good practice for carrying a baby around. Provided Melody accepted him back into her life.

When he came back downstairs, he picked up the bag from Mrs. Smith and held it out to Melody. "Delayed delivery."

Her brow furrowed, but she took the bag. "Of what?"

"The box from Mrs. Smith."

Her gaze jerked up to meet his. "The box? I'd forgotten about this."

"Mrs. Smith didn't. She intercepted me when I was leaving the fundraiser. Then I forgot it as well."

She was quiet for a few moments, one hand stroking the top of the box through the bag. Eventually she nodded and set it back down on the table. "Thank you. We should get going."

Melody was driving, so they got settled into her truck. He waited until she'd backed out of the driveway before turning to her. "I ordered some things."

She glanced at him. "I should care, why?"

"Because they're going to be delivered to your house, to your attention."

"I'm not a courier service, Caputo. Or should I say Dewitt?"

There was a bite in her tone, but at least she hadn't kicked him out of a moving vehicle. "Stick with Caputo for now. No one else in town knows who I am, and both Zach and my attorney want it kept that way. And the items aren't for me. They're for you."

He watched as her grip on the steering wheel tightened, but she kept her eyes on the road. "Trying to buy me off?"

"No. Just trying to make your life a little easier. My attorney and his wife have a couple kids. I asked him to find out what she liked when she was pregnant."

"Your attorney knows I'm pregnant?"

Her tone was tight, which meant she was keeping her temper barely leashed. Between Melody and Damien, he'd be lucky to survive until the case against Robert came to trial. Neither was happy with him, and Damien had been especially pissed when he'd been told the news. "This isn't something I could keep from him. Whatever your decision regarding custody, I'll make sure he knows I want you and the baby fully supported. You won't have to worry about anything."

"I can care for my kid. On my own."

He watched the main strip of Sunflower Falls go by as he picked his words carefully. "You absolutely can. But I can provide a solid base so you're never spending extra energy worrying about finances. If you don't want me in the baby's life, I want to help ease at least the money burden of making their life as full as possible. I don't want you ever worrying you'll never have enough money for their activity of choice or if they need additional educational support."

Melody remained silent until they were past town limits. The doctor she'd chosen for the pregnancy was a good hour away from Sunflower Falls. He didn't like how far away it was in case anything happened, but he also knew better than to argue with her decisions regarding her own health care.

"What kinds of boxes should I be expecting?"

"I'm not sure, but Aspen recommended a particular brand of peppermint tea for when she got queasy. And since winter's coming up, she also recommended this fuzzy heated blanket for when you wanted to just chill out on your couch."

Melody nodded, but kept her attention on the road. A few miles down, she flicked a glance at him. "No furniture?"

"No. I have no clue what you'd want, and I also would consult with you first on that large of a purchase." Mainly because while he had the feeling she'd accept things like specialty tea and cozy blankets, she'd find a way to chuck a piece of furniture she hadn't asked for at his head.

Melody kept conversation to a minimum for the rest of the drive, so Tony let his mind wander to what other helpful things he could get past Melody's guard.

The practice's office was brightly lit and filled with soothing blues, greens, and yellows. There were even a few containers of fresh yellow mums strategically placed in the room. Melody checked in and the clerk gave her intake forms to work on. Tony sat next to her as she did so, surveying the others with them in the waiting room. There was one other couple together, but every other person in there was in a more advanced stage of pregnancy and seemingly there on their own.

He and Melody only had to wait maybe five minutes after she turned in the forms before they were called back and placed in an exam room.

The physician's assistant ran through the initial exams

such as weight, height, blood pressure, and had Melody go to the bathroom and take another pregnancy test.

Twenty minutes later, the doctor came in. They appeared to be around his age and wore their hair close-cropped with makeup that highlighted their features.

They first greeted Melody. "Welcome to our practice. I'm Dr. Kelsey Naylor. I prefer she/they."

Melody blinked for a moment, then smiled. "Melody Keller. She/her. This is...Tony."

He smiled at the doctor and held out his hand. "He/him."

Dr. Naylor raised their eyebrows. "Partner?"

Tony watched Melody struggle with how to answer, but it needed to be her choice, so he kept his mouth closed. Finally she let out a sigh. "Father of the baby at the very least."

Dr. Naylor nodded and left it at that. "And are you comfortable with him being here? Tony can sit in our waiting room if you choose."

"It's fine."

"Okay." The doctor began running down the information Melody had provided on the forms. When they got to the point regarding birth control, Melody made a face.

"We always used condoms, and I was on birth control."

Tony cleared his throat as he thought back to the hotel room in Niagara Falls. Both Melody and Dr. Naylor looked at him. "There was that one time?"

Melody frowned. "What one time? You've never gotten in here without a condom on." She used both hands to point to her pelvic area.

All Dr. Naylor did was rub their hand over their mouth. Tony had the impression they were trying to hide a smile.

"No, but I came on you right above that area."

"That's still not in me."

Dr. Naylor coughed. "Yes, well. As they say in the classic dinosaur movie, life finds a way. You are pregnant, and based on the information provided, you're likely six or so weeks along. This is typically the earliest you'd notice if you weren't trying."

Melody snorted at that, but shook her head when Dr. Naylor glanced at her.

"But I got my period. I thought those stopped when you got pregnant."

Dr. Naylor nodded. "You'd be surprised how many people continue to menstruate after becoming pregnant." They made a note on the forms and continued on. "The first ultrasound to confirm the fetus's age is generally around eight weeks, so I'll have our staff arrange an appointment for you in two weeks when you check out today."

Dr. Naylor then went over a proposed care plan with Melody. Tony kept quiet other than to answer the question regarding if he planned on being with Melody for appointments.

"I plan to for as long as she'll have me and my schedule allows. I may need to return to California for some projects I have in the works there."

He caught Melody's side eye when he described the case as projects, but Dr. Naylor didn't need to know anything beyond his schedule as he knew it. They made another note in Melody's file and continued on.

Once Melody had asked all her questions and had them answered to her satisfaction, Dr. Naylor stood and shook their hands. "Again, welcome to our practice. Feel free to call us at any point. My partners and I rotate on call for non-emergency questions, and it's never the same person who's on call for emergencies. Since you're over in

Sunflower Falls, definitely call 911 first if you have an emergency. The faster you receive care, the better."

Melody nodded. "Will do. And you're sure I can work on site?"

Dr. Naylor grinned. "I'm positive. Just stay away from the areas where chemicals are being used, even when it's well-ventilated. When you get to five months, we'll discuss again to see how you're feeling in your body."

Melody nodded. "And next appointment is the ultrasound?"

"Yes. We'll schedule the next in-office appointment to be the same week so we can go over the results, but you'll be able to get your baby's first photo at the ultrasound itself." Dr. Naylor winked at them. "Just watch out for the ultrasound staff trying to sell you the glam effects package."

That got Melody to laugh, which had his gut heating. He wanted to be the one making her laugh like that. It was her laughter that had first attracted him, and every time she laughed near him, he was like Pavlov's dog.

When they were back out at her truck, he did a quick check of what was in the area on his phone's map function. Finding what he was looking for only a couple miles away, he glanced over at Melody. "Do you mind if we head over to the store? I need to pick up a few things, and we can get some of those items Dr. Naylor recommended."

Her expression gave nothing away, and as she'd put on her sunglasses, he couldn't read her eyes. "Target? Sure. Anywhere else?"

The fact she was even offering to take him around and not dumping him back on Zach was a good sign. Right? "I don't think so."

Ten minutes later, he grabbed a cart and offered to buy

her something from the coffee stand. She took him up on a bottle of water, and he counted it as another win. As they began wandering the aisles, he felt himself relax even more.

This was one of the small pleasures he never took for granted. Back when he'd been on the show, he'd been well-known enough that anytime he'd stepped foot into any store, he'd either been accosted by fans or photographed while inspecting medications for athlete's foot or something equally not anyone else's business.

The temptation to reach out and take hold of Melody's hand ate at him. That wasn't a level of contact she'd be open to now. But he could let a little corner of his mind imagine that instead of still being at odds, they were happy together. And even more happy to be on a mini date after the first doctor's appointment for the pregnancy.

Holding hands as he guided the cart around the store. Sneaking kisses. Some with a bit of tongue. Him pointing out the sexy lingerie for her and matching silk boxers for him. Her rolling her eyes at him, but a sparkle in her eyes.

When Melody stopped for a moment to examine a display of maternity tops, he looked around. This early in the day, the store was close to empty, but there were more than enough people wandering around the aisles.

He took the chance. "Are you mad?"

"Hmmmm...what was that?"

He moved a little closer so he could lower his voice when he spotted a man with two small kids in a cart coming down the aisle toward them. "I was wondering if you were mad."

This time, her attention lasered in on him. She cocked an eyebrow. "About what? There are so many options."

"About the baby."

Her expression immediately softened. "Oh." She turned

back to the display and reached out to finger one sleeve. He wondered if she was going to answer him at all. The man with the kids caught his eye as they passed, and he did a little head bob in Melody's direction and grinned. Tony lifted a hand and smiled back.

Finally, Melody let out a sigh. "I'm not mad about the baby. Not exactly." She dropped the sleeve and walked around him. He followed with the cart. "I am mad that you lied to me. I'm sad I can't be more excited about the baby coming because of that. I'm pissed at my dad for being such a conniving bastard that I'm having a hard time getting over you lying to me."

She went silent at that, and after they passed another section of the store, Tony reached out and lightly rubbed her arm before letting go. "I'm sorry I didn't find a way to tell you sooner. You're right. I should have found a way."

Melody didn't look at him, but lifted one shoulder. "You should have. And I appreciate you apologizing again. As much as I don't want to give you any credit at all, I get why you were lying in the first place. Rationally, I get it. But feelings aren't rational. You're not my dad, but..."

After Melody had been released from the urgent care clinic, he'd gone over to her house and explained everything. Her mom had been there, too. If it hadn't been for Nina, he didn't think he'd have been able to get through to Melody. It was also Nina who had suggested that he accompany Melody for the first visit to the doctor. For the rest of his life, he'd make sure Nina had absolutely everything she ever desired just for helping him have the opportunity to repair his relationship with Melody.

"I understand. Like I said, I can't promise to always be here because of the case, but I will be here as long as I can. And if I have to leave, I will come back." He watched as

Melody poked through the display of graphic onesies. "I'd also love it if you came out to LA with me at some point."

She glanced at him. "For the case?"

"No. Just to see where I live."

"Why?"

He leaned his forearms against the cart's handle. "I know we can't go back to the way we were before you found out. That wasn't solid ground. But, I'd like the opportunity to build a new foundation with you." He nodded at the onesies. "Even if it's only for the baby's sake."

She was quiet for a moment. "I'll think about it."

He let out a low breath when she turned back to the onesies. She hadn't rejected him outright. Which meant he had a chance to convince her. Standing back up, the design on a onesie caught his eye, and he laughed.

Melody looked back at him. "What?"

He pointed at the display of Halloween-themed onesies. "That one."

It took her a moment to spot the one he meant, but when she did, a slow grin formed on her face and she laughed, too. "Too bad they don't have a daddy and baby matching set."

A warm glow built in his chest as he went over to the display. He did the mental math and plucked three size options of the one with bloody vampire teeth and script below them that said "Red's My Favorite Candy" from the display and threw them in the cart. "For next year."

She cocked an eyebrow at him. "Turning your kid into Undercover Immortal, the Return?"

He locked his gaze on her eyes. "Gotta watch out for us vampires. We'll always find a way to win your heart."

*texts*

MELODY

I need help.

ANA

Always.

With what?

I'm assuming it's not heavy lifting because
you call Eric for that.

...

Melody?

Mel?

MELODY!!!

MELODY

Chill. Button got into the garbage.

ANA

Oh.

Did she eat anything?

I thought you put a baby lock or something on the can?

MELODY

Are you okay?

ANA

I'll be fine. You wanted help?

MELODY

Yeah. It's weird.

ANA

:gif of Carrie Bradshaw blinking fast:

Try me.

MELODY

Tony sent me some things.

ANA

Oooookay.

What things?

Sexy things?

MELODY

NO!!

Comfy things. Expensive things.

ANA

DIAMONDS?!?!?!

MELODY

NO!!!!!

Comfy things which are also expensive. I looked them up online.

ANA

I'm not seeing a problem?

MELODY

Do I need to reciprocate?

ANA

I'm coming over.

MELODY

Why?

ANA

Because I need to test these things out if you're asking if you need to reciprocate so I can tell you the level you need to reciprocate with :grinning devil emoji:

MELODY

Just tell me if a verbal thank you is enough or if I need to send him a card or something.

ANA

Can't hear you. Getting in my car. See you in a few.

MELODY

The hell?

ANA

# *ten*

AFTER DROPPING Button off with her mom a couple days later, Melody drove down the main road of Sunflower Falls. She stopped in at the diner and picked up her take out order of a breakfast sandwich.

Nancy herself walked the order out from the kitchen. Standing a good six inches taller than Melody with shoulders broader than Eric's and craggy features, Nancy was an intimidating figure. Her hair was pulled back into a neat bun under her hairnet. She handed over the bag and looked Melody up and down. "You doing okay?"

"Yeah. Thanks for letting me do take out."

Crossing her arms against her chest, Nancy frowned. Her voice, when she spoke, was a comforting rumble. "Your mom and Ana are worried about you. You need anything, you let me know. I haven't seen your dad around, but if I do, I'll kick his ass back out of town."

Melody laughed. "Thanks. I haven't seen Dad in a couple months."

Nancy grunted. "You let me know. You and Eric do good

work here. Can't have you running off thinking we don't appreciate that."

Touched, Melody leaned in and gave Nancy a quick hug. She'd been one of the most solid, supportive people Melody had known. Nancy shifted and patted Melody's back. "Get going. Can't let anyone else's food burn while I'm out here jabbering with you."

Melody headed back out and drove down to the beach. She had a little bit of time before Eric and the crew expected her on the site, and she wanted to enjoy her breakfast sandwich and do some thinking.

Being around a part of Tony brought up feelings. Ones she wasn't ready yet to deal with as she still needed to sort through the feelings brought up at the doctor's appointment and subsequent shopping trip.

She parked at the beach, grabbed a work blanket and her breakfast, and headed for the sand. Some people were out exercising, or walking their dogs, but other than a few waves, everyone left her alone.

Once she got settled, she took a large bite of her sandwich as she watched the waves roll in.

It soothed the part of her that still felt rocked by the other day. The experience had awakened the bloom of hope in the deepest part of her soul that being with Tony had nurtured before the lie was revealed. Every time he'd been over since they got back from Niagara and he'd had his shirt off or undone, she'd gotten a thrill at seeing the ring she'd placed on his finger hanging from a chain.

One night she'd been playing with it after sex and asked him about it.

"Simple. This ring is your claim on me. The marriage is secret, but I keep your claim close to my heart."

When she'd overheard him that day at Geraghty's, she'd thought the bloom had died like the hope she'd once held of having a father who actually loved her. But it was still there, sturdier than it had initially appeared, but a bit withered.

If she nurtured it again, and something else happened, she didn't know if she could be the person she had to be for Peanut. She didn't want her baby to have a broken parent for a mother, but this fear had deep roots.

She also couldn't deny that she still had feelings for Tony. Warm, positive, sexy feelings. It was so hard to reconcile the man who made realize she could be a better person, a man she could still see, and the one who'd knowingly lied to her.

The alarm on her phone chimed, so she quickly finished her sandwich and headed back to her truck.

Once she was at the job site and out of the truck, she drew in a deep breath of air scented with lake water and fresh sawn lumber and drywall. This was home. Her foundation.

Eric had parked his truck up against what would be the house's front entrance. The decking was simple in design as Tony wanted the back deck and patio to be the main gathering area, but this would still be an enjoyable area for a morning coffee.

It had taken some doing—and money—to get the house that had previously stood on this property cleared. They'd been lucky in that, because of the lot's location, there was no basement or cellar space to also clear. The existing foundation slab had been easy to rip up and truck out.

They'd also been lucky with the timing of when they'd poured a new slab to fit the new house's configuration. The weather had cooperated, and they'd been able to let it cure for three whole weeks. A full month would have been ideal, but with needing to get the exterior framing up and closed in before the onset of winter, they needed to squeeze the schedule where they could.

When she heard her name called from the roof, she looked up and spotted Mike and Patty, the primary roofers on their crew. She waved. "Eric up with you?"

"Down in the house. I already beat his ass for the Halloween party pick." Mike grinned down at her.

"Fuck."

"That's what I said, too." Patty flipped Mike the bird when he did a little happy dance.

"I'll leave you to it. Patty, don't throw him off. We don't need the insurance company upping our rates."

Patty let out a sigh loud enough to be heard over all the other work the crew was doing. "Fine. If you insist. Good thing I like his wife and don't want to make her a widow."

Mike did another mini dance. "Malort for everyone."

Melody rolled her eyes and headed inside. At least she had the perfect excuse to get out of drinking Mike's disgusting favorite liquor from his hometown.

How Chicago had gotten a reputation as a food destination, she had no clue. Besides deciding that bread pie covered in sauce and cheese constituted the ultimate in pizza, they also had to inflict the worst tasting liquor ever on the world.

After making sure her hard hat was firmly situated on her head, she went inside. Eric was standing over a table with blueprints unrolled and held down with a hammer and a tape measure on the loose ends.

She dropped her work bag on the floor next to him. Her brother just continued to stand with his arms crossed against his chest and study the prints.

"How could you let Mike win?"

"Libby called."

"She knows better than to call during the first day of roofing."

He finally looked over at her. "There's an offer on the table."

Melody frowned. "Offer of what?"

"Our own show. Greer's got some family issue going on, or she would have been the one to call."

She drew in a deep breath through her nose, and let it back out through her mouth. Back in August, while Libby was still down in the city dealing with her father's shit, she and Eric had filmed a concept reel for Greer, their media agent and Libby's business partner, to send out.

It helped that she and Eric had both appeared as guests on Uncle Stef's shows more than a few times, but they'd been wanting to bring more focus to helping revitalize small towns by doing a mix of a single, season-long house rebuild, as well as highlighting the work being done in Sunflower Falls and other small towns they'd research.

"Who offered?"

"Triple H for one of their streaming networks."

Home, Hearth, and Holidays was Big. In addition to the multiple cable networks they'd built up, they'd been expanding into the streaming market with even more niche networks. "Does Uncle Stef know?"

Eric pulled at his lip. "Not yet. I wanted to tell you first."

Melody looked around. While most of their crew was on site today, they were spread out in other areas of the house. The electrician was also due in today to finish installing the last of the outlets. She'd likely be here any minute.

But for now, it was just the two of them. Melody placed

a hand on her lower stomach. "How does this affect things?"

Eric shrugged. "It doesn't have to. We either do this together or not at all." He slung an arm around her shoulders and pulled her in tight to his body. "You know I'll support you all the way. What's most important to me is that you and the nibling stay healthy and safe."

Melody leaned into him and let her head rest on his shoulder. Eric had always worked to protect her from the worst of their dad's shit. He hadn't always been successful, but he'd tried. "You're a good brother."

He leaned back and looked down at her. Then put the back of one of his hands on her forehead. "I didn't hear sarcasm in there. Are you running a fever?"

She snorted and pushed him back. "Fine, I won't be nice to you ever again."

"There's the baby sister I know and love."

"I'm over thirty, and I'm about to become a mom myself."

"Not for another nine months, and I don't care how many kids you have. You'll always be my baby sister."

She stuck her tongue out at him, and then evaded the punch he aimed toward her shoulder. "What's on the agenda for today?"

Eric ran down the checklist for the day and then flipped to the part of the plans focusing on the top floor. "Tony called yesterday to see if we could adjust the plan for the bathrooms upstairs."

"What about them? I've got the tile guy coming in later this week to do the final measurements so we can order everything."

"He wants the shower in the secondary bathroom changed to a tub situation."

"What? Like one in the primary? There's not enough space for a free-standing tub in there. That's why we're putting in the shower." And it was a nice shower with lots of fancy jets and a rain shower head. She'd had fantasies about the configuration.

"Not free-standing. A typical, but nicer tub. He said he wanted the house to be more family-friendly."

Melody's eyes narrowed. "Family-friendly?"

Eric glared right back at her. "Don't take that tone with me. I don't know what's going on with you two at the moment, but he didn't say anything about you. For all we know, he's decided to change how to market this as a rental. And you know damn well that having a full tub in the secondary will make this more marketable to families looking to rent in the area."

"They can use the free-standing tub."

Eric got that "you're irritating me" look on his face that he always got when she chose to be stubborn about something that made sense except for her having a grudge against someone. "Pretend to be you from the future. Do you want to be bending over the wall of a free-standing tub in order to give your kid a bath?"

She hated it when he used logic against her. Why couldn't she ever just hold her grudges tight and ride them out? She poked at his chest. "You're irritating me."

"We're even then. Answer the question."

She wrinkled her nose. "How hard can it be?"

Eric looked up at the ceiling. "Why?"

"No one up there to answer you." Melody hip checked him out of her way so she could look closer at the plans. She pointed to the area where the shower was sketched in. "We could get a standard sized tub. It won't be as deep as the shower, but it should fit length-wise. If anything, we might need to build a small bump out to make up the difference, but that could be used as a storage shelf for whatever he'd want to keep in the shower."

"Yeah. I wanted to run it by you first before I confirmed with him it was possible. I asked him if he had a specific style in mind, and he said he was fine with whatever you picked out since you know the style he's going for."

Melody chewed on her nail. "Okay if I go home and trawl through the design catalogs?"

"Go for it. Don't forget that we're meeting at Geraghty's at five."

"Do I have to?"

"And you wonder why I constantly refer to you as my baby sister."

Melody stuck her tongue out at him, but knew she was pushing it. Tony had been the one to organize the meeting at Geraghty's and had made it clear it was a group thing, not an under-the-table date with her. He was making an effort. She had to give him that, even if it went against her nature to do so.

"I'll be there. Do you need me to do anything at the office?"

"Need to, no. But if you want to head over there, go right ahead. Libby said it was time for us to hire a part-time office assistant as she couldn't give us any time right now."

"It's your bad filing habits she's talking about. I keep my space in pristine condition."

Eric just grunted. "Get on out of here."

Melody grabbed her work bag and headed out. The crisp fall day was calling. She could go home and sit on her deck while she perused the design catalogs. If she went into the office, she'd be tempted to do other things. Like organize Eric's desk.

Decision made, she swung by the motel to retrieve Button even though she'd dropped her off not even an hour ago. Her mom was surprised, but was busy with guests checking out, so Melody was able to get Button without argument or explanation.

Back home, she grabbed her laptop and the latest catalogs from their main suppliers. The paper catalogs were anachronistic, but sometimes were better for her thinking process.

She flipped through a few and tagged possibilities.

Around lunchtime, she got a text from Ana.

ANA

You going to Geraghty's tonight?

MELODY

Yes. You knew this.

ANA

...

Mom's acting up.

MELODY

Need me to come over? Pretend we're going out to sleep with random guys?

ANA

This isn't high school. I'm an adult and allowed to sleep with any random guys I want to.

Melody snorted. Ana had never slept with a random guy. As much as Melody had encouraged it, that had never been her best friend's way.

MELODY

Sure. What's Helen going on about now?

ANA

I have no clue. She's been in a spiral since
Jillian announced she and Frank were
getting divorced.

Ana's oldest sister Jillian had been a near mythical figure in their house growing up. She'd been an only child until their brother had shown up when she was ten. Five years after Hank, Bethie had arrived with Ana following a year later. Jillian had gone off to college when Ana'd been a toddler and treated them more like distant cousins than her younger siblings. Melody had only vague memories of Jillian because she'd been around so rarely.

MELODY

Her perfect child is no longer perfect?

ANA

Jillian's only failure prior to the divorce was
in not giving our mother picture perfect
grandchildren. Probably for the best,
though, with the divorce.

Floating dots appeared a few more times, but Ana never came back. Melody let it go as she didn't particularly care one way or the other about Jillian. Ana did, but Ana's family, other than Bethie, was fucked up.

After eating some lunch, she dove back into the catalogs. She got another hour in before her phone blew up again with texts. This time from Libby.

LIBBY

I need you to come over.

Eric's still over at Tony's, and I need help.

Now.

Frowning, Melody grabbed her phone and got Button into her harness. She thumbed out a response as she opened the driver's side door of her truck and got Button hooked up into the puppy restraint system.

MELODY

Should I be calling emergency services?

Libby typically had her head screwed on straight, so if emergency services really were needed, she'd call them instead of texting Melody. But it never hurt to check.

LIBBY

No.

That was it.

Trying not to get freaked out over why Libby needed her help, but refused to tell her why, Melody drove the few blocks over to Eric's house.

Libby's car wasn't parked in the driveway as it usually was.

MELODY

I'm here, but I don't see your car.

LIBBY

...

Office

Of course. Melody blew out a breath and then turned her truck around to head downtown. She parked next to Libby's car behind their office space. Button recognized where they were at and was wriggling as Melody unhooked her.

Once they were out of the truck, Button strained at her

lead to get into the office. She probably smelled Mayzie in there.

It took a couple moments for Melody's eyes to adjust to the lower light of the office. As soon as they had, she froze in the act of unhooking Button from her lead.

Libby sat at Eric's desk with a gorgeous woman sitting across from her. Mayzie was in the pen area they'd left up after the rest of Button's littermates had been given over to the veterinarian's office to arrange their adoptions. Two young kids, a boy and a girl, were sitting on the other side of the fencing watching Mayzie chew on one of her toys.

"Uh, hi." She picked Button up. Her dog was not happy with not being able to play with either the kids or Mayzie. As they passed the pen, Melody saw Mayzie's eyes track them and she swore Mayzie let out a relieved huff when Melody kept Button in her arms rather than setting her down into the pen.

The strange woman grinned. "Hello. You must be Melody. I've heard...some things about you. Not enough. I'll have to ream out Anthony next time I see him. Libby was telling me about what you and your brother do. It's so fascinating. I looked up some episodes of your uncle's show on the way out."

"Mom. Breathe."

Melody looked behind her and saw the kids hadn't taken their attention away from Mayzie. But one of them had called their mother out, who was indeed taking a deep breath.

"Sorry. Sorry. I'm just so excited. It's been forever since Anthony talked about any woman, and now..." She froze. Her eyes jumped between Melody and Libby. "Sorry. My mouth sometimes gets away from my brain."

Weirdly, this strange woman kind of reminded Melody

of Ana. Kind, but overly enthusiastic when something caught her attention. "You're a friend of Tony's?"

She grinned and nodded. "From California. We used to work together."

Melody's brows rose, and she saw Libby's quick glance out of the corner of her eye. Shifting Button to her other side, she held out her hand. "Melody Keller."

The woman shook her hand. "I can be so scatter-brained. Aspen Brandon. And those are my kids, Hannah and Kieran."

"Nice to meet you...Aspen? Wait a minute." The way the light coming in from the plate-glass windows looking out onto the street hit her face and the angle of Aspen's grin struck a memory. "You're Lily Whitting."

Aspen grinned. "I am! And my husband is Anthony's attorney. He finally let me bring the kids out to find out who Anthony's hiding from him."

Melody's stomach dropped. If Tony's attorney was interested in her, and sent his wife who knew Melody was pregnant, then nothing good could be happening. Even if his wife was a freaking award-winning actress.

# *texts*

LIBBY

You will never believe who I met today.

GREER

Please tell me someone fun.

Also fuck my family.

LIBBY

Awww. HUGS.

I know you love your family.

GREER

Not when they're being assholes.

LIBBY

Is your cousin at least there?

GREER

No, she's at work. But Auntie Hetta's
arrived.

LIBBY

Did you call her auntie?

GREER

Bet your ass I did. Her latest boy toy's with her and she tried to make like she's a barely older-than-me cousin and not my mom's older sister.

Forget my family. Who did you meet?

LIBBY

You cannot breathe a word. Not one.

GREER

Give me a moment.

Okay. In the bathroom away from my family. Go.

LIBBY

Lily Whitting!!!!

GREER

You're shitting me.

How the fuck did you meet Lily Whitting?

LIBBY

I can't tell you.

GREER

Excuse me? We're business partners. Best friends. You can tell me anything.

LIBBY

…

I can't with this. Seriously. Not yet. As soon as I can, I will. But she came to Sunflower Falls. And I met Lily Whitting!!!

GREER

As soon as Nonna's out of surgery and I know she's okay, I'm coming up there, getting you drunk, and making you spill everything.

**LIBBY**

Eric will protect me.

**GREER**

😂😂😂

**LIBBY**

Seriously, though, keep me updated about Nonna.

**GREER**

Will do. Snuggles to my best girl Mayzie because I know she would never leave me hanging with how SHE met Lily Whitting!

# eleven

TONY SCANNED the parking lot as Zach parked his SUV outside of Geraghty's. He spotted both Eric and Melody's trucks near the back of the lot. Even recognized Ana's little sedan. They were the last ones here thanks to a call he'd gotten from the DA's office.

"You know you have to tell her."

"Not yet. I want to have tonight with her."

Zach rubbed the back of his neck. "Why do you keep trying to put things off?"

Tony snorted. "Maybe I'm an optimist thinking everything will just work out if I avoid the hard stuff?"

Zach pinned him with a glare. "Seriously, man. I've never known you to put things off like this. When you caught Robert, we were meeting with the cops and DA's office within forty-eight hours."

Tony let his head fall back against the headrest and stared at the car parked across from them. "I told her not even a week ago that I had at least a month to be here with her. If I leave now..." He cleared his throat as something had gotten stuck. "If I leave now, I don't know that she'll ever let me back in. She's giving me space to make it up to her, but it's because of her mom. And probably Ana. I can't lose her, Zach."

"Then let her know that. Be honest with her."

Tony snorted again. "Being honest with her is one thing. Her believing me is a whole other thing."

"Come on. We'll get you a burger and a beer, and you'll figure it out."

As they were walking in, a text notification beep came from his phone. Tony looked down and read the text from Damien. Swore. And realized Zach was also swearing.

He looked up and tracked Zach's line of sight to where Aspen was sitting with Eric and Libby, Melody, and Ana. The kids were racing around the pool table, rolling a couple balls into the middle of the table.

The rest of tonight's diners at Geraghty's ignored what was going on. Kids horsing around were a regular occurrence this time of day, but it was like no one recognized Aspen. Admittedly, she'd dressed in a graphic t-shirt advertising a beloved hot sauce and jeans, and had her hair pulled back into a ponytail. But the woman still radiated charisma.

How anyone missed the fact there was an award-winning actress, one who routinely showed up in the tabloids whenever she left the sanctuary of her home, he couldn't figure out.

Aspen spotted them and waved. Hannah saw what her mom was doing and looked over. "Uncle Anthony!"

She had her mom's lungs and projection skills.

Zach rubbed his hand over his face. "I'm going to kill Damien."

Both Hannah and Kieran ran over, and Tony crouched down to pick them up in his arms. They kept getting bigger every time he saw them. Everyone said kids grew like weeds. He swallowed down the thought of seeing his own kid so infrequently that he noticed how much they'd grown every time he saw them.

"Hey guys. What are you doing here?"

Hannah's expression clearly communicated how tired she was of dealing with mortals. "To bring you home. At least that's what Daddy says. Mom says we're here to scope out your love life and get you back on track."

Off to his side, Zach tried to cover a snort with a coughing fit.

"I promised Daddy to keep Hannah from getting arrested."

Tony glanced down at Kieran. "Really?"

"Yep. He says that Mommy can handle things, but I think Hannah still needs a reminder."

Hannah rolled her eyes and pushed away from Tony. He set her down, and she stomped over where Aspen waited with her arms held out. Tony shook his head and then looked back at Kieran. "You know, bud, sometimes we're not supposed to let the women in our lives know we're watching out for them because they can handle themselves just fine."

Kieran shrugged. "Daddy said the same thing, but if Hannah knows I'm watching, she tries better."

Tony swallowed his own snort and set Kieran down. The little guy reached for his hand, so he let his fingers twine with Kieran's as the kid skipped over to where everyone waited for them. Including Harry.

"What's everyone having?"

Aspen looked up. "Do you have a kids' menu?"

"Kids' menu is chicken tenders or a burger with ketchup only. Both come with fries."

Aspen grinned. "Can we have one burger without the ketchup and an order of the chicken tenders?"

Harry nodded. "What do you want?"

Aspen looked around at them. "Anthony?"

"She'll have the same as me."

Harry nodded again. "Everyone else good with the usual?"

Everyone chimed in with yeses, and Harry headed back to the bar to put in the order. Aspen grinned at him. "This is so fascinating. I love it."

Tony let his frustration bleed through. "I've been to your cabin. There are a few places like this in that town."

Aspen's grin widened. "But this place is on a lake. Not up in the mountains."

He grabbed the open chair next to Melody and sat down. Feeling the brush of her leg against his as she shifted in her seat soothed the anxiety he was feeling. One day, he wanted to walk into a situation like this and pull her into his lap for all the world to see. "What are you really doing here, Aspen?"

His friend's eyes twinkled. "I figured I'd take the kids on a little adventure, and find out more about the place you've been staying."

Getting into a fight with Aspen was always a losing proposition. Mainly because she never fought back. She didn't consider fighting worth her time, so she didn't do it. She just steamrolled over you if she thought it was in your best interests.

He looked over at Melody who had one eyebrow cocked at him. "Having fun?"

She nodded. "Aspen's been very informative."

He looked between the two women and covered his face. "Shit."

Aspen leaned in. "It could be worse. I could have been your parents."

Cold settled into his gut. "You haven't been in touch with them, have you?"

Melody shifted next to him and he glanced over at her to see her brows raised.

Aspen shook her head. "It's been a couple weeks since I talked with your mom. The last time I talked with her, she was taking a day trip up to Milan to talk with a few designers."

Tony gave a silent prayer of thanks. If his parents showed up, he wasn't sure what they'd try to do in the interests of "helping out". He didn't want Melody feeling overwhelmed because he damn well knew what would happen then.

She needed to be given as much space as he could manage without completely disappearing. And he wasn't sure how to explain to her he wouldn't be exactly disappearing tomorrow morning.

But he was going to be gone.

Aspen helped Hannah down from her lap as Harry returned with a tray of drinks. There were a couple waitresses working the room, but whenever their group showed up, Harry inevitably took over the service of their table.

He set down two glasses full of water next to the beer Aspen had apparently ordered. "For the kids."

She grinned up at him. "Thank you. You have a lovely establishment."

Tony thought he was hallucinating, but he caught Melody staring at Harry, too. The man was blushing.

"Appreciate it. Your kids want to play pool?"

Tony caught Zach's eye and did his best to not burst out into laughter. Harry's rules regarding the pool table were legendary. The fact he was offering it up to kids, and kids he didn't know was both a surprise and not. It was rare for someone to not fall under Aspen's spell.

She glanced over her shoulder to where Kieran and Hannah had gone back to rolling the balls that had been left out. "Thank you for offering, but I probably shouldn't be putting sticks in their hands. Hannah would just as likely try to start a sword fight as to figure out the physics of a perfect run."

Harry blinked and then grinned. He slapped Aspen on the shoulder. "You're welcome back anytime."

She grinned back up at him. "Thank you. I definitely need to bring my husband with me if we're ever back in the area." She stared dead at Tony when she said the last bit.

He picked up his own beer and avoided her gaze. He hadn't exactly told Damien that not only had he married Melody under his assumed name, but he'd also been buying property while he was here. That at least was all under the holding company he and his parents owned, so there was no reason to amend any of the legal documents.

"Food will be out soon."

After Harry left, Aspen propped her elbows on the table and rested her chin in her hands. "Anthony, why have you been holding back from me? This town is lovely."

All his friends were now staring at him. Even Hannah and Kieran had stopped pushing balls around to stare at him.

The only way to block Aspen was to fight fire with fire. "Does Damien know you and the kids are actually here?"

She waved one hand. "He arranged for the jet."

Eric choked on the beer he was sipping. "Jet? You flew a jet here?"

Libby patted his hand, then leaned in to whisper something in his ear. His face went pale, and Tony guessed he hadn't realized who Aspen really was beyond being a friend of his from California until now.

Aspen smiled at him. "It was the most direct route, and I find it easier to manage the kids, especially Hannah, when it's just me traveling with them. Please, tell me what each of you do here." She pointed at Ana who got a deer in headlights look on her face. "You first. Ana, right?"

Ana cleared her throat. "I'm sure someone, anyone, else would be more interesting than me."

Aspen winked at her. "Everyone's fascinating in their own way. Did you grow up in Sunflower Falls?"

"Yes. I've lived here all my life. Went to the county's community college and then got my bachelor's through an online program."

Aspen's brows rose. Then she looked at Melody. "Did you do the same?"

Tony felt the muscles of Melody's back tighten. Not a good sign, but when she spoke, her tone was even. "Not quite. I also got an associate's degree, but then I followed Eric and went to trade school."

"Interesting. There probably weren't many women in trade school, were there?" The thing about Aspen was that her interest was always genuine. She counted every interaction as possible research for a future role. People noted her interest and relaxed around her. Except maybe Melody.

"More than when I was a kid and told my uncle I wanted to be a carpenter."

Eric laughed. "Even then he knew you wouldn't be interested in finish work."

Melody scowled at him. "I like pounding nails in. I pretended they were Dad's face. Better than therapy."

Eric sipped his beer. "Sounds like you need to call your therapist again."

Melody flipped up her middle finger.

He leaned in. "Kids, Melody."

Aspen waved her hand. "Don't worry about it. They see me do that to their dad all the time. You two remind me of him. Well, him when he's with his brothers. It's so nice to have siblings, right?"

Libby turned to Aspen. "Do you not have any siblings yourself?"

"My dad raised me alone. It would have been nice to have someone else take his attention off my back."

A snort erupted from his right side, and, at first, he thought it had come from Melody. Then Ana spoke up. "Speaking as the youngest of four, I can tell you that my mom gets on all our backs. Siblings don't help."

Tony saw Zach raise his head and stare at Ana. Before he could say anything, though, Harry returned with the first round of food. The kids rushed back over and dug into their dinners. He wasn't sure how they weren't crashing as they must have gotten up before the crack of dawn this morning.

"Where are you all staying?"

"The motel. It's so cute. And Mrs. Keller," she looked at Melody, "your mom, right?" When Melody nodded, she continued on. "She was so sweet considering we arrived without a reservation. Luckily there was a room immediately available, so the kids could have a nap. Then we got to meet the dogs."

He stroked Melody's shoulder. "Where are the dogs?"

She shrugged, but didn't dislodge his touch. Minor progress. "With my mom."

Harry was back with the rest of the food, and they all dug in. Melody paused at one point when Hannah reached out to him with a pickle in her hand. "Here you go, Uncle Anthony."

Melody looked at him while he took an exaggerated bite of it. "Pickles?"

He winked at her. "I like things with a kick."

And under her breath, she said loud enough so that only he could hear. "Anthony?"

He bent his head to press a kiss behind her ear. "Told you, only the people around here call me Tony."

She frowned at him and then bit into the burger she'd ordered. When he began stroking her back again, she turned to Ana to talk about something that had happened at the library but didn't shake him off.

Aspen caught his eye, and when she shifted her gaze between Melody and him, then cocked an eyebrow, he knew exactly what she was asking. He didn't know how to answer. Despite making some progress, things weren't settled with him and Melody, and the clock was ticking down.

He had to tell her. Tonight. Not only was their plane scheduled to leave JFK first thing in the morning, but he had no clue when he'd be back. Or if he'd even be allowed to contact her while he was gone.

When everyone had finished eating, he leaned down to Melody's ear. "I need to talk to you."

"You can talk here."

"This needs to be private."

She sighed. "Fine. Come over later."

"How about I catch a ride with you?"

"I need to pick Button up, and then walk her."

"I can walk with you."

"You're not letting this go, are you?"

"I can't." He checked around the table. Everyone

seemed to be paying attention to them, while also trying to give them some level of privacy. "Things are happening."

Melody jerked her head back. She opened her mouth, but must have thought better of giving into her initial reaction. "Fine." She waved across the table. "Zach?"

He looked up from his beer. "Yeah?"

She pointed at Tony with her thumb. "I'll give this one a ride home. He have a curfew?"

Zach looked at him and sighed. "Ten. At the latest."

Melody nodded and looked back at him. "Finish eating and we'll go."

Conversation flowed around them, but neither spoke much, and no one tried to force it. Tony assumed everyone was feeling the tension between him and Melody. The kids, as usual, ignored it all as they focused on eating their own dinners and trading a phone back and forth to pick videos to watch.

When she was done with her dinner, Melody stood. "I'll see you all later. Nice to meet you, Hannah and Kieran." She paused, then continued on. "You, too, Aspen."

She didn't wait for a response. Tony stood as well and tossed his wallet at Zach. "Get this for me."

Zach caught the wallet and saluted. Tony ran after Melody because he damn well knew she wouldn't wait long for him. Once they had gotten in her truck and headed down the road to the motel, she ground out her question. "What things?"

# *texts*

ANA

Is everything okay?

MELODY

Yeah.

We're just going to talk.

ANA

Call me if you need anything.

MELODY

I will.

But I can handle him.

ANA

I know you can.

Also, how could you leave me alone with
LILY FREAKING WHITTING?!?!

How many times have I watched Ghosts of
Ourselves?

MELODY

I don't know and I don't want to know.

I'll call you later.

ANA

Love you.

LILY FREAKING WHITTING!!!!!

MELODY

Muting you.

*twelve*

MELODY CLIMBED INTO HER TRUCK. A minute later, Tony was sitting next to her. She waited until he closed the door to ask the question she didn't want the answer to because if it was what she thought it was, she needed to make a decision sooner than she wanted to.

That bloom of hope quivered under the weight of reality striking.

When he'd stroked her back in Geraghty's, it had taken everything in her not to crawl into his lap. He not only actively tried to make her life easier, just his touch made her feel more settled. The bloom had filled out a bit at the withered edges. Despite everything, that was a sensation she didn't want to lose. "What things?"

He looked over at her. There was something mournful in his expression. It wasn't something she'd ever really seen on his face. Other than when he'd been on the show. "Let's get Button, and we can talk at your house."

"Afraid I'll kick you out of the truck?"

"Frankly? Yes."

Appreciating that bit of honesty, she nodded and

started the truck. Twenty minutes later, they were back at her house. Tony had been the one to get Button from her mom which had given her a chance to respond to the texts Ana had sent her right after they left.

Tony got Button from her travel harness in the back seat and met Melody at the front door. "You said she needed to be walked. I can do that."

And he would. He was making the effort. Which meant she needed to as well. "Give me a moment and I'll go with you."

His shoulders lowered, and he smiled. "Great. I'll keep her entertained out here."

She ran inside and took care of what she needed to. It was amazing how small her bladder felt now. Peanut was just about the size of a raspberry, but her bladder sometimes acted like they were much bigger.

After grabbing the reserve container of dog bags and a flashlight from Button's basket by the front door, she went back out to meet Tony. She stood in the doorway and watched as he played with her dog. Both of them were doing the play pose, and then Button jumped onto him. He laughed and wrestled with her.

Would he be like this with Peanut? She couldn't ever remember her dad playing with her, unless he'd convinced her that the con he was running was only a game. That had happened more times than she liked to remember. And he'd been smooth enough that none of them had realized what he'd been doing until she had stopped finding it "fun."

Tony looked up and caught her eye. "Ready?"

She held up the little bone-shaped container. "Yep."

He got hold of the loop end of Button's leash. "Come on, Button. Mommy needs a walk."

She snorted. "You're in a mood."

His expression turned serious, and when she stopped before him, he reached up and brushed a lock of her hair behind her ear. "I don't want to forget this."

She cocked her head. "What?"

Button whined next to them, and he looked down. "Let's get her walked. If no one's around, I'll tell you as we go."

Melody blew out a breath. The continued secrecy rubbed at her even though she'd been the one to originally ask they keep their...situationship and then supposed marriage a secret from everyone, but she at least understood the reason behind it. They headed down her street, in the general direction that would lead them downtown and to the beach.

A few of her neighbors were out despite the encroaching night. Some with their older kids who were running around their yards. Probably trying to wear them out for bed. She'd be one of them at some point. When she tried to picture it, though, she couldn't tell if Tony would be standing there with her watching as Peanut played with Button.

The bloom quivered again and grew some more. She wanted him to be. Tony's joy in life and way of finding the fun in experiences balanced her. She wanted him in her life. Not just for Peanut, but for herself.

She reached out and took his hand. He didn't say anything or try to put his arm around her shoulders, but squeezed her hand.

As Button sniffed and periodically marked her territory, they stayed silent. But it was an easy silence, all things considered.

At this time of year, it was nearly full dark but there was enough ambient light from the houses that they could see where they were going. At one point, Button squatted and did her business. Melody shined the flashlight on it so she could pick it up as soon as Button finished. But when she got the bag out from the container, Tony plucked it from her hand. "Keep the light on it."

She did, and he had it picked up and the bag knotted in no time. Button yipped and pulled at the leash, but Melody called out a command. "Sit."

Button plopped her behind on the grass. "Stay." She looked over at Tony. "We're not far from the beach entrance. You good with carrying that?"

"Absolutely."

"I can take her."

He reached down and rubbed behind Button's ear. Her dog canted her head and had a look of absolute bliss on her face. "We're good. Aren't you a good girl, Button?"

Despite the darkness, Melody felt a blush bloom on her face. Tony had called her that in bed sometimes. With a much different tone, but the words had her remembering his fingers tangled in her hair as she sucked him off.

He looked over at her right then, and she began walking away.

"Something I said?"

She heard the suppressed laughter and flipped him the bird over her shoulder. He stopped holding back, and his rich laugh filled the air around them. His hand brushed over her shoulder when he and Button caught up to her.

"Thanks. I needed that."

She slid him a look. "Can you tell me now?" They were on the outer edges of the downtown area, but at this time of night, it was quiet. She spotted lights on in Secrets and Whimsies, but that was usual as it was Mrs. Smith's monthly inventory period.

He touched her back as they crossed the street. "If you're good with it, I'd like to sit on the beach one last time."

She jerked her face up so she could see his. "Last?"

His jaw tightened. "For now. I hope."

Melody cupped her stomach. This was the answer she'd been expecting. Fearing. She'd promised to give him a chance to prove his case, but his time wasn't up yet. But the look on his face earlier, and his choice of words made her realize maybe it was.

Soon they settled on an empty stretch of the public beach. The waves from the lake provided a steady drone so that even if anyone else was on the beach, they shouldn't be overheard. Button was tired from the walk, so she settled down between the two of them and rested her head on her paws.

Tony clasped his hands together on his knees. "Zach and I are flying back to California tomorrow."

Even though she'd suspected that's what he had to say, it still felt like a punch to the gut. "When did you find out?"

"This afternoon. I was told that if I wasn't in California by five their time tomorrow, I'd be held in contempt of court and a bench warrant issued for my arrest."

She blinked, then turned to look out at the lake. "They can do that?"

"Easily. The man I'm supposed to testify against is still missing, however no one thinks he's dead at this point. Don't know where he is, but my attorney told me that the police aren't the only ones looking for him."

Melody drew in a deep breath. "Do they think he's coming after you?"

Out of the corner of her eye, she saw him shake his head. "No. Robert's primary resources were the other people who are now searching for him. Damien thinks he may have stolen from them, and they finally discovered it. Wouldn't surprise me. If that is the case, Robert had better hope the police are the ones who find him first."

She opened her mouth to ask the question hanging in her mind, but she couldn't get the words out. Swallowing the lump in her throat down, she forced them to leave her lips. "Are you coming back?"

Tony's sigh was long and deep. Partway through, Button lifted her head from the sand and laid it on his knee. He chuckled and rubbed her head. "Thanks, Button." He was silent for a moment more. "I don't know. I don't want to make you another promise I can't keep."

Tears pricked her eyes. Mentally she poked at the bloom, but it stood firm. If this was going to be her last night with him, she didn't want to waste it. Her capacity for hope wasn't large, but it wasn't nonexistent. If they were going to make it, she had to nurture that bloom.

Fuck the ticking clock and his having to go back to LA.

She was going to make sure they both had orgasms to remember.

Turning back to him, she lifted her hand to his chin, and brought his face down to hers.

"Melody?"

She answered by pressing her lips against his. He groaned and gripped her wrist. Sweeping out with her tongue, she tasted him. It had been so long, and she didn't know when she might have the chance again.

If ever.

"Baby. Please. Don't give up on me."

The taste of him became salt kissed, and she realized she'd started crying. "I don't know what I'm doing." Relationships were not her strong suit, and she still wasn't sure how to fix the foundation of the one she wanted to build with him.

He kissed her and brushed her hair behind her ear. "You're going to continue baking our baby, conquer the world of home improvement, and keep faith in me. Please. I'm sorry I'm asking you to be strong for us. I should be here pampering the hell out of you for as long as you'll let me."

She rested her forehead against his even as Button wriggled out from between them. "You know I wouldn't let you do it for long."

He laughed. "Every minute you'd let me would be a win. You don't have to be the strong one all the time."

"Told you I have a reputation as a badass to maintain."

His fingers traced her jaw and lifted her face so their eyes met. In the moonlight, shadows and the beard he still wore made his face dark and menacing, but the look in his eyes was beyond soft. "Your armor's strong, but I know your heart is pudding for the right people and I want to be one of those people. And I know I still haven't earned it."

"Tony..."

He kissed her. "Let me finish."

She squeezed her eyes closed and nodded. A few more tears leaked out.

He brushed his thumbs against her cheeks, pushing the tears away. "I don't know how long this is going to take. Getting to trial can take years. They can't keep me holed up the entire time. I don't think. But I can't make any forever promises to you until this is cleared up."

"Will it ever be?"

He wrapped his arms around her, and she curled into his shoulder as Button sniffed the surrounding sand. "It's got to be. One way or another. Robert's not the big fish they want. He's just an avenue to their primary goal. But having me available puts pressure on Robert to get him to flip or whatever they're looking to get out of him."

She hated the idea of him never coming back into their lives because he wasn't allowed to. That was the difference with her dad. He chose to leave them and only came back when it benefited him.

Checking her watch, she saw it was nearly nine. Time was racing away. She pushed away from him and stood up.

"Kicking me out already?"

"Just get moving. Button." Button came over immediately, and Melody grabbed the leash.

Tony stood up and brushed the sand from his jeans. "I'll walk you home and then head over to the house."

She grabbed his hand. "Stop dawdling." She tugged on his hand and set a fast pace toward her home.

"Melody?"

"You're wasting time." Refusing to let go of his hand and not caring who saw them, she hurried across streets and intersections as soon as any cars were clear. Button saw it as a game and ran and jumped, playing with her leash.

Tony said nothing for the rest of the walk, keeping pace with her. As soon as they were back in her house, she pushed him toward the stairs. "I'll put Button to bed."

He looked over his shoulder, his gaze dark. "Are you sure about this?"

Taking a deep breath, she nodded. "Yes."

He bent and picked up Button. "I can put her to bed."

"I don't want to think."

He turned and crowded her up against the wall. "I promise to turn off that gorgeous brain as soon as this one is in her crate."

Button yipped and licked Melody's face. They both laughed, but Tony moved to the stairs.

Melody followed up, doing her best to turn her brain off herself. The decision felt impulsive. But right. They had little time left. She wasn't sure if she would have ever given him another chance were it not for Peanut, but she wasn't making this decision for Peanut. It was for herself.

They might still crash and burn, and he might not come back which meant she'd have to make a life on her own. But she knew deep in her gut that if she chose against the possibility of them being a Them, she'd regret it.

She went into her room and began stripping out of her clothes. Her arms were over her head, tangled in her t-shirt, when warm hands skated across her skin before they settled over her belly.

Warm lips pressed a kiss to her shoulder, next to her bra strap. "Maybe I should keep you like this."

She worked to free her hands, but before she could, he had her shirt fully wrapped around her hands, binding them together, and spun her around so that she faced him. "What's gotten into you?"

"You." He kissed her, stealing her breath. With his body, he guided her back toward her bed.

# *thirteen*

THE SECOND TONY had spotted Melody stripping out of her clothes, he knew he couldn't let her go. He needed to tie her to him. Convince her they belonged together like he'd known deep in his gut from the beginning. Yeah, they were having a baby, but a woman didn't need a man, especially one with the baggage he was carrying around, to raise a kid.

No. Melody needed to make the choice of being with him on her own, and for herself. The pregnancy had given him some space to persuade her he was worthy of being her partner. But the ultimate decision was one she needed to make for herself.

He laid her back on the bed carefully as he made sure her hands were still tied up in her shirt. A smirk tugged at her lips as she watched him with a cautious gaze. She moved her still-bound hands. "Going to let me go?"

"Not if I can help it."

Her gaze darkened. They hadn't played too much with this side of sex. Maybe they should have. Something for him to look forward to while cooling his heels in California.

Melody didn't untangle her hands, but she didn't lie there quiescent. She was incapable of not trying to control the situation, and that was something he loved about her. In and out of bed.

Her hips shifted, and then her legs were wrapped around his waist. They both still had their pants on, and he had to concentrate hard on not letting her movements drive him past the edge of control.

Reaching under her back, he undid the clasp for her bra and moved the cups off her breasts. He rubbed her nipples with his thumbs and then pinched them. Her back bowed up off the bed.

"Tony." The breathlessness with which she said his name soothed the animal clawing inside of him.

"You're such a brat."

"You never complained..." He pinched again, and she shuddered. "...about that before."

"We don't have much time."

She opened her eyes and glared at him. "So fuck me."

"Always trying to control things."

"Now you're the one wasting time."

Fully aware of the second hand ticking away, a locust chomping away at their time together, he stripped off her pants and then undid his jeans.

He pulled a condom out of his back pocket and was about to rip it open when Melody sat up, her legs wrapping once again around his hips and her bound hands resting on his chest.

"I don't think we need that."

He blinked. He'd never had sex without a condom. The only time he'd even come close to getting inside a woman without one on had been when he'd likely gotten Melody pregnant, and he still wouldn't have tried to go in bare. "What do you mean we don't need one?"

She laid back down, arms over her head and her legs splayed open. "I mean, I'm already pregnant." She cocked an eyebrow at him. "You haven't been sleeping with anyone else, have you? Do I need to worry about the other reasons for you using a condom?"

"No." He stroked his hands along her thighs, enjoying the firm muscles under the skin. Melody was someone who worked hard and didn't shy away from doing the work needed. Even if that meant hauling boxes of ceramic tile or assisting with fine finishing work. "It had been nearly a year for me."

"Then I think we're good."

"What about you?"

"My last partner?"

"Yep." He traced the fine skin along the joint of her inner hips. Her eyes darkened, never leaving his gaze.

"Two years."

"Why so long?" He moved one thumb to trace her open pussy.

She drew in a deep breath. "Do we have to talk about this now? Remember, you turn into a pumpkin at ten."

He laughed. "I guess not." After swiping his fingers down her pussy to get them wet, he wrapped his hand around his cock. "We're doing this?"

"How many times do I have to tell you to fuck me?"

Even while they were taking a step that felt like jumping off a cliff, she could still make him laugh. Guiding the head of his cock to her pussy, he reveled in the first touch of skin to skin.

"I want to touch my breasts. Make you fuck me faster."

He jerked against her, his whole cock rubbing up and down her wet pussy. "Jesus, Melody. Next time I'm gagging you along with restraining your hands."

"I'd prefer to gag on your cock."

This woman. When she went all in, she went ALL in. He notched his head in her entrance and pushed. Not slowly. Melody had made it clear she didn't want slow. But he also didn't want her thinking this was a fast fuck and done.

Fast, yes. Done, never.

Even as he powered in and out of her, his one thumb rubbing against her clit to get her to climax as fast and often as he could in the next ten minutes, he bent down to kiss her. She nipped his lips with her teeth, and then settled back, inviting him in.

She moved her arms so that her bound hands were behind his neck, holding him to her. He groaned, and as he did so, her hips jerked up.

Melody's eyes rolled back, and he realized she was coming. "That's it, baby. Be a good girl and give me your orgasm."

Her hips jerked again as he powered into her. She groaned low and long. He tried to hold off, but the tight clenching of her pussy on his bare cock was too much. As he spilled into her, the thought of claiming her, marking her with his seed had the power of his own orgasm ratcheting up.

He barely managed to not fall on top of her, instead, landing to her side. Once he'd pulled out, he moved the hand he'd been using to massage her clit down to cover her pussy. He pressed kisses to her shoulder, timing them to the continued aftershocks he felt fluttering through her groin.

Melody untangled her hands from her shirt and

brought them down, running her hands through his hair. "I need a moment before the next round."

Again she made him laugh. "Unfortunately, I have a feeling Zach would be over here to haul my ass out of the house before I was ready."

"Please. You don't have to have an erection to take care of me."

He licked her shoulder, enjoying the taste of sweat and satisfied woman. "I want to take care of you even if I'm never capable of erections again."

"Bite your tongue, that's what Viagra's for."

Burying his face into her arm, he couldn't help the chuckles bubbling out of him. He'd always considered himself a good-natured guy, but even as he was preparing to leave her for an indefinite amount of time when he really didn't want to, she gave him joy in the moment.

He looked over at the clock she had sitting on her side table. He had fifteen minutes to get dressed and back to the house he and Zach had been sharing.

"I need to go."

Her hand paused in the stroking of his hair. "I know." She blew out a long breath. "What do we do next?"

"I don't know. Once I talk with Damien and find out what the next steps are, I'll let you know. I'll do my best to text you, call you when I can." He pushed up on his elbow so he could look her in the eye. "I want to know about the baby. Make sure you're both okay. Send me photos of the ultrasound?"

She swallowed, opened her mouth to say something, but then just nodded.

He pressed his forehead against hers. "I'm sorry I can't be there with you. I want to be. So badly."

She stared at him. "Why? I mean I know I'm a great lay and all."

He could hear the pain underlying her attempt at humor. "Oh, Mel. I've done a shit job if you don't know you're the one for me. Even if the baby wasn't in the picture. You just made me laugh after some of the hottest sex of my life, when I'm being forced to leave you. How can you not be my person?"

Melody closed her eyes, and he wasn't sure if it was to close him out or something else. But she threaded her fingers into his hair and pulled him down for a kiss. Instinctively, he knew that if he said he loved her, she wouldn't welcome it. Not when he was also getting ready to leave her. Declaring love meant commitment. An acknowledgment of a future. Together.

He couldn't commit to her, but he could love her. Even without saying the words.

She broke the kiss and pushed at his shoulder. "You should go."

Tears leaked from the corners of her still closed eyes. "Want me to call Ana? Have her come over and stay with you?"

Melody opened her eyes, stared at him, and then rolled her eyes. "No. If I need company, I can call whoever I want myself. Seriously. Zach probably is on his way over."

Tony bit back the growl of frustration building in his chest. He needed more time. But he didn't have it. "As soon as I know what's happening, I'll let you know."

"Fine. Get going. I don't need Zach coming over."

Tony got dressed, and headed back downstairs. He had his phone out and was shooting a text to Zach when he felt a rush of air against his skin a moment before Melody gripped his biceps and turned him around. She pulled his face down for one more kiss. He tried to sink into it, but before he could, she stepped back. She pulled the short silk robe she'd thrown on tighter to her body. "Be careful. Please."

He reached out and pushed her hair behind one ear, savoring the feel of it one more time. "I won't take any stupid chances. That I can promise you."

She blew out a breath and nodded. "Get going."

He saluted her. "Yes, boss."

She rolled her eyes again. "If only."

He waited to leave her doorstep until he heard the click of her locks. Then he hit send on the text she'd distracted him from. As soon as his text app showed it had been delivered, a bubble popped up indicating Zach was composing a reply.

ZACH

Am I supposed to come pick you up?

TONY

It'll be faster than me walking. Melody's not exactly in a state to be driving me over.

ZACH

TMI, asshole.

TONY

I'm going to start walking. Where should I meet you?

ZACH

Just walk straight down toward town and I'll stop when I see you.

TONY

Five minutes later, headlights swooped across the yards

and road Tony was walking along. Zach pulled up next to him. "Get in. Flight's changed."

Tony climbed into the SUV. "When did that happen? And to when?"

"About a half hour ago. I've already got my stuff packed. As soon as you're packed, we're out of here."

Tony twisted in his seat. "What time is the flight? We were already leaving ass early."

"They moved it up by an hour. As it is, we'll just make it."

He scrubbed his face with his hands. Neither he nor Zach had gotten any sleep today. Zach might have while he'd been gone, but that wasn't enough for a nearly six-hour trip down to JFK. "Wait, it's still out of JFK, right?"

"Yeah. And what's working in our favor is that we're driving in the dead of night, so little to no traffic to block our way."

"Bite your tongue. I don't want to get locked up because some asshole crashed his car and block the Tunnel."

Zach pulled into the driveway of the house they'd been staying at. A light in the living room was still on, giving the house a sense of welcome. Tony went in and packed while Zach did what he needed to close up the house. On their way out, he locked the door and then dropped the keys in the mailbox. His mom would be by later this morning to gather what they'd left behind and for the final closeout.

They climbed back into the SUV, and Zach drove through the downtown area of Sunflower Falls to hook onto the county road. Tony looked over as they passed the block where Keller Construction had a storefront that acted as their office. He thought about the pen they had set up for Mayzie's puppies when Libby had been caring for them over the summer.

Would Melody bring the baby into the office with her? Or would she just work from home when she needed to be in an office environment? A vision of Melody wearing a little baby in a carrier with the baby wearing a bright purple mini hardhat had him laughing.

As they passed the Sunflower Diner, Zach looked over. "What's so funny?"

Tony shook his head. "Nothing." He'd have to remember to tell Melody about it, though. She wouldn't ever bring a small baby onto an active construction site, but maybe he could find a mini hardhat somewhere to get as a gag gift.

They passed the sign inviting visitors to come back to Sunflower Falls, and Tony hoped it would be true.

Eight hours later, he and Zach were in the air headed to Los Angeles. They had barely made the flight before the doors closed as there had indeed been an idiot on the road, but thankfully their first-class seats hadn't been given away so they could both sack out for at least part of the flight.

Before he settled down for a nap, he shot a text to Melody.

TONY

In the air. Miss you already.

MELODY

Are you going to be sappy about this?

He pulled out the chain he'd been wearing around his throat since the day they arrived back in Sunflower Falls from Niagara and took a picture of the ring hanging from it. He knew she'd noticed it, but she'd never commented on it.

**TONY**

Always have been, always will be.

**MELODY**

**TONY**

**MELODY**

**TONY**

**MELODY**

Glad you're safe. Keep it that way.

**TONY**

Planning on it. Will text when we arrive.

The flight attendant came around to see if he wanted anything to eat or drink. He requested a bottle of water and then took advantage of the lie-flat bed.

Nearly six hours later, they were landing at LAX. Still groggy despite sleeping almost all the way, he got his carry-on bags sorted so they could quickly deplane. They were among the first off, and as soon as they exited into the baggage claim area, he spotted Damien, dressed in a full dark blue suit and lime green tie, waiting for them.

He went over and shook his hand. "What are you doing here?"

Damien briefly looked over at Zach and then turned his gaze back to Tony's. "The DA's requested you remain in your house. It's not an official court order, but they said they would submit one if necessary."

Tony looked between Zach and Damien. "They can't do that, can they?"

Zach shrugged. "I'm not the attorney."

"They can. And not only can they have you confined to your house, they can request GPS monitoring to ensure you don't leave. Come on, I'm driving."

Shifting his bags over his shoulder, Tony followed Damien out to the parking garage. "Can we at least stop for a burger? I slept the entire flight and have only had a little snack bag since dinner last night."

"You can have it delivered when you get home."

Damien's tone was all lawyer, not even a teasing hint of friend seeping in. "So my house? I'll order now."

Damien looked over his shoulder as he turned down one of the garage's ramps. "We're headed to the courthouse first. Both the judge and the DA want to see you in person."

"I need food, man."

Zach snorted. "You might as well. I can tell he's going to be a whiny baby about this."

Damien held out his key fob, and the lights of an SUV a few cars down from the start of the row flashed. "Fine. Drive-through only and you will like what I select."

"Why do I feel like one of your kids right now?"

Damien shook his head, but climbed into the driver's seat. Tony tossed his bags into the cargo area and waited while Zach did the same. "Is this bad?"

Damien shouted from the front seat. "Yes. Get in."

Zach pressed the button for the gate to lower and lock. "We'll talk later."

As they exited LAX, Tony took a picture of the palm trees lining the road. Pulling up his text app, he sent it to Melody.

TONY

Can't wait to show you these myself in person.

MELODY

Glad you arrived. Dealing with a situation. Text later?

TONY

Sure.

He touched the screen and let the words out he wanted to say to her in person but was too afraid she'd run from. "Love you."

# *texts*

MELODY

Why am I getting messages from vendors about possible partnerships? And they're saying you referred them?

TONY

Forking out. Sex later.

Duck.

Fuck.

WORKING out. TEXT later.

MELODY

You could have just not replied and let me think you were still sleeping. Don't hurt yourself.

## TWO HOURS LATER

TONY

Sorry about that.

I just emailed a couple places I've worked with in the past and asked them about anything new they had and maybe mentioned seeing some of your work and how our moms are friends.

They took it from there. Cross my heart.

MELODY

Friends? Isn't that stretching things?

My mom met your mom once. I don't think that constitutes friends.

TONY

You should check them out. These people do great work and they'd be great features for some of your higher end designs without breaking the budget.

MELODY

I thought you were supposed to be staying quiet and lying low.

TONY

I am. Pinky swear. Zach's running everything through something that makes them think I'm possibly over in Europe with my parents.

I haven't left the house since the day we got back.

I might be a bit bored.

MELODY

:photo of boxes piled up in living space by entrance door:

Shocking news. You can stop now. I don't have space for all of this.

TONY

Donate what you don't want to whoever
needs it most.

MELODY

How am I supposed to explain donations of
baby clothes and other stuff when no one's
supposed to know I'm pregnant?

TONY

Have Ana do it?

There should be a few orders of diapers in
there. I wasn't sure which kind would be
best or if you'd want to do cloth or not.

MELODY

You realize this baby's not arriving for
another eight or so months, right?

TONY

Being prepared is never a bad thing.

But, again, may be a bit bored.

MELODY

:photos of house under construction:

We've got the house closed in, and we're
starting with the main floor for installing
cabinetry and flooring.

We had to go back to the county for an
amendment to the permitting because of
the design changes to the secondary
bathroom, but we should have approval for
that soon since most of the plumbing won't
be materially affected.

TONY

Excellent. Sorry about causing a delay, but a tub's going to be much better in there, right?

MELODY

Your house, your design. You get what you want.

TONY

...

Are you okay?

MELODY

...

I will be.

Just tired.

Didn't sleep well.

TONY

Do you need me to send more peppermint tea?

MELODY

I can buy my own peppermint tea if I need more, but I'm still well stocked.

I'll be fine. Seriously.

Just lay off trying to make connections for me when I didn't ask for them? Please?

TONY

Sure.

I just want to make your life easier.

I'm sorry.

MELODY

Thank you.

Go work out some more. Or whatever. I
need to get back to work.

TONY

MELODY

Bye.

*texts*

MELODY

:photo of the backs of Hannah and Kieran with Button walking to the side of them on a hiking path:

Apparently Aspen likes hiking? But Damien doesn't let her go without supervision? So she recruited me and Libby?

TONY

…

I'd forgotten about that. I think it has to do with how they met.

MELODY

…

Aspen says hi.

So do Hannah and Kieran.

TONY

What about Libby?

MELODY

She says hi, too.

184

TONY

And you?

MELODY

:selfie of Melody giving him the middle finger:

TONY

😍

MELODY

I do not get you sometimes. It's like you're masochistic for wanting to be with me.

TONY

😘 You balance me.

MELODY

What are you doing today?

TONY

:photo of feet up on a recliner and a late morning news show on a wall-mounted flat-screen TV:

MELODY

Still bored?

TONY

SO BORED.

And you told me to stop buying you stuff.

:selfie of Tony making a pouty face:

MELODY

😶

TONY

Even Zach's getting annoyed with me.

MELODY

This is news?

TONY

He's a trained bodyguard.

He's not supposed to get annoyed at clients.

And tell them.

I don't tell my demanding talent what assholes they're being when we're on set.

MELODY

Do you need water? Food? A nap?

TONY

You don't have to treat me like a toddler.

But maybe a nap?

MELODY

I'm viewing this as practice for Peanut. Gods help me.

TONY

I can't even work on any film projects right now. If I read something I like, I'm going to want to bid on it.

I have been reading up on pregnancy stuff. Are you having any food aversions? Breast tenderness?

MELODY

I...

No.

I'm okay. Still can't drink coffee. But that's the only thing. I'm not commenting about the breasts.

TONY

You can test them and send me the video?

:gif of man waggling eyebrows:

MELODY

Pervert.

I have to herd two other women, two children, and two dogs. Bye.

Maybe later.

# *texts*

TONY

:link to a real estate listing:

MELODY

Are you thinking about moving?

TONY

No! Why would you ask that?

MELODY

Because you just sent me a listing for a
house in the LA-area? I'm assuming since it
says views of the Pacific in the headline.

TONY

No. I thought you might like it?

MELODY

...

Why?

TONY

As a project house.

That's an area with a lot of potential.

MELODY

A house with views of the Pacific is in an area described as having "potential"?

That, and the price, means LA is not for me.

TONY

You haven't even come out here.

MELODY

...

Give me a few minutes. Crisis with a supplier. Maybe an hour.

TONY

:link to Santa Monica Pier:

:link to Getty Villa:

:link to Academy Museum of Motion Picture:

:link to Duke's Malibu:

That one's one of my favorite restaurants.

:link to tour of landmark homes in Los Angeles:

:link to Instagram page of taco truck:

That's my favorite taco truck, but it'll have to wait until I can go back outside.

I wonder if I can get Zach to do a taco run for me...

MELODY

Did you...

Did you just link bomb me?

TONY

Uh.

Maybe?

Sorry?

Just thought you might like some options of what we can do when you get here.

MELODY

A. If I come visit you anytime soon, it doesn't sound like you'll be able to leave the house.

B. That's a lot.

TONY

There's a lot to do here.

But tell me whatever you want to do and I'll make it happen.

MELODY

Yeah, we need to find you a hobby.

Right now I just want to focus on getting your house here finished and deal with doctor appointments for Peanut.

TONY

The ultrasound is Wednesday at nine your time, right?

MELODY

Yeah.

TONY

Let me know if you need anything.

I'm also happy to make any decisions about the house if you need them?

MELODY

No. The last time you made a decision, we ended up having to delay some things. Remember?

TONY

That moving ahead?

MELODY

Yeah. We got the amended permit this morning.

I've got to go.

No more link bombing.

*texts*

MELODY

I'm watching Undercover Immortal.

Which I haven't done since it first aired.

TONY

:clutches chest:

You haven't watched my magnum opus
since it first aired? I thought you were a fan.

MELODY

💀

I didn't want to ruin the memory in case it
didn't hold up.

It does…mostly…for the record.

TONY

I'll be sure to frame this conversation for
display on the refrigerator.

MELODY

…

Be honest with me.

TONY

About anything.

MELODY

You wished you could have sparkled, too. Right?

TONY

Sparkling would have been a bad idea since I was supposed to be undercover and all.

MELODY

That's not a direct answer. You promised to be honest.

TONY

Fine.

…

Super secret pinky swear you won't ever tell anyone?

MELODY

I'm waiting.

TONY

Yes. I wish I had sparkled.

# *texts*

MELODY

:video of Melody testing her bare breasts:

They are tender.

TONY

Warn a guy next time.

I almost started playing that with Zach sitting next to me.

MELODY

You asked.

TONY

I did.

Thank you.

Can I return the favor with anything?

MELODY

…

Jack yourself off for me.

TONY

:video of Tony lying naked on a bed and masturbating until he comes:

…

Sorry.

Had to edit that as the whole video wouldn't send over text.

MELODY

:photo of Melody with a glassy eyed expression kissing her fingers which are glistening:

Thank you.

TONY

Fuck.

I can't wait to see you do that in person.

Miss you so much.

MELODY

Miss you, too.

*texts*

MELODY

I'm scared.

TONY

Hey. Do you want me to call?

MELODY

...

No. I need to get to sleep.

TONY

I've been told I have a soothing voice.

MELODY

...

...

TONY

What are you scared about?

The ultrasound?

MELODY

Yeah.

196

What if they find something wrong?

TONY

If they do, you call me immediately and we talk about it. With whoever's there with you.

That's what speaker phone's for.

MELODY

I don't flip out like this.

TONY

…

I'm glad you texted me. I'd rather be there with you. So much.

I'm sorry I can't be there for you.

MELODY

Ana's going with me.

TONY

Good. You should have someone there with you.

Everything will be okay.

Whatever happens, good or bad, we'll figure it out.

MELODY

Thank you.

TONY

If they offer the glam shots, get them. We're going all out for this kid.

MELODY

TONY

Believe me, if they offer a glam shot and my mother finds out we didn't get it, I'll never stop hearing about it.

MELODY

Good night.

TONY

*fourteen*

ALMOST TWO WEEKS after Tony had returned to California, Melody sat in the waiting room for baby's first ultrasound. Her phone pinged, and Ana looked over from where she was texting away on her own phone.

"Are you going to look at it?"

"No."

"Why not? It could be Tony. He knows today's when you've got the appointment."

"I'm sure it's Tony. Or my mother. I don't want to deal with either of them at the moment."

Ana blinked at her. "Excuse me?"

Melody handed Ana her phone. "You deal with it. Whoever it is."

Ana cocked her head. "What the hell crawled up your ass? Do I need to get you a protein shake?"

Melody closed her eyes so she wouldn't have to look at all the other pregnant people in the waiting room sitting with their spouses. There were three other couples, and a pair that looked like mother and daughter. The daughter was in a uniform from one of the area's ritzy high schools.

Both of them were furiously typing away on their phones, too.

"Maybe. I'm hungry." She looked around, and it felt like if anyone was aware of their conversation, they were ignoring them. She lowered her voice anyway. "And I'm pissed. I want Tony here."

Ana swiped Melody's phone from her hand. "Progress at least."

Ignoring the smugness in Ana's tone, Melody closed her eyes and rested her head against the wall behind their chairs. Her brain had been spinning the last few days between missing Tony and also thinking that he must be thrilled to be back in Los Angeles and away from Sunflower Falls. Rationally, she knew that wasn't true considering how many times he mentioned being bored since he was stuck at his house when they had talked or texted. But brain weasels were going to brain weasel.

A nurse with a tablet in hand opened the door to the exam area and called out a name. A Black couple stood up, the man carrying his partner's designer bag. Melody admired the woman's ease of movement when she had to be at least six months along, and in heels.

Barely two months along and she was feeling clumsy, even in the work boots she wore when on site. The other day she had tripped over literally nothing.

Moments after they disappeared behind the door, another nurse appeared and called out another name. This time it was the high school student and her mother. The nurse said something, and the daughter shot a glare at her mother and said in the loudest possible voice without actual shouting, "No. The father will not be joining us."

As soon as they disappeared behind the door, she looked

over at Ana and widened her eyes. Ana pursed her lips and shook her head. "Drama we do not need to be around for, thankfully. Tony said to remind you he wants any photos you can get to share. Preferably the glam package?"

Melody scowled. "What are you talking about?"

Ana tossed her phone back. "You told me to take care of it."

Melody opened her phone and scrolled back through her text app.

Thank the gods Tony hadn't sent anything inappropriate. This time.

After one sext session they'd had, he'd sent a photo of how he'd been feeling the next morning and she'd been in the middle of a conversation with the plumber, showing him the product pages of the ordered fixtures for the secondary bathroom on her phone.

She found the start of this morning's thread.

TONY

Thinking of you today.

Attached was a photo of the sunrise over the pool in his gods damned backyard. A few days after he'd left, he'd video chatted her and gave her a tour of the house. She'd known Tony had to be well-off from his own efforts, let alone anything his parents had given him.

She hadn't expected him to live in a house on the California coast with views of the Pacific Ocean and enough land to have both a decently sized lap pool and an athletic court of some kind. His house probably was worth as much as the entire lakefront of Sunflower Falls.

At least Ana'd had the decency to identify herself when responding.

MELODY

It's Ana. Melody gave me her phone to deal with you. Pretty sunrise. Shouldn't you still be sleeping?

TONY

I know you and Zach are texting.

Melody whipped her head around to look at Ana. Who sank down a little in her seat and pulled her phone close to her chest.

"You're texting Zach? Why?"

"Because he caught my mom reaming me out one day and told me to text him any time I got too frustrated by her. He said he'd be a neutral sounding board, and that I shouldn't have to do time for matricide."

"What has your mother done now?"

Ana waved her hand. "Not something I want to talk about before you go in for your first ultrasound. We can deal with it later."

Melody made the "I'm watching you" hand gesture. Ana responded with a middle finger scratching the side of her nose.

Going back to the text conversation with Tony, she saw more photos of the sunrise. And then the breakfast he was making in his, of course, gourmet kitchen.

TONY

Tell Melody these are the ingredients for the smoothie I was telling her about the other day.

Her mouth started watering.

"You told him about the seal?"

Ana shrugged. "It's really cute. Kieran's got excellent taste."

"I still can't believe Aspen bought that."

Ana shot her a look and then opened her mouth. Before she could say anything, a nurse opened the door to the exam area again. "Melody Keller?"

Melody stood up and headed to the nurse. "That's me."

Ana followed, and the nurse looked over at her. "Is this the other parent?"

Melody shook her head. "The father's out of town. This is my friend. I was told that it would be okay to bring another person with me."

The nurse smiled. "You're perfectly fine. Our ultrasound technicians just like to make sure they're speaking appropriately when explaining the process."

They followed the nurse back to a room where the nurse took Melody's blood pressure. "And you drank the recommended amount of water prior to arriving?"

"Yes."

"Great. Your blood pressure's good, so we're all set." She

went to a tall, narrow cabinet and pulled out a folded item. "If you'll change into this gown, the technician will knock in a few minutes. As it will be a transvaginal ultrasound, you'll need to remove your underwear, too. You can draw the curtain over there for privacy." She pointed to the back corner. "Any questions?"

Melody shook her head. "Thank you."

"The technician should be here in a couple minutes to give you enough time to change."

Once the nurse left, Melody went behind the curtain and changed. She wasn't sure which way wearing it would be easiest for the technician, so she went for her own comfort and pulled the gown on like a dress shirt, holding the front closed. She left her clothes on the stool behind the curtain and climbed up on the table in the middle of the room.

Ana came over and touched her arm. "You doing okay?"

Melody let out a long breath. "As good as can be expected."

"Want me to invite Tony to a video chat?"

Wincing, Melody shook her head. "No. I'm sure he'd love that, but I don't want this broadcast if you know what I mean." No one needed a visual record of what was going to happen next.

Ana nodded. Before she could say anything more, there was a knock. Ana moved to the front of the table to block the view of anyone passing by the door.

"Come in."

The technician, a woman with dark tan skin and her dark brown hair pulled back in a tight French braid, pushed a cart with several machines on it into the room and smiled at them. "Good morning. I'm Lupe Gottfried, and I'll be your ultrasound technician today."

Melody smiled at her. "Nice to meet you."

Lupe rolled the cart over to the table where Melody sat. She pulled a tablet from one of the carrier bins on the side of the cart and tapped at the screen. "If you could confirm your full name and date of birth?"

Melody did so, and Lupe nodded. "The nurse informed me the father will not be joining us today. Would you like his name on the record for the ultrasound? It will show up on the images we provide."

Swallowing, Melody nodded. "Yes. Please."

"What's his name, and how do you spell it?"

For a moment, she wasn't sure how to answer the question. For so long, she had thought of him as Tony Caputo. With him back in Los Angeles, she felt like she was in a split reality. "Anthony. Anthony Dewitt." She spelled out both names.

Lupe typed it in, then paused and looked back up at Melody. "Isn't that the name of that actor who was in that vampire show?"

She knew her smile was weak, but Melody did her best. "He gets that a lot."

Lupe laughed. "I'm sure he does." She began typing on the screen again and then handed it to Melody. "This explains the procedure and the risks involved. I'll need you to read it in full, and sign at the bottom if you'd like to proceed."

Melody took the tablet and read through the form which thankfully included illustrations like you'd see in textbooks. It was fairly straightforward, so she signed with her finger in the box at the bottom and handed the tablet back to Lupe.

Lupe tapped on the screen some more and then put the tablet back into its slot. "The lube I'll put on the wand will feel chilly at first, but it'll warm up a bit from your body heat as we begin the procedure. You'll be able to watch on the screen here." She pointed to a surprisingly small screen. "I'll point out what features I can see, but I'm primarily looking for indicators that the fetus is developing as expected. I cannot diagnose anything if there are any issues. The scans will go through our regular review process, and the gestational age of the fetus will be determined then."

Melody nodded and reached a hand out to Ana. Ana immediately gripped it and squeezed.

Lupe looked at them and smiled at Melody. "Ready for this, Mama?"

Blowing out a breath, Melody nodded then laid back down on the table. Lupe helped her position her feet in the stirrups. The clinical nature of the procedure was offset by the poster of a multitude of babies of all skin tones taped to the ceiling.

Lupe placed one hand on Melody's thigh. "I'm going to insert the wand. Are you ready?"

"Sure."

As soon as Lupe placed the wand against her vulva, Melody sucked in a breath. Lupe hadn't been kidding when she'd said the lube would be chilly. Lupe pressed it in, the pressure firm, but gentle, until she bumped up against Melody's cervix. Shifting a bit, Melody tried to get comfortable. At first, the room was quiet. But as Lupe moved the wand, a strong, rhythmic whooshing sound filled the room.

Melody turned her head and watched as the grays of the screen gained definition. There was a lighter gray on the edges, and then a darker gray filling most of the screen, with lighter again in the center. Tears filled her eyes. "Hey, Peanut."

Lupe grinned. "An excellent name for the little one. They're strong." She pressed something on the machine and then pointed to the dark gray. "That's the embryonic sac." She then pointed to the slightly more bulbous end of the lighter gray in the center. "And that's the baby's head."

Melody reached out, but didn't touch the screen as she didn't want to accidentally break anything. "Baby's first picture."

"Yep." Lupe began moving the wand again. As she did so, she talked through what she saw.

Ten minutes later, they were done with the screening. Lupe gently wiped the lube from Melody's vulva. She then handed Melody another towel and a pad. "If I missed anything, you can use this and toss it into the green bin. There's a bathroom down the hall you can use before you leave. You might want to wear the pad for at least a few hours. We'll have all the images, along with a confirmed due date, added to your patient portal by the end of the day. You'll be able to download the images and then share them with whoever you care to."

Once Melody finished dressing and checked out, she and Ana headed back into the sunshine toward Ana's compact. Melody slipped on her sunglasses.

"Do you want to stop for something to eat?" Ana held up her car fob and unlocked the doors.

"Can we get drive through? I want to get back to Sunflower Falls. There's some paperwork I've been putting off, and Eric's getting on me about it."

"Sure. How's Eric doing? Libby said that he's been surly lately."

Melody shrugged. "He's been mostly fine, but he's been the one primarily talking with Greer and Triple H."

"What's the deal with your mom? Why didn't you want

to deal with her if she had been the one texting instead of Tony?"

Melody tapped her fingers on her knee as Ana pulled out of the practice's parking lot and headed toward her favorite fast food breakfast place. "She's been sending me a lot of baby advice stuff. I mean, it's my mom and not yours. And I'm not forgetting that conversation, for the record. But I told her to back off a bit, and then she sends me meal plans for pregnant women."

Ana looked over, a small smirk on her lips. "So, boundaries?"

Melody laughed a little. "Yeah. I know it's her first grandchild, but I didn't think she'd be like this. She's never bugged Eric or I about getting married or giving her grand-children to spoil."

"Well, the good thing is that you can take a short break from her, have a conversation about your bound-aries, and she'll likely listen to you and respect them. Unlike my mother." Ana pulled into line for the drive through. Fifteen minutes later, they were back on the road. As Melody unwrapped her sandwich, Ana sipped at her coffee. Melody sniffed the air, trying to see if she could get a caffeine high just from the smell of the latte.

Melody bit into her sandwich and sighed. She'd felt like she would have gnawed off her own arm if she hadn't gotten food soon. "What's the deal with your mom now?"

"The usual. Why haven't I gotten married? Given her grandchildren. Though, she wouldn't spoil them. At least not any kids that come out of me. She treats Bethie's kids better than she treated any of us growing up, but I still wouldn't say what she does with them as 'spoiling.' The last thing she told me was that I should quit the diner because, and I quote, no one's going to want the soiled goods of a waitress."

Melody held up her hand to catch the bite of food she'd just taken. "What the fuck?"

"Yeah." Ana shook her head. "I have no explanation for her."

About to say something that probably couldn't have been taken back, Melody frowned when her phone started ringing. She dug it out from her pocket and saw it was Eric. Frowning even harder since he was supposed to be on site today, she answered. "What's wrong?"

Eric's sigh was long and cartoonish. "Why does anything have to be wrong for me to call you?"

"Because when you call me instead of text, something's usually wrong."

Eric grunted. "Nothing's wrong. Exactly. I just finished a call with Greer and Triple H."

Melody adjusted the seat so she was leaning back a bit. She missed her truck. "Okay. What's the issue? They don't like our proposal?"

"No. They like our proposal fine, but they want to talk with someone in person. In California."

Melody blinked. "They've got offices in New York. How about we go meet with whoever's there?"

"According to the Triple H people, their main New York person for this division is out on extended leave, and their schedule can't accommodate sending someone out to the East Coast at this point."

It was Melody's turn to growl. "If they're going to make us jump through these hoops, do we want to work with them? Are they at least offering to pay for everything since they're the ones insisting on the meeting and the location?"

Ana looked over, taking her attention from the road, but

Melody waved her hand, finger pointing back to the road. They didn't need killer deer jumping out from the woods and Ana not noticing until it was too late.

"Yeah, they're offering to pay."

"So go. I can take care of what's left of Tony's place and get started on the Wilson cottage. Donna's back from vacation, so it's not like we won't be without a site manager for double coverage."

"That's the issue."

"What? You don't trust me?"

"No, brat. While I was on the phone with Greer and Triple H, Libby got a call from her attorney. The FBI and some other federal agencies want to interview her. They said it was likely to be a multi-day thing. I need to be there with her."

"So we put off Triple H."

"No. Uncle Stef's going to be on break from his show in a few days. I already texted him and he said he can help Donna oversee the crew while I'm in New York and you're in California."

Melody sucked in a breath. "I can't."

"Why?"

The response had been instinctive. Triple H's headquarters were in Los Angeles. She could possibly see Tony. But the brain weasels were back in force, telling her he might have decided after being back in LA that he didn't want to be with the woman who had tied herself to small town living, even if she was giving birth to his baby.

Her phone buzzed. "Eric, hold on."

It was a notification of a text, but it disappeared before she do more than see it was from Tony. She put the phone back to her ear. "Eric, I'll call you back. I need to check something."

"Don't worry about that. Just come into the office when you get back."

"Sure."

She hung up the call, told Ana Eric needed her at the office, and switched over to her texting app.

TONY

Everything okay? Miss you and Button

He'd attached another photo. This one of a buzzy bee dog toy.

She choked back a laugh as she remembered the dog show movie they'd watched together one night early in their situationship when she'd unexpectedly gotten her period. When she'd greeted him at the door and told him to go home because nothing fun would be happening, he just shook his head and introduced her to a few of his favorite movies.

She bit her lip.

MELODY

Miss you, too. I'll send the images as soon as I get them.

TONY

Call me when you have a chance? Even if you don't have the images yet.

Thinking about what she wanted to say, she saw bouncing dots pop up.

TONY

I know you're thinking too hard. Text me when you're home for the night, and I'll call you.

When they were actually talking with each other, she had few doubts. But they couldn't talk twenty-four/seven.

Ana remained quiet the rest of the drive back to Sunflower Falls. She didn't say anything until they passed the welcome sign on the edges of the downtown area. "Want me to drop you off behind the office?"

"No. Drop me off in the diner's parking lot. I'll walk the rest of the way. I need to clear my head."

Ana glanced over at her, but did as she asked. "Are you okay?"

"I'll be fine."

"That's not an encouraging answer."

Melody shrugged. "It's the only one I've got."

A horn double honked behind them. Melody looked over her shoulder and saw Ralph Winters, one of the county maintenance guys, in his pickup behind them. His pet pig Bacon was in the passenger seat. "Thanks for the ride. I'll talk with you later."

"Melody..."

Before Ana could try to pressure her into something, Melody climbed out of the seat. She waved at Ralph. Bacon started pushing at the window with his snout, so Melody tapped it as she passed.

She turned down the block and shoved her phone into the pocket of her jacket. For mid-October, it was still warm, but there was a breeze off the lake adding a chill to the air. As she walked by Secrets and Whimsies, she saw a display of wooden toy tools. Remembering the set that Uncle Stef had gotten her and Eric when they were kids, she smiled. It would never be too early to start Peanut in the family business if they wanted to join in.

Pushing through the door, she took a deep breath. The

scent in the air wasn't the expected pumpkin spice, but something with more vanilla and a dark floral tone.

"Melody." A little girl's voice piped through the store, but Melody couldn't see the source. Then Kieran barreled into her legs. He wrapped his arms around them. Hannah was right behind him. She snuggled up to her other side.

Melody wasn't quite sure how, but Aspen's kids had decided she was their new best friend. Aspen turned around from where she was chatting with Mrs. Smith as the older woman wrapped up whatever Aspen had bought.

There was a tug on her jacket. Kieran was looking up at her and gesturing for her to move closer. He still hadn't let go of her leg, so she did her best to bend down without dislodging him.

"What's up, K-man?"

He giggled, but leaned in so his mouth was near her ear. Even so, his whisper wasn't as quiet as he probably intended. "Did the baby like the seal?"

"Shhhhhh. Mommy said we're supposed to keep that secret."

Melody looked over to the register area. Aspen was doing something dramatic with her hands, but she had the feeling that Mrs. Smith had still heard exactly what Kieran said. Weren't older people supposed to lose their hearing at some point?

Mrs. Smith must have finished whatever she was doing and handed Aspen a bag with a bow tied on top.

They both came over to where Melody stood with the kids.

Mrs. Smith smiled at both children and then Melody. "How can I help you, dear?"

"The toy tool set. Is it sold yet?"

"No."

"I'll take it."

When she said nothing further, Mrs. Smith let out a light chuckle. "I'll get it wrapped for you. Come over when you're ready to check out." She left them alone.

Aspen had her hands on her hips and was tapping her fingers against them. "What have I taught you both about projection?"

Hannah struck the same pose as her mother. "Even whispers carry."

"Exactly."

Kieran hung his head. "I'm sorry, Mommy."

Aspen bent down and kissed his forehead. "I'm not the person to apologize to, kiddo."

When he looked up at her with an adorably confused expression, Aspen pointed to Melody. He looked at her with puppy dog eyes, and Melody had to restrain herself from cracking up. This kid was way too much like his mother. "I'm sorry for telling your secret so loud, Melody."

Melody held out her hand. "Thank you for the apology. We're square."

He frowned but gave her hand a solid little kid shake. Then he and Hannah wandered off to look at something else.

Aspen lifted a brow. "How did it go this morning?"

"Fine."

Aspen waited for her to say more, then frowned when she didn't continue. "Was there something about the ultrasound? I can listen if you want. I've had a few myself." She gestured to where Hannah and Kieran had begun a game of keep away. "Hannah, put that back this minute."

Hannah did exactly what she was told.

Melody rubbed the back of her neck. "You know Tony."

Aspen's eyes widened. "I do. Is there something wrong with him?"

"I might have to go out to Los Angeles in a few days for a work thing. Will he want to see me?"

Aspen blinked. Then clapped her hands. "You're coming to Los Angeles? When? I'll fly you!"

Melody held up her hands and laughed. "Chill. I don't know exactly when. A production company Eric and I have been talking to wants to have an in person meeting, but Eric needs to be with Libby for something. I don't know anything beyond that."

Tilting her head, Aspen kept her gaze on Melody even as she shifted so she could also keep track of the kids. "Why are you worried about Tony? Of course he's going to want to see you. Damien told me he's been getting twitchy. Staying home isn't his modus operandi."

Melody pointed a finger at Aspen. "That's exactly what I mean. He's used to city living. Maybe I was just a fun fling while he was stuck in a small town. At least that's what the brain weasels keep telling me. Intellectually, I know and understand his reasons for keeping his identity secret, but the fact he lied to me is always there in the background waiting to jump on any doubts."

Aspen whipped her head around. "Excuse me? Damien was also telling me how Tony keeps bugging him about when he can come back here. Have you two not been talking?"

Blowing out a long breath, Melody shrugged her shoulders. "We've been texting, some calls, but it's not like what we have here in Sunflower Falls is all that exciting. I mean, yeah, he bought the house and everything. But it's not going to be anything like that house he has in California. He has a private freaking sports court."

Aspen nodded. "He does love that court. But Tony won't decide you're not worth it just for a sports court."

"And a lap pool."

"Or a lap pool. Melody, honey." Aspen wrapped one of her elegantly long arms around Melody's shoulders and squeezed. "I've known Tony since just after he left Undercover Immortal. He's had a social life, but I've always had the feeling he was searching for something. Maybe not consciously, but still searching. I didn't feel that at all from him when we all had dinner together that night I arrived. He couldn't take his attention from you. He found what he'd been looking for."

Melody shook her head. "Guys who spend that long searching like the chase more than the capture. My dad's always chasing the next con. It's hard when I've had someone lie to me in a way that reminds me of my dad."

Aspen hugged her again. "You find out when you need to be in California and let me know. You'll fly out with us on the jet, and we'll talk. I promise you. Tony has been searching for the one person he could see himself with for the rest of his life. How could he not want a committed relationship when he had his parents as role models?"

Melody took a deep breath. Aspen's confidence was chipping through the wall of fear that had erected itself around her heart. "I'll talk to Eric and I'll let you know."

Aspen grinned. "We're going to have so much fun."

# *texts*

ASPEN

Get the house ready.

DAMIEN

Why?

ASPEN

We're headed home!

DAMIEN

Good. The kids need to get back into the
school routine. Their tutor asked me when
we wanted to start up again.

ASPEN

And we're bringing a special guest!

DAMIEN

Do I need to do a background check?

ASPEN

You've already done it. It's Melody.

DAMIEN

Does Tony know?

ASPEN

No. And you're not telling him. I want to surprise him. Meet us at his house after work tomorrow.

DAMIEN

Does he know you're coming over?

ASPEN

Again, surprise!

DAMIEN

I'll warn Zach at least.

# fifteen

TONY DODGED A PUNCH FROM ZACH. But not the swipe of Zach's leg. He hit the mat with his back, and his head bounced a bit. Zach stood over him, hands on his hips and sweat dripping down from his face. "We definitely need to be working out more."

Out of breath, all Tony could do was nod. He didn't want to admit the reason he'd gotten his ass handed to him by Zach, even worse than usual, was because he wasn't paying attention. All he'd been able to think about for the last couple days was Melody.

She'd sent him an email with the images from the ultrasound, and then went radio silent. He figured something had come up with a project the first day. But they hadn't gone more than twenty-four hours without communicating since he'd left Sunflower Falls.

When he hadn't heard from her by this morning, he'd texted Eric who'd said that Melody was fine and she'd contact him when she was ready.

If he could have jumped through time and space, he would have so he could yell at Eric for that non-response.

Then Eric had followed up that he was in New York with Libby because of some interview with federal agencies about her father and hadn't seen Melody the last couple days either. Tony had still wanted to yell at Eric, but all he'd done was wish Libby luck.

Ana wouldn't answer his texts either, so he tagged Zach to see what he could find out. Which was nothing. Tony had been ready to prison break out of his own house at that point and head to LAX so he could fly back to Sunflower Falls. Zach had finally talked him down and into a sparring session. Where he had proceeded to kick Tony's ass and then some.

Tony held up a hand, and Zach pulled him up. Working to catch his breath, he met Zach's gaze. "I need to call Damien. I need to find out what's going on."

"With the case?"

"No. With Melody. I need to get back there."

"And I told you, your ass is staying here. Ana would have told me if anything was wrong. When Melody's ready to contact you, she will."

His doorbell rang at that moment, and Zach began walking out of the room. "Probably the food delivery."

Tony frowned because he didn't remember Zach ordering any food. He had a private chef service for when he was in Los Angeles. The service ordered all the food.

Zach waved over his shoulder. "Come on. I'm going to need your help."

Grabbing his water bottle from the stand near the door to the indoor gym, Tony followed. "What did you do? Order a pallet of protein powder or something?"

Zach didn't bother replying as he walked through the hall to the front door. After checking something on his phone, he opened it and stepped aside.

Expecting to see a delivery person at the door with some massive food order of some kind, Tony's mind went blank when he saw Melody standing there.

She gave him a small wave. "Uh, hi?"

He ran over and pulled her into a hug. She was okay. She was fine. She was here. In Los Angeles. He breathed in the scent of her shampoo. She was really here.

"Surprise!" He looked over Melody's shoulder to see Aspen doing jazz hands with the kids on either side of her grinning at him.

"We kept the secret good this time, right, Mommy?" Kieran grinned up at her.

Aspen laughed. "We sure did, honey."

Tony rocked with Melody in his arms. He didn't want to ever let her go.

Zach coughed behind him. "I suggest you all come inside. I heard from your one neighbor's security detail that the paparazzi's started hanging around because your neighbor's breaking up with her flavor of the week."

Aspen nodded. "We saw them. Poor woman. She really needs to stop picking influence chasers for lovers."

Tony finally loosened his grip on Melody and pulled her into the house. "You can go advise her on your way back home."

Aspen pushed the kids ahead of her. "Like I'd leave you two alone right now after we've been in a plane for over five hours."

"I can call Damien."

"He's meeting us here later. He went into the office today since we weren't home yet. I also have food on the way."

Tony looked down at Melody. He'd refused to fully let her go, so he tucked her under his arm as Aspen and the kids trooped into the house. "Are you hungry? I can put something together. I think. I don't remember what's in the fridge."

"I could use some food. Maybe some ginger tea first?"

"Ginger? Are you okay? Did you get airsick?" Grabbing her hand, he started pulling her to the kitchen. He didn't know if he had tea of any kind at all, but he'd order a rush delivery of it if necessary.

She squeezed his hand and pulled back a bit. He finally slowed down.

"Just a little queasy. I'm fine. Aspen gave me some dry snack crackers on the plane, and that helped. Since traffic wasn't too bad, we came here straight from the airport, and she had Hannah submit an order with some delivery service."

Aspen passed by them. "It should be here in about thirty minutes. Okay if the kids hit the pool? I want them wiped out for bedtime."

Tony drew in a deep breath. "Sure." He pulled Melody back into a hug and rested his cheek against the top of her head. "You're here. You're really here."

She wrapped her arms around his waist and squeezed hard. "I'm here. Can we go somewhere else for a moment?"

"Yeah." Tony looked over at Zach. "Can you keep Aspen occupied?"

"As long as you promise you're not going for a quickie or anything."

Melody snorted. "Believe me, I'm not in the mood at the moment."

Concerned she wasn't feeling well, Tony pressed a kiss into her hair. "Promise. But we need some privacy."

Zach waved and then headed to the kitchen where Aspen was already going through his cabinets.

Tony led Melody to the small room off the entryway that he used as a study. One wall was lined with books and framed photos. The seating was limited, but there was a long couch for when he wanted to sack out for a quick nap. After closing the door, he led her over to the couch, sat down, and gathered her into his arms.

"This was a surprise."

"A good one?"

The doubt he heard in her voice cut at him. He'd thought they'd been progressing, even with him being in Los Angeles and her in Sunflower Falls. Would she always doubt him when they were separated? He kissed her head. "Very good. I was telling Zach that I needed to get back to Sunflower Falls since I hadn't heard from you." He swallowed, understanding that she needed the reassurance. "Ask him. He'll probably tack on that I'm a whiny bastard when I don't get my way."

Melody laughed, and then let out a long breath. Her body relaxed even more against him, and he was thankful for the small indicator.

"Why did you come out? Is everything okay? Do you need to go to the doctor?"

She tilted her head back, and he did the same so he could meet her gaze. He really didn't want to let go of her now that she was here. "Are you going to be this hovery?"

"Is that a word?"

"Stop trying to deflect."

He pulled the raised eyebrow. "Excuse me? Kettle meet pot."

She scrunched her nose at him and lightly elbowed his stomach. "Still deflecting."

"Takes one to know one."

"Just answer the question."

"Am I going to be hovery? In what sense?"

"Over me? During the pregnancy?"

He bent his head and kissed her. The feel of her body in his arms and her lips on his was something he'd gone to bed every night craving. "If me wanting you near me every second of the day possible and making sure you're as comfortable and taken care of as possible is considered hovery, then, yes. I'm going to be hovery. But not just during the pregnancy. This is forever."

"What if I need space?"

He shifted so he was sitting up straight and maneuvered her until she straddled his lap.

It was her turn to give him the raised brow. "You know this isn't going to be possible when my belly gets huge with the baby."

He placed a hand over where the baby was growing inside her. "I don't care how big your belly gets. Baby or no baby, I will always want you straddling my lap." He waggled his brows at her. "We'll be in our 90s in one of those assisted care places and I'll be begging for lap dances from you."

Melody rolled her eyes and laughed. He watched as even more tension drained from her shoulders. She wrapped her arms around his head and bent down to kiss him. Soon, the fire that never really went out when they were in each other's orbit flared high, and he was twisting their bodies to lie down on the couch.

A knock on the door had them breaking apart.

Hannah's muffled voice came through. "Uncle Anthony, Zach says Melody needs to come have a smoothie he made."

Melody snorted. "He's going to think I'm a liar."

He gave her another brief kiss. "No. He just knows me

too well." He got up off her and held out his hands to her. She took them, and he pulled her up.

She was looking over his shoulder and froze. "Tony?"

Frowning, he glanced over her shoulder to see what she was looking at, but all he saw were the family photos. Looking back at her, he lifted a hand to her cheek. "What? Are you okay?"

She moved around him and reached up to touch the latest addition to the collection. He hadn't even thought about it. "I had them rush the frame job."

She turned back to him, tears in her eyes. "You really want the baby." She ran back to him and hugged him hard.

"The baby. You. Forever. Look at the photos next to it."

She did, and he watched a couple tears well over. The first one was a photo that Ana had sent to Zach who'd forwarded it to him. They'd been in public, so hadn't been doing anything as obvious as touching. But they'd been looking at each other, daring each other. The other was from their wedding day. One of their witnesses had snapped it with his phone. The expression on Melody's face was bemusement mixed with heat. He was looking down at her as if she'd hung all the stars in his heavens.

There was another knock. "Uncle Anthony..."

Wrapping his arm around her, he led her back to the door. He opened the door to see Hannah standing there, her hand raised, and Kieran next to her sucking on one of the rocket ice pops he kept in the freezer year round for him. Both of them were in their swimsuits. Kieran grinned at him, red residue lining his lips.

"We're coming."

Both kids cheered and ran back to the kitchen.

He steered Melody down the hall, but before they'd gotten far, the entryway door behind them opened.

In a split second, he had Melody behind his back. A moment later, he was wrapped in a hug and cloud of his mother's favorite Baccarat perfume.

"Mom?" He looked over to the door, where his father stood, arms loaded down with bags. "Dad?"

"My baby. We came the moment we heard. You're locked up here all alone."

His father rolled his eyes as he set each bag down in the hall and closed the door behind him. "Vicky. He's perfectly fine. Let him go and let's get some food. I'm hungry."

His mother whirled around, hands on hips and chest out. "It's always with your stomach, Leo. I need to care for my baby who's being horribly abused by our legal system."

Even that had him rolling his own eyes as his dad met his gaze, brows raised. "You see what I have to put up with. I swear she slept on the flight over." His dad came over and kissed his mom. "As you can see, our baby is perfectly fine. Like he has been for the last thirty-six years. He may not like being cooped up at home, but the legal system is not abusing him."

Tony frowned. "Wait a minute. How did you find out?" He stared at his dad. "Did you cut filming short? I thought you had another week?"

"We do have another week. I'm flying back in two because our lead went and got drunk the other night and got in a bar fight because he was told he wasn't as pretty as he looked on screen."

A snort came from behind him, and his parents froze. His mother scooted around him. She clapped as soon as she saw Melody. "I didn't know you'd be here."

Tony looked down at Melody who appeared as shocked as he was. "Um, hi?"

Moving his gaze between his mother and Melody, he

voiced the suspicion forming in his mind. "Do you two know each other?"

Aspen chose that moment for her entrance. "My darling Vittoria!"

"Beautiful Lily!"

The two golden statue winners did the air kiss thing they always did even if they'd seen each other only the day before.

There was a tug on the shirt he wore. He looked down at Melody. She pushed up on her toes and whispered. "I don't know your parents. I swear."

She wasn't as quiet as she thought. Plus, his father had excellent hearing. "But we are looking forward to getting to know you better. Aspen's reports have been highly entertaining."

Melody swallowed and held out her hand. "Nice to meet you, sir."

"Leo, please."

"Melody."

Tony's mom came back over and wrapped her arms around Melody. "And call me Vicky. Everyone who matters does."

Pushing down his panic at what Aspen might have reported to his parents, Tony hugged his dad. "Welcome home." He looked over his dad's shoulder at Aspen. "I'm very interested to hear what Aspen reported to you."

His mother released Melody to reach up and pinch his cheek. "Only that you started dating someone. And that her husband had been unable to argue his way out of having you under house arrest."

"Mom. Damien's an excellent attorney. It's not his fault."

She humphed, but grabbed both his hand and Melody's

and pulled them to the kitchen. "I need to know everything. Tell me how you met. Was it love at first sight?"

Tony gently, but firmly, stopped his mother. "Mom. I love you dearly, but Melody just arrived with Aspen and the kids. I was training with Zach right before they arrived. We both need showers. How about you and Dad figure out where you want to order from for dinner, my treat, and we'll put in an order as soon as we come back down?"

"Come on, Vicky. Let's leave them alone. I could use a nap myself after that flight."

With the distraction of his dad wanting to go to bed early after what had to have been an ass-long flight since his parents flew nonstop whenever possible, he and Melody escaped. He grabbed the bag Melody had left in the entry-way, and directed her up the stairs.

"Turn left and head all the way down the hall."

Following her, watching her body move, he wondered if he could talk her into a joint shower. He definitely needed one, but she might want to just refresh herself or whatever. "I know I told my mom you needed a shower, but do you?"

"Probably. If it's cold enough, it'll wake me up, which should help with the jetlag."

Cold enough for that would be too cold for sexy fun times. "You take my shower, and I'll use the one in the guest room."

Melody glanced over her shoulder. "Isn't Zach using your guest room?"

His step stuttered, and realized that while he'd given her a video tour of the more public parts of his house, he hadn't shown her the upstairs. "I actually have four guest rooms. Plus my suite."

It was Melody's turn to stop mid-step. "Suite? Your bedroom's big enough to be called a suite?"

He placed his arm around her shoulders and led her around the corner and through the door to said suite. Expansive windows on the left had a clear view onto the Pacific Ocean.

Grinning down at Melody, he watched as her mouth dropped. "No fucking way. And you're building a house in Sunflower Falls? Why?"

"I enjoy investing. It's a pretty property. And we'll need some place to live when we're there."

She blinked. "When we're there?"

"Yes. We're going to need a house when we visit."

She blinked again. Stepped back. Fuck.

"Melody?"

"I think we need to talk. I am going to take a shower. In one of the guest rooms. And stay there. We'll use my time here, when I'm not in meetings, to discuss this further. But not right now."

Realizing that saying anything more would only shove his feet farther down his esophagus, he nodded. "Sure."

He turned and led the way back out of his room. Zach's room was next to his for security reasons, but if he could kick Zach out, he would. He showed Melody the room next to Zach's. It overlooked the pool in the backyard. It wasn't exactly pool weather, but both Hannah and Kieran were doing cannonballs into it with his mom and Aspen looking on.

When he'd bought the house, one of the draws had been that every guest room had an en suite bathroom. This one only had a shower, but he'd had it renovated last year to bring it up to date. He opened the door and let out a relieved breath that it didn't need any cleaning. "It's got a rainfall shower head, but all you have to do is..."

Melody placed her hand on his arm. "I know how to work a bathroom. Of all designs."

"Oh, yeah. Right. Sorry."

She had a little smile on her face, so hopefully she wasn't completely shutting him out. "You go get your shower, I'll get mine, and we'll meet back downstairs."

"Sure. Fine."

He left the room, and she closed the door on him. He tried hard not to feel like she was pulling back again, but with her wanting to "talk", it felt like he was again at the bottom of an uphill climb.

Taking one of the fastest showers possible, he got dressed in jeans and one of his favorite concert t-shirts. Shoving his feet into a pair of comfortable sandals, he went back downstairs.

"Anthony."

He froze. It felt like he was a teenager, sneaking back into the house after curfew. Again.

"Yeah, Dad?"

"Come here."

He realized his dad was in the study. Shit.

When he walked to the study, he found his dad staring at the framed photos. "Yes?"

His dad took one from the shelf, turned, and held it up. "Do you have some news to share?"

His mother's perfume reached him before she did. "Leo, Anthony, we're ready to place the order..." She came into the room behind him, and froze next to him. Her gaze locked on the image from the ultrasound. "What's this? Leo?"

"That's just what I asked our son. It was on his family photos shelf. It looks like a recent addition."

His mom looked up at him, tears in her eyes. "Anthony?"

# *texts*

MELODY
What am I doing here?

ANA
Is this supposed to be a philosophical question?

MELODY
Why did I let Aspen talk me into coming to see Tony?

ANA
Because you wanted to see him?

MELODY
This was a mistake.

I should get on a plane home tonight.

ANA
Uh, also meetings with Triple H?

MELODY
This was a bad idea.

I'm booking a flight

ANA

Damn it. I'm doing a desk shift. I can't call you, so you had better listen up.

You are not going to panic fly home tonight.

First, back-to-back cross-country flights are probably not good for the baby.

Second, I'm supposed to be the friend who spins out and you're supposed to be the friend who grounds me.

MELODY

There's one for only a thousand bucks. I can do that. Mooch meals off my mom to pay off the card.

ANA

MELODY! You're not listening to me.

MELODY

Can you come pick me up in Buffalo?

ANA

DO NOT BOOK THAT FLIGHT!

Give me a second. I'm going to pretend there's a reference question outside and call you.

## *sixteen*

MELODY DRIED her hair with the thick towel that had been in the bathroom. The reality of the wealth Tony had access to was crashing into her. She was extremely tempted to crawl into the bed and stay there until her meetings with Triple H on Monday. That, or ask Aspen to take her to a hotel.

But that would be cowardly.

Kind of like trying to book a flight home leaving tonight before Ana had talked her down.

Running her fingers through her mostly dried hair, she gave herself a moment to feel the overwhelm, and then shook it off. Facing what people said about her dad had never been easy, but it had allowed her to carve out a life for herself separate from him and his exploits.

Up till now, she'd been the person who kept both feet firmly planted on the ground, not letting out-of-reach dreams tempt her into doing stupid things. Then she'd met Tony. How he treated her, his open-to-anything approach to life had made her think maybe some dreams weren't so bad. That maybe finding someone to love her as she was, no matter her family history, was possible.

The pregnancy? Something she'd never expected. But so welcome. Even if the hormones had her emotions spinning out of control. And the one emotion that she was most afraid of was hope.

As she'd learned time and time again, hope couldn't be trusted.

But being with Tony had made her want to hope again. If he broke that for her, she wasn't sure she'd be able to try again.

She finished getting dressed and made her way back downstairs. Voices came from both the study and the kitchen. She turned to the kitchen. Letting herself do the small cowardly thing soothed the kid inside of her.

Aspen was standing at an island with Zach as he prepared some snacks. She'd never gotten that smoothie she'd been promised now that she thought about it.

He nodded at her. "It's in the fridge."

"Thank you." She looked around the room and realized that whoever had installed the appliances had applied veneers to blend them in with the cabinetry. Going over to the most fridge-like doors, she opened one and was rewarded with a smoothie that had a sticky note with her name on it.

Taking it out, she took the first sip. Very green, but exactly what her stomach needed. She toasted Zach with it. "I appreciate it."

Voices came from down the hall to the kitchen, but before she could decide on hiding somewhere else, Aspen cheered. "Food's here."

Zach held out his hand. "Give me your phone. I'll get it."

Apparently used to the demands of bodyguards, Aspen handed him her phone and then came over to Melody. "I know we ordered food already, but Anthony's ordering again from a restaurant for his parents. Do you want to order more adult food from there?"

Melody thought about it and realized now that she had something in her stomach, she was ravenous. The order of chicken nuggets and fries she'd requested from the place Hannah ordered from would probably feel like an appetizer. "Sure. Is there a menu?"

Before Aspen could reply, Tony's mother swept into the kitchen, arms wide open. "Melody, my darling, darling girl. Helping to give me my greatest desire in the world." She flung her arms around Melody and hugged her. Hard. The woman's head was barely at Melody's shoulder, and she was slim, but she could give a bear hug that rivaled the ones from Harry.

Melody looked over at where Tony stood in the doorway with his father. His dad's eyes were watery and Tony was rubbing the back of his neck. When Tony met her eyes, she widened them and mouthed 'What. The. Fuck?' at him.

He opened his mouth, but Vittoria, Vicky, beat him to it by releasing her and then reaching up to squeeze her cheeks. "My very first grandchild. You don't know how much I've looked forward to this day. We must go shopping for the baby."

Melody caught Tony's gaze again. "You told them?"

"Not exactly."

Her eyes widened even further. "Not exactly?"

His father came over and pulled Vicky back into his embrace. "Not Anthony's fault. I was in his study and discovered the image from the ultrasound."

She closed her eyes and nodded. She'd been surprised as well to see it in such a place of prominence.

"We're thrilled for the both of you. Are your parents happy? We'd love to meet them."

Melody looked over at Tony, who shook his head and gestured at her.

"I think you already know my mother. Nina Keller. My uncle is Stef Keller from To The Bones."

Vicky covered her mouth with her hands. "Little Melody? Nina's baby? I thought you were in college."

Not willing to get into what might have caused that misconception, Melody shook her head. "Nope. I got an associate's degree and then headed to trade school. No college for me." Was that something they'd stick their noses up about?

Vicky came back over to enfold her in a hug. "Nina's little Melody and my Anthony. Giving me a baby. I'm going to be a Nana." She looked over at Leo. "And you're going to be a Papa."

Leo grinned at the both of them.

"Mom. Chill. You're overwhelming Melody. Give her some space."

Thankful he'd finally spoken up, she stood still as Vicky gave her another squeeze and released her.

It was clear both Leo and Vicky were excited about the baby. They were obviously a tight unit as a family, and it left her feeling unmoored. Her mom had been happy, but Melody would be ecstatic if she could ensure that Peanut never met her own dad. She'd assumed that Uncle Stef would step in as Peanut's grandpa-figure, but Leo's reaction made it clear he welcomed the role.

Zach came back in the kitchen at that moment, hands

filled with bags. He looked around the room, but just nodded at Aspen. "Want me to get the kids?"

Melody had forgotten Aspen was even there, but looked over at her. Aspen's eyes were suspiciously bright and was grinning. She waved her hands. "I'll get them. Give me a couple minutes."

The food from the first order was soon distributed, and they were all seated around the gorgeous black walnut dining table in Tony's formal dining room. Uncle Stef would drool over the craftsmanship. Tony came in, placed a giant bottle of ketchup in front of the kids, and then sat down next to her. "Do you need anything?"

She gestured to the sauce packets that Hannah and Kieran had piled in front of her as the kids refused to use them. "I think I'm set."

He reached for one of her nuggets and she tapped his hand. "You've got your own food coming."

"We didn't order yet. Remember?"

The doorbell rang again. She cocked a brow at him. "If you didn't order, then who's that?"

Tony frowned and looked over at Zach. "I don't know. Do you?"

He was getting up from the table. "Yeah."

Zach said nothing further, so Melody went back to her nuggets. Tony pulled out his phone and placed it down next to her after unlocking the screen. "Here's the menu. What would you like?"

Moments later Zach returned with Damien following him. He went straight for Aspen, bending down to kiss her. It was a bit weird to witness because Melody could tell that if there hadn't been other people there, the kiss would have gotten a lot more explicit. He then kissed the top of each kid's head. Neither Hannah nor Kieran bothered to stop eating while receiving affection from their father.

Melody blinked. When she'd been their ages, if her dad had done something like that, she would have stopped everything she was doing to bask in it. But Hannah and Kieran acted as if this was a regular occurrence.

"Leo. Vicky. I thought you were supposed to be in Italy."

Leo gave a tight smile. "Marcus."

Damien gave a curt nod. "Of course Marcus. He's going to pull the wrong move one day and find himself only able to book commercials for low-T medications. Well, good that you're here so you can hear the news first-hand."

Tony froze next to her, and then she felt him slowly relax. As if he consciously had to do it. "How about we order dinner first, and then you can share this news my parents will want to hear? We're going to order from Le Cochon de Lait."

Melody looked closer at the menu. All the item names were in French. This was not like ordering take out from Harry's. Maybe she'd stick with the chicken nuggets and fries. At least she likely knew what those ingredients were. She tried to pass back Tony's phone. "Here."

He looked down. "What did you decide?"

"I'll stick with this." She picked up one of the sauce packets, tore it open, and squirted it onto the flattened bag.

Tony frowned at her. "That won't be enough."

She was about to argue, but her stomach chose that moment to rumble. "It'll be fine."

Narrowing his eyes at her, he leaned closer so his mouth was next to her ear. "I bet I can choose the perfect meal for you. If I win, you eat it with no arguments. If I lose, you get to ream me out in front of my parents."

She leaned back. "I would never do that." The idea of fighting in front of anyone else sent ants crawling over her nerves.

He cocked an eyebrow at her. "Afraid that I'm going to win?"

Melody bit her tongue to stop the instinctive agreement to take on the bet. He was determined to feed her, so she may as well let him try. "You order it. If I'm in the mood to eat it, I will. Otherwise someone else can have it. I'm not betting you."

He stared at her for a long moment which made her want to squirm in her seat, but he finally nodded. "I'll take that."

The others gave him their orders, all in perfect French, and she felt even more out of her element.

Tony rubbed her back. "You okay?"

She nodded as she bit into another piece of chicken. How could she tell him she felt completely out of place here? Working in construction, and specializing in renovating and building homes, she worked with people of varying incomes.

Some people were barely making things stretch to afford a necessary home improvement. While others like the Sullivans who'd been the project they'd finished up over summer had money for high end options. Even with Tony, she'd known he'd had access to money before she'd known exactly who he was because of what he'd chosen to do with the house in Sunflower Falls.

But that wasn't casually ordering dinner in perfect French. That wasn't owning a home where the primary suite had an entire glass wall overlooking the Pacific Ocean. This was a completely different culture than what she was used to.

Feeling more and more like a puzzle piece plopped down in the wrong puzzle, she steadily ate the nuggets, fries, and finished the smoothie. When the kids were done with their dinners, they tried to leave the table for the playroom they'd been in earlier after swimming, but Aspen had them clear their places first. Once they'd completed that task, they ran for the playroom.

Aspen laughed. "They're going to be out cold in five minutes."

Damien lifted his wrist and tapped on the screen of his watch. "Setting the timer."

Tony leaned back in his chair, a finger stroking up and down her neck. The action had shivers running through her. She fought the urge to go hide out in the playroom with the kids. She wanted to hear whatever news Damien had, too.

Showing that he must have been reading her mind, Tony spoke up. "Do we need to save this discussion until after we eat because it will ruin our appetites or is it good news?"

Damien leaned his arms on the table. "It's mixed. Nothing that should turn your appetite, but it's nothing to celebrate."

Leo pushed away from the table. "I'm going to get a beer. Anyone else want one?"

Damien and Zach shook their heads, but Aspen and Tony raised their hands.

Vicky got up, too. "I'll help. Melody, do you want something sparkling?"

"Um, sure." Ginger ale would have tasted great, but she doubted Tony had that on hand. Maybe she could find a regular grocery store somewhere and get some things tomorrow.

Leo and Vicky soon returned with Leo carrying a tray filled with drinks. Vicky handed them out, and Melody was surprised to see the familiar blue bottle of a popular New York-local brand of sparkling water among the beer bottles and a champagne glass. "Thank you."

Vicky grinned. "I fell in love with it when we did To The Bones, and I've made Tony keep it on hand for me ever since."

Feeling comforted at the bit of home even in this piece of very rich California and the care that Vicky had put into trying to make her feel welcome, she twisted off the top. The water fizzed on her tongue, and was refreshing after the nuggets and fries.

Once they were all settled around the table, Damien leaned forward. "This isn't to go past this room." He looked over at his wife.

She widened her eyes at him. "Who would I tell?" Then batted her lashes.

He scowled at her. "You're lucky that Vicky and Leo are here, because we both know damn well that if you had found out this news and they weren't here, you would have texted her immediately."

Aspen waved her hands at Melody and Tony. "But he's her only, baby son." The gesture, along with the words, was so over the top comical that Melody tried to cover her laugh with a cough.

"And it would have been up to Tony to share with them or not." He held up a hand when Aspen opened her mouth. Probably to argue. "Moving on. They still haven't found Robert. Besides an arrest warrant for the added charges the cops had been sitting on, the judge has now issued a bench warrant."

"Does that give them any additional help in finding

him?" Tony reached out and twined his fingers through hers beneath the table. Melody felt the tension in his hand. Unable to resist offering him a small comfort, she rubbed her thumb along his little finger.

Damien nodded. "In addition to the cops looking for him, now the sheriff's deputies will be on behalf of the court, too. I've also been informed there are likely federal charges coming soon."

Leo snorted. "That's going to be a clusterfuck. Depending on who gets to him first, who knows what will happen."

"That's a concern. The reason I know about the federal charges is that an agent approached me outside of court today after the status update call." He looked over at Tony. "They want to talk with you."

Vicky paused, her champagne glass almost to her lips. "Why do they want to talk with Anthony?"

"I'm not sure. Until I see the actual charges filed, I don't know what exactly they're investigating Robert for."

Zach cleared his throat. "Which agency did you talk to?"

Damien frowned. "The one who spoke identified himself as IRS, but there were multiple agents there, and none of the others introduced themselves."

"Well, that's not good." Leo tapped the table with his knuckles. "I can tap some of my contacts. See if they can find where Robert has gone to ground. It's been, what? A month or so now?"

"Over six weeks. And we shouldn't get involved, Leo."

"You're not my attorney, Damien. There are already so many people looking for him that another person or two won't matter. I promise that if my contacts find him, all they'll do is contact local authorities and keep an eye on him until said authorities arrive. With the baby on the way, we can't have Anthony tied up in this any longer than necessary."

Damien sighed, shook his head, and then sat back in his chair. "All I ask is that you don't tell me or your son who you're contacting. If anything goes wrong, we need plausible deniability."

Leo's grin reminded Melody of a shark, and she realized she recognized it as something Tony had often done on Undercover Immortal. "There won't be any issues."

Melody had no doubt that whoever Leo contacted would be aware of his fatherly wrath if something endangered his son. The contrast to her father—who would have left her to her own devices if anything had gone wrong with some con he'd been running in order to save his own skin—had never been clearer. Thank the gods for Uncle Stef.

Her feelings about Tony being in potential danger were clear, however. She was not a fan. As rocky as everything else felt, she knew that she'd be beyond pissed if anything happened to him. They deserved to have a chance to work out their issues. One way or another. Someone taking that chance from them? No.

The conversation must have taken longer than Melody thought as there was a ping from Tony's phone. He looked down, then squeezed her hand. "Delivery driver's here with dinner."

Zach stood up. "I'll get it."

Leo and Vicky headed back to the kitchen and returned with utensils and drink refills. Zach came back in, loaded down with branded insulated bags.

Melody soon realized that this group had done this before. Everyone seemed to have a role in the dance of serving dinner, but for her. As Tony placed what he'd ordered for her on the table, he kissed the top of her head. "I think you'll enjoy this."

The restaurant staff had individually wrapped each meal in thick boxes that she realized had kept them warm. She opened hers and found a sandwich with a separate well filled with creamy mashed potatoes topped with three caramelized cloves of garlic and another with glazed carrot medallions.

She picked up the sandwich and looked at it. Marbled rye topped what looked to be shaved roast pork, and some chopped veggie slaw. She grabbed a fork and tried the slaw. The crunch was sharp, but so was the spice kick. Groaning, she placed the top slice of bread back on and bit in. The pork damn near melted on her tongue, and her eyes rolled back at the experience in her mouth.

Refusing to look at Tony since she knew he'd be grinning at her as if he'd won an actual bet, she focused on the food. Before she completely filled up with the sandwich, she tried the mashed potatoes and carrots. Both were also ridiculously good.

Forcing herself to swallow before talking, she cleared her throat and looked over at Aspen. "What's the name of this place again?"

She grinned and held up what looked to be a bacon-wrapped stuffed date. "Le Cochon de Lait. The Tasty Pig."

Tony offered her a fry. "We can order again if you'd like. The owner's a friend of mine."

Damien snorted. "The owner's a friend, and Anthony's an investor. You'll never have a bad meal."

The food was too delicious to ignore, but Melody tried to push down the feelings of inadequacy. She and Eric were building their own business. Building a life for themselves separate from their past. But they'd never be the type of people to invest in a restaurant with a fancy French name. The Tasty Pig? Yes. Le Cochon de Lait? Never in a million years.

She took another bite of the sandwich and looked around the table as she chewed. What had she gotten herself into by having what she'd thought was only a summer fling?

*seventeen*

ALL THROUGH DINNER, Tony felt Melody pulling further away. He knew he'd fucked up somehow earlier, but other than Damien talking about Robert pissing off the feds in addition to the local cops, he wasn't sure why she'd be pulling back.

Was it his parents finding out about the baby?

Something else?

Was she sick? Did they need to go to the hospital? She had finished the sandwich.

He, Zach, Damien, and his father cleared the table. His mom went with Aspen to gather up the kids, who were likely sacked out on the couch in the TV room. He paused to check on Melody, but she shook her head at him and went to the door that led out to the pool deck.

"Anthony."

"Coming, Dad." Fighting off the urge to follow her out and swear to slay all her dragons, he took the remaining trash into the kitchen.

Zach was loading the dishwasher, and Damien was replacing the bag in the garbage container. His dad held out the mostly full bag, and Tony dropped what he carried into it. While his dad took it out to the garage, he looked over at Damien. "How worried do I have to be that the feds want to talk with me?"

Damien leaned back against the counter. "Let's wait for your dad to come back."

A minute later, his dad came in and went to the sink to wash his hands. He looked over at Damien. "How worried do we have to be about the feds wanting to speak with Anthony?"

With a snort, Damien shook his head. "I'm not saying you shouldn't be worried, but I didn't get the impression that Anthony was a target of any kind. They just want all the information they can get from him about Robert and anyone Robert may have brought with him."

"Do I need to send Melody back to Sunflower Falls? I don't want her getting mixed up in anything."

Damien frowned at him. "She just got here."

"And I don't want her or the baby to be in danger."

"You realize she's here for more than just you, right?"

Tony thought back over the hours since Melody arrived. "She didn't say anything about why she came out."

Zach turned and shook his head. "That's because you never gave her the chance or asked. You have your head so far up your ass."

Scowling at his friend, Tony crossed his arms against his chest. "What?"

"Anthony Michael."

He winced. His dad pulling out the middle name was never a good sign.

"What did we teach you about communicating with your partners?"

Zach leaned against the counter next to Damien. "Can't

blame him too much. Melody's not the most communicative person either."

His dad sniffed. "She's not my child." He jerked a thumb in Tony's direction. "He, however, is. You make sure your partner is always on the same page. Making assumptions of what they want or understand is only going to lead to heartbreak."

"I'm not making assumptions."

Zach crossed his arms against his chest. Damien blinked. And his father snorted.

"Son. It sounds like you are most certainly making assumptions. Go out there and speak with her. I know I would very much enjoy being a part of my grandchild's life, and your mother will make your life hell if you do anything that prevents her from doing the same. I won't stop her. Melody seems like a nice woman, and I'd like to get to know her better. That's not likely to happen anytime soon if you screw this up."

"Are you trying to direct me?"

His dad snorted. "Hell, no. I'm trying to father you. But being your father absolutely helped me become a better director."

He scowled at his dad. "You're welcome."

His dad jerked his head back to the living space. "Go speak with her. We'll get the rest of this cleaned up."

Damien nodded. "I'll call you tomorrow. I need to get Aspen and the kids home, anyway."

In the living room, he could hear his mom and Aspen talking as they got the kids moving. Melody's voice wasn't in the mix, so she hadn't come back in and joined them. He looked out to the pool deck where she'd been headed and saw the glow of a phone screen in the darkness.

Heading out there, he didn't try to muffle any of his

movements. But when he sat down on the lounger next to Melody, she jumped and dropped her phone.

He picked it up and handed it to her. There was a photo of Button lunging for a camera, mouth open, on the screen. Laughing, he met Melody's gaze. "Who's taking care of her?"

"Ana. My mom's got Mayzie, and the motel's all booked up for the county fair."

"That's right. I'd forgotten about that."

Melody paused in the act of taking her phone back, then nodded. "Of course you did. Why should you remember things like county fairs? People who order from fancy French restaurants don't go to county fairs."

He frowned. "Hey. What's going on?"

She shook her head. "Nothing. It's nothing."

He reached out and took her hands in his. The feel of her skin against his soothed the part that was getting worried about the direction this conversation was going in, but only a tiny bit. His dad had been right about kicking him out here. "It's not nothing. You're obviously worried about something."

She blew out a breath. "It's...just..." She bit her lip. "Look. We're from different worlds. We should never have hooked up."

Alarmed, he moved to sit next to her. He put his arm around her, but from the stiffness in her back and shoulders, he didn't try to pull her deeper into his embrace. "Melody. Just because we had different experiences growing up..."

She exploded into action, getting up and pacing the pool deck. "Different? Try solar systems apart. Your dad's an award-winning movie director. My dad has spent time in multiple jails for fraud. My mom runs a motel. Your mom hosts fundraisers that people give millions to." She held up her hands palms out toward him. "I've done everything from laying tile to clearing out septic systems on jobs as needed. Your face was on my wall as a teenager."

"Okay. You've done manual labor. I have, too. Both my parents taught me you do whatever's needed on a production to make it happen."

She raked her hands through her hair. "You're not getting it."

He heard the frustration in her tone. Telling her he wasn't because she was keeping it all bottled up in her head wouldn't do anything to help. He leaned forward, hands clasped and elbows on his knees. "I'm trying to. I really am, Melody. Can you break it down as if I was a small kid? Because that's how I'm feeling right now."

Instead of answering, she walked down to the end of the pool and then turned to follow the edge. He realized she needed to let the energy out. Even though she'd flown out with Aspen and the kids on a private jet, she wouldn't have had much room to move. Melody needed movement. Action. She did a lot of the office work for the business, but she was out on the site about as often as she was in the office.

And he realized what he'd been trying to do. Melody wasn't one to be contained. Ever. And he'd been trying to contain her. Mold her. His idea of pampering and caring for her would just look to her like he didn't accept her for who she was.

He let out a long breath as he watched her move around the pool. When she got to the doors leading back into the house, he worried for a moment that she'd just head back in and demand to be taken anywhere else.

She continued walking the edge of the pool, back

toward him. Stopping in front of him, he could see the burning edge in her eyes as she stared at him. "You really want to understand?"

He nodded, not wanting to break the moment, and then realized she needed to hear his words as much as he needed the same from her. "Yes."

Melody looked over her shoulder, and then sat down on the lounger he'd originally sat down on. "When I was growing up, things were rough."

She paused again, her gaze on the pool. After a few moments, he reached out and laid his hand on hers. Relief hit him in the gut when she turned her hand over and gripped his.

"I need you to know that my father never hit me." She went silent again. Then she drew in a deep breath. "But when I was in high school, my mom finally divorced him because he got into a fight with Eric. I wasn't there. I'd been over at Ana's. But when I came home, Eric had a bunch of ice packs on his face and hands with Uncle Stef checking him out, and Mom was on the phone with an attorney. That's why I do all the self-defense courses. First Uncle Stef and Eric wanted to make sure I could handle it if my dad ever came back and lost it with me. I kept doing them because I liked the exercise and it helped me feel more steady with everything."

He squeezed her hand. "I'm sorry, Melody. I figured out things weren't great with your dad. I didn't realize that had happened."

She swallowed. "The thing is, I'd seen him, Dad, earlier in the day. I'd given him a key to the house. I'm why he and Eric got into the fight. He wouldn't have been there if I hadn't given him the key."

"Melody..." He started to get up, but she shook her head and held up her hand.

He watched the shadows on her throat undulate as she swallowed. "Dad could always talk me into doing anything he wanted help with. I wanted him to love me, us, so much that he'd stop getting into trouble. I always hoped that this time I'd do the thing that was just enough. And then Eric got hurt because of me."

He squeezed her hand, unsure how to respond in a way that wouldn't invalidate her feelings or experiences. He also didn't want to stop her from feeling like she could share with him.

"I know you're thinking I should probably go to therapy. I have. It helped. Intellectually, I know it's not my fault. My dad could have found another way into the house. He could have just waited outside the door until one of us came home. But I've never been able to fully unload those feelings of guilt. They're as real to me as the fact Earth is round."

Tony cleared his throat. "I understand. I do. If I hadn't agreed to bring Robert on as a partner in the production, he wouldn't have had access to the actors and crew and subjected them to his behavior. I didn't give him permission to do what he did, but I gave him that access."

She looked at him. "When I found out you'd been lying about who you were, I felt like I was fourteen again. Finding out that I'd been stupid enough to believe someone who said he'd loved me just so he could take advantage of me. Hurt my family."

Tony's heart broke. If he could have kicked his own ass, and then her dad's, he would have gladly done it. "I am so sorry. I will forever be sorry I didn't tell you sooner."

Melody nodded. "Growing up, I always thought people weren't giving my dad a chance. If they were just nicer to him, he wouldn't feel like he had to do what he did." She let out a quiet laugh, but he heard the pain in it. "Thing is, my dad always chose to do what he did. My mom and Uncle Stef shielded us from a lot, but I found out later he had fucked up my grandparents' finances. Everyone in town knew. It really sucks being known as the child of the town fuck up who'd screwed over his own parents. I'd sometimes overhear Ana's mom talking about me, and how I'd probably be a bad influence."

Scowling, Tony moved to sit next to her again. This time, she allowed him to pull her into his embrace. "Well, that's just shitty. Didn't she realize you could have heard her?"

She snorted. "She probably meant for me to overhear. Ana's mom, to put it kindly, is a bitch. That's the thing about small towns. A lot of the stereotypes are true because some people want them to be. Ana's mom wants to be the queen bee of Sunflower Falls, so she makes that happen, at least in her own mind, by putting people into the places she assigns them. My dad maybe doesn't want to be the town fuckup, but he also doesn't care about how his actions affect others. And he keeps coming back because he's like a damn homing pigeon."

He looked out over the pool to the darkness of the Pacific Ocean. The vast expanse had always made him feel small, but secure in this tiny part of the world. It was a steady presence that would be there long after he left this world. "But you love living there."

She nodded against his shoulder. "I do. Because for every one of my dads, for every one of Ana's moms, there are also people like Nancy, Harry, even Mrs. Smith. They make the town better. They give me an anchor in knowing there are good people who will take you as you are, and give you a safe space to land when life gets really shitty."

They sat in silence for a few minutes. Melody periodically would rub her head against his shoulder. At one point, he looked down and saw her eyes were closed. "Melody?"

"Yeah?" Her voice was soft. She was drifting off to sleep, which wasn't surprising considering the long ass day she must have had.

"Why did you come out here?"

"Hmmm? Oh. I've got a meeting on Monday with Triple H."

He really was an ass. Why hadn't he thought of that? "Need anything from me?"

"No. Since you can't leave, I'll just use a car app to get there."

Even half asleep, Melody put him in his place. She didn't need him. And if there was anything she did need, she'd find a way to get it on her own. "Let's get you up to bed."

"Not sleeping with you."

He let out a small laugh as he stood and tugged her up. "Not tonight. You're already mostly asleep."

"Jet lag's worse than Ana's mom."

This time his laugh went deep to his gut. "Some day, you'll have to tell me the story of Ana's mom."

Melody frowned as she stood and wobbled a bit. Once she'd gained her balance, by leaning into his side, she looked up at him. "I don't know that anyone knows the whole story of Ana's mom. We've never figured out why it's like she doesn't like Ana. I always thought the baby of the family was supposed to be the best loved one. But other than Bethie, and sometimes their dad, Ana's family mostly ignores her if they're not treating her like crap."

"Definitely a story for another day, then." He led her back into the house and up the stairs to the room she'd claimed earlier.

But instead of heading into the bathroom to do whatever, she face-planted onto the bed.

He bent down and pulled her shoes off her feet. She sighed and rolled over. Then patted the bed next to her. "Come here."

Melody's eyes were closed, so he let out the grin. "I thought we agreed. No sleeping together tonight."

"I'll sleep. You hold me. I'm the person growing your baby."

Letting out a small breath of relief, he toed off his own shoes and climbed into the bed from the other side. She rolled over again and scooted over and plastered her back to his front. He wrapped one arm around her hips and rested his hand on her stomach. She hummed, and then he heard her breathing even out.

Pressing a kiss behind her ear, he closed his eyes. "I'm sorry, Melody. I'll be better."

She mumbled something and rubbed her ass against his cock. It began to harden, but he fought off the natural reaction to having her so close against him after so long. They needed to talk more. Tomorrow.

He'd find some way to show her he was both better than her father, and that he'd place her first instead of assuming he knew best. He closed his eyes and drifted off.

# *texts*

ANA

:photos of Button asleep on her back on a dog bed with a toy hanging from her mouth:

LIBBY

Like daughter, like mama

:photo of Mayzie asleep on her back on a bed with a toy hanging from her mouth:

ANA

When are you getting back to Sunflower Falls? We need a girls' night out.

LIBBY

Still not sure.

I'm meeting with my lawyer this morning before my next meeting with the feds.

ANA

I'm sorry your dad's such a shithead.

LIBBY

So am I.

Eric says that if we do a girls' night, I'm not allowed to drink Melody's share of wine.

ANA

WAKE UP, MELODY!

Unless you're having sex with Tony.

Carry on, then.

Also, tell me all the details so I can live vicariously.

LIBBY

Eric also says that he would like to not be anywhere near where Melody may or may not be discussing her sex life, so I'm going to mute notifications in case she wakes up :winky face emoji:

<h1 style="text-align:center">eighteen</h1>

MELODY SURFACED from the dream she'd been having. She'd been so warm, floating out in the sea with the sun shining above. The sense of peace she'd felt had been so profound.

She couldn't remember the last time she'd woken up feeling so rested.

Then she realized Tony was damn near wrapped around her. His breath puffed evenly against the back of her neck. Slowly reaching down so as not to disturb him, she confirmed that she'd slept on top of the bedcovers, and was still in the clothes she'd changed into after her shower yesterday.

Trying to think back to last night, all she could remember was patches after completely emotionally unloading on him. At least she hadn't cried. She preferred to do that in the shower where the water washed away all evidence of it, thank you very much.

"Mmmmmm..." Tony hummed in his sleep, but then his hand started moving down her stomach to the waistband of the leggings she'd put on.

She placed her hand over his, tangling their fingers together. A flash of him trying to leave, and her telling him to hold her because she was growing his baby bloomed in her memory.

He'd stayed. He could have left easily after she'd fallen asleep. But he'd stayed. Even after everything she'd told him last night. The bloom of hope unfurled further.

She'd given him only the highlights of life with her father. But he'd stayed.

"Love you, Melody."

She froze and turned her head to look at him. The angle was bad, but she could see enough that his eyes were still closed, and his breathing was still easy. He was asleep, or at least in that in-between stage between sleep and wakefulness, but he'd said he loved her.

Swallowing past the lump in her throat, she gave voice to the secret she'd tried to keep buried even from herself. "I think I love you, too."

Eyes still closed, he grinned and began nuzzling the back of her neck, pulling her in closer to him. She felt the stirring of his cock against her ass. Unable to help herself, she began grinding back against it.

His hand moved down again. Instead of stopping him, she guided him below the bands of her leggings and panties. He growled against her neck as their fingers hit her pussy.

He stroked her mound, slipping his fingers lower into her slit. She shifted her legs to make space for him. She felt his tongue against her neck, and she couldn't help but let out a small sound of pleasure.

"Yes. Give me all your sounds." He put his thumb against her clit, circling it as he moved two fingers into her.

"All your pleasure belongs to me. Even if you're getting

yourself off when I'm not around, I want you to tell me all about it. Everything you do."

The possessive words lit up parts of her brain she'd never experienced before.

"Tony." Even she heard the trepidation as she whispered his name.

He moved his fingers deeper, pressing harder with his thumb. "You are mine to care for. Mine to give pleasure to. Mine. But I will never contain you. Never. Tell me what you need, Melody."

Hearing the words broke something inside of her and the tears began flowing. "You. Give me you."

He pulled her in tight to his body even as he began pumping his fingers, coaxing an orgasm from her. She cried out, but he moved so that his mouth covered hers.

When the waves of pleasure eased a bit, he pushed her leggings down to her knees. "Is your pussy ready for me? Like this? No condom. Because we don't need one. We've already got a baby planted in you. I'll keep planting as many babies in you as you want."

Gods. Why was her brain lighting up like this? She pushed her ass back against him as he undid the fly of his jeans and pushed them down enough to bare his cock.

"That's it, baby. Tell me how much you want your cock. It's only for you. Use it however you want."

Her brain was melting, the only thing she could think of was him getting inside of her and filling her up. With everything. "Inside me. Now."

He lifted her upper leg so that her calf rested against his, giving him just enough space to enter her pussy. Her breath caught at the feeling. With all the constrictions, he felt bigger than he ever had before. She was wet from the orgasm, but he still had to work the head of his cock inside of her.

"You're so tight like this. So tight. But I'm not going to come until I'm all the way inside of you. Just going to sit inside of you. Filling you up. Marking you so that you never forget what it feels like to have me there. With you. All the time."

She reached down to her clit and began stroking it.

"That's it, baby. Make yourself wetter." He pushed in. It was like one of those post drivers they used on sites. Inexorable.

She started coming when he was maybe halfway in her, and she couldn't stop it. He moved his hand so that his fingers continued stroking her clit. "Keep coming. Give me everything. You're going to suck me dry aren't you?"

Her head fell back, and he sucked on her neck. "You are the most beautiful person. Inside and out. Thorns and all. Never forget that. I. Am. Yours."

He gave a short pump with each of the last three words, and she felt warmth flooding her as he came. Another orgasm hit her so hard that she curled in, gripping his wrist as she tried to process everything.

"Fuck, Melody." His fingers dug into her skin and she thought he might leave bruises. The idea of being marked by him, in her most intimate area sent more sparks flooding her brain.

Unable to move after having her world rocked off its foundation, she laid there soaking in the connections both physical and the tiny golden threads of emotions she imagined winding around them.

Tony's cock eventually softened a bit, and he pulled out of her with a groan. As he did so, he placed a kiss to the back of her neck. "You okay?"

She let out a shuddering breath. "I will be. Just a lot of emotions."

He moved from behind her, and she flopped to her back. He propped himself on his elbows so he hovered over her. "Was that too much?"

She reached up and pushed his hair off his forehead. It fell back down immediately. Tenderness she didn't realize she was capable of had her caressing his face. "No. It was just right. I..."

When she couldn't continue, he bent his head down and kissed her. Another tear leaked from her eyes. She wrapped her arms around his chest and hugged him to her.

"I'm sorry, Melody."

She shook her head against his chest. She had to get the words out. "No. No." Swallowing, she fought against the vault door in her mind that wanted to keep her safe. "That was amazing. I never thought I would have liked the whole 'I'm going to get you pregnant with all the babies' vibe. But I did. A lot."

He shifted them again until he was on his back and she was curled up onto his chest. It felt awkward with her leggings still halfway down her legs, but he stroked up and down her back. "I liked it, too. It's not something I've done with anyone else."

She traced a pattern in the hollow at the base of his neck. "So it's just ours."

He pressed a kiss to the top of her head. "Looks like. If you're good with it."

She nodded. As she opened her mouth to tell him she was really good with it and wanted to maybe try it again, there was a knock on the door.

"Breakfast's ready. Your mom's threatening to come get you herself, so get moving if you don't want her barging in on you." Zach's voice faded away with the last few words.

Melody lifted her head to look at Tony. "Would your mom really do that?"

He grimaced, but nodded. "Mom's got boundaries. And I bet she sent Zach up with that message not intending to follow through, but she would absolutely do her best to embarrass me if she thought it would serve her greater plan."

Not wanting to get the bedspread any dirtier than it already was, Melody did her best to scooch over to the side and get off the bed without touching it. Having her leggings at her knees did not help at all. "What greater plan?"

"I don't know. Maybe just feed us breakfast?" Tony sat up and swung his legs off the bed before helping her to get her leggings back on in a walkable manner because no way was she free balling it into the bathroom in this particular post-sex state.

When she was finally somewhat back in order, Tony stood up, got his own jeans done up, and kissed her. "Take your time. I'll run to my room for a shower, and then go down and placate her." He cupped her cheeks and stared into her eyes. "When we're done with breakfast, we'll kick my parents out for the day and talk. Okay?"

She nodded. "Yeah."

He bent down so that his forehead rested against hers. "I love you, Melody. I know you're not there yet, but we've got something good even beyond the Peanut between us."

She wrapped her arms around him again and hugged him. "Thank you."

"For what?"

"For not getting pissed off at me. For not leaving. I know I've got a lot of baggage. It's not for everyone."

He hugged her back and then leaned back and tipped up her chin so she was looking into his eyes. "Everyone's got baggage. Thank you for finally letting me in on how much you've got. We'll do what we have to figure out how to carry the load together."

She bit her lip. "And, maybe, after we talk, we can do some more, uh, playing around?"

He waggled his brows. "Playing around? We can definitely do some more playing around. I'll drink a protein shake with breakfast."

Surprised she could laugh after everything, she smacked his arm. "Go get a shower. We do not need your mom barging in here."

He kissed her again and then left the room. Melody locked the door behind him, though she had a feeling Vicky really wouldn't barge into her room. Tony's probably, but she had the sense that Vicky was doing her best to make sure Melody understood she was welcome in their circle.

Letting the shower sand down the rest of the rough emotional burrs in her mind, she remembered she needed to text Ana and her mom. She should also touch base with Greer before the meeting with Triple H tomorrow.

At first, she'd thought the meeting was a convenient excuse to see Tony. But now? With their relationship feeling like it was moving in a solid direction, she was ready to take on the big ass media company and take no prisoners. She and Eric had a vision, and if Triple H wasn't the right place for them, they would find someone else to partner with.

Revved up for the day, she turned off the shower and wrapped herself in one of the luxurious towels that Tony put out for guests. It made her wonder what he had in his own shower.

After getting dressed, she found her phone on one of the

side tables. Tony must have plugged it in to charge because she certainly didn't remember doing so. There were notifications from Ana, Libby, and her mother. The ones from Ana were more photos of Button to a group chat, and Libby's were replies to that. The one from her mom just said "Call me when you're up."

She opened her contacts and called the motel's number. After a few rings, her mom answered. "Sunflower Falls Motel."

"Hey, Mom. I'm up."

"Melody."

Relief colored her name, and she frowned.

"Can you hold? I have a guest checking in."

"Sure."

The motel's hold music filled her ear. She got up and went into the bathroom to grab her clothes. They'd have to be laundered before she packed them. She wondered where the laundry room was hidden in this house.

"Melody, are you still there?"

"Still here, Mom." She dropped the clothes on top of her suitcase. "What's up?"

"Your father called yesterday. He mentioned how you'd gone to California."

Melody's gut clenched and then anger burned through her veins. "He did, did he?"

*nineteen*

ON HIS WAY past Melody's door, Tony heard her speaking to someone, and then realized she was probably on the phone with her mother or Ana. Leaving her to it, he headed downstairs. His own mom was turning the corner of the railing when he was about halfway down.

"I'm coming."

She sniffed with her nose in the air like she'd been doing since the television period drama she'd been in. And won an award for. He chuckled and bent to kiss her cheek. "Melody's taking care of a few things, and then she'll be down."

He wrapped his arm around her shoulders and guided her back to the kitchen. His dad was standing at the stove, pushing around something in a pan. As he passed behind him, Tony snagged one of what turned out to be sliced pieces of sausage.

"Hey. Make your own breakfast."

"No need. I already made it for him." His mother went over to a plate where his favorite breakfast of French toast was sitting. She uncovered the butter and pulled a butter knife from the drawer. As she had since he was a very small kid, she began buttering the French toast thoroughly, one slice at a time.

His dad scowled at his mother. "Why do you spoil him?"

"Because someone needs to spoil him. You push him, I spoil him. He's a well-balanced child."

He leaned back against the counter next to the sink as his dad gave him the stink eye over his shoulder. "We should probably be glad we didn't have any surprise grandchildren before now."

Tony grinned at him. "You taught me well. I always made sure my partners and I used protection."

His mom clapped, flinging speckles of melted butter over the cabinets and him. "You planned this baby? Oh, Anthony, I'm so happy for you."

Grimacing, he licked a fleck of butter from his hand and then rubbed the back of his neck. "Yeah, well, no. This baby wasn't planned. But it is very welcome."

His mom tugged on his arm until he turned and faced her. She cupped his face and brought it down to her level. She beetled her brows at him. "Not planned?"

"No." When she was like this, pure honesty was the best way to deal with her.

"And Melody knows all her options?"

"Yes. We discussed that. I was very clear that I supported her decision. Whatever it was."

She nodded and released his face. "Okay, then. Do you think she'll want to go shopping for baby clothes with me today?"

"And now you're spoiling our grandchild?" His dad moved the sausages over to a paper lined plate and then poured what Tony realized was scrambled eggs into the pan.

His mom pointed the butter knife at his dad. "I will spoil this grandchild as much as Melody will allow."

Tony grabbed a piece of the French toast and bit into it. "Don't I get a say?"

"How many times have I told you not to speak while chewing? And, no. I spoiled you, so I will spoil your children. You deserve spoiled children."

He covered his mouth so he didn't spit out the French toast as he began laughing. "Thanks, Mom."

The sound of a clearing throat had him looking over at the hall entrance to the kitchen. Melody stood there, an uncertain look on her face.

He grinned at her. "French toast?"

"Normally, I'd be all over that, but my doctor wants me to increase my protein."

His mom whirled around. "Any morning sickness? I can make some tea, if you'd like."

Melody smiled at his mom. "Thank you, no. Just water for now, I think. I'll find something in the fridge."

His dad cleared his throat. "I'm making scrambled eggs. I'd be happy to share. Also have chicken sausage if you'd like that."

Melody opened her mouth, but paused before responding. "Sure. That would be great. I guess not many people can say they have The Leo Dewitt making their breakfast for them."

Grinning, his dad turned back to the stove. "Only family. Anthony, get Melody some water. This will be ready in a minute. We can sit at the dining room table."

As he was getting a glass, he saw Melody frown and look around. "Where's Zach?"

Tony stopped as he realized he hadn't seen Zach either.

"Oh, he stepped out to take a call. He's probably back by the pool." His mom waved to the living area.

The kitchen windows had a view of the ocean instead of the pool, so Tony couldn't see if that's where Zach was. But he also didn't hear his friend, so he had to be outside somewhere. "Should we make him breakfast?"

His dad grabbed another plate out of the cabinet. "He was finishing up when your mother and I came down. Order up."

Tony held onto the glass of water for Melody and grabbed his own plate before following his mother and Melody out to the dining area table. After Melody sat down, he set her glass down next to her and pressed a kiss to the top of her head. His dad sat down on her other side and handed her plate to her.

"Thank you. This looks delicious."

"Can't go wrong with chicken sausage and eggs. Even better, my doctor hasn't told me to lay off them yet."

"Melody, before you came in, I was asking Anthony what he thought about taking you shopping for baby clothes."

Melody looked up at him. "You can leave the house?"

He cut into a slice of French toast and shook his head. "As far as I'm aware, I'm still required to stay here. This would be just Mom and you."

Blinking, Melody turned to his mom. "Um, that would be nice. But Tony and I need to talk about some things today. And I have meetings tomorrow. And I'm supposed to fly home on Tuesday."

Tony froze. "Tuesday?"

She speared a slice of sausage and some eggs. "Yeah. We're still working on your house, and there are a couple of other projects starting soon. Eric and Libby are still in the city. I need to text him to see what his schedule is, but I'm point person until they're free to come back to Sunflower Falls."

Remembering his promise to not try to contain her, he gave a quick nod and dug back into his food.

"If you're leaving on Tuesday, then we most certainly need to carve out some girl time today. Though, I might be able to go back to New York with you. It's been ages since I spoke to your mother."

He realized Melody had frozen along with him at his mother's words. He looked over and saw Melody was blinking. Melody was usually the one steamrolling people, so being on the other end was probably more than a bit disconcerting.

"Uh..." She turned to Tony, widening her eyes. Her lips mouthed the word "help."

He shrugged.

"We can go over to The Grove. Leo, would you make some calls?"

His dad sighed. "Remember, we hired Alyssa to be your assistant."

"She's on vacation as she should be."

Leaning over, his dad kissed his mom on her cheek. "As she should be. I'll call Norma, and she'll make the calls for you. Let me know which stores you want to go to."

"And we'll need a car." His mom looked at her watch. It was the same elegant gold band watch she'd been wearing for most of his life. His dad had given it to her as a wedding present as she'd been late to nearly all their dates. "Eleven? That will give you two a couple hours to talk and do whatever you need to do."

His mom really was in steamrolling mode today. "Mom.

Chill. I don't know how long it will take us. When we're done, if there's time, you can arrange for a car then."

She sat back in her chair and tapped her fingers together in front of her lips. She'd always wanted to play a villain mastermind. "Four hours and we leave at one."

While his mother was notorious for losing track of time and getting ready for dates, she also had a reputation as a tough negotiator. Stories were still whispered about her time in the union's leadership. He placed his hand on Melody's. "It's up to Melody. If she wants to just lay out by the pool and chill out in quiet, that's what she gets to do."

"Of course. Melody?"

Melody, being a lot more polite than he could be, finished chewing before answering. "Let's see how I'm feeling later?"

His mom clapped her hands together. "Absolutely. Leo, call Norma."

His dad opened his phone, pulled up a contact, and then handed the phone to his mother. Tony could hear the call ringing, and then his father's executive assistant answered. Joy filled his mother's expression as she got up from the table. "Norma, darling. It's Vicky. I have a small favor to ask."

Shaking his head, his dad went back to finishing his breakfast. "Norma's going to love this as much as Vicky."

Melody froze. "Wait. Is Vicky going to tell her about the baby?"

Both Tony and his dad froze and then looked at each other. His dad scrambled up from the table and ran after his mom. A few moments later he came back, shaking his head. "Sorry about that. I caught her just in time. Norma would keep quiet anyway, but if you don't want word getting out, no one outside of family and who you choose to tell will know."

"Thank you." Melody went back to eating and soon finished her breakfast.

Tony finished his a minute later.

He was gathering up their plates and utensils when his dad waved at him. "I'll get those. You two go talk. Your mom's going to want to go shopping as soon as you give her the green light, so the faster you can work out whatever it is you need to work out, the better."

"Thanks, Dad."

His dad chuckled. "Believe me, it's as much for me as for you."

Before he could lead Melody outside to the garden area he thought she'd like, Zach came back inside. He spotted them immediately. "Good, you're here. That was Damien. The authorities have found Robert."

Tony blinked. Melody grabbed his arm. Tugged on it. "That's a good thing, right?"

Zach nodded. He looked straight at Tony. "This doesn't mean you're free to leave, however. There's a conference scheduled for tomorrow. You need to be at the courthouse, but Damien will meet with the judge and both sets of attorneys. If you're needed, you'll be called in. Damien expects you to be called in."

"Will Robert be there?"

Zach shrugged. "Damien didn't say."

"Where was he?"

"On his way across the border."

"Tijuana? Seriously?"

"Wrong border. He somehow thought no one would look for him if he went into Canada."

"Robert hates the cold." It was a nonsensical thing to say, but this whole situation felt nonsensical.

"Yeah, well, he decided to not only drive into Canada, but cross the border in Minnesota. That's at least partially why he's been off the grid for so long. And before you ask, I'm not sure what else he's been doing in all that time."

Tony shook his head. This whole thing was becoming farcical. All they needed was some rural county sheriff from Minnesota to show up at the trial looking and sounding like Frances McDormand in Fargo. "Anything else?"

"Damien's going to be over in a few hours to further discuss tomorrow. We'll need to leave for the courthouse by six to avoid traffic."

He looked down at Melody. "Where's your meeting with Triple H? Maybe we can drop you off?"

"At their headquarters. I don't know where that is in relation to here, though."

Zach looked up from his phone. "They're in City West, so not anywhere close to the courthouse. When's your first meeting?"

"Nine."

"You'll probably want to leave by six, too. If you get there early, there are a few coffee shops over by them. I'll call my office to arrange a driver."

Tony looked over at Zach. "Thanks." Then he realized what else Zach had said. "Damien's coming over?"

"Yeah. He didn't say how long he expected it to take, but I'm betting at least a few hours."

Blowing out a breath, Tony nodded. "Fine. Thanks."

Zach headed back into the house, and Tony reached for Melody's hand.

She tugged him back when he started for the garden. "What's wrong?"

He rubbed his face with his free hand. "I don't want to rush this conversation, but with Damien coming over now, and then both of us in meetings or whatever tomorrow and you leaving on Tuesday?" He opened his mouth to continue, but no words came.

Melody squeezed his hand. "I get it. We've got time now, so let's talk. Where?"

He bent his head and kissed her. "I love you. Please don't ever doubt that."

She ducked her head. "I'm getting there."

"I've got this garden I think you'll like. It's got this secluded patio space." He led her to a corner of his property that butted up against his neighbor's storage garage. Her maintenance staff primarily used it, and since it was Sunday, they were unlikely to be around. He drew in a deep breath. Most of the plants had gone dormant at this time of year, but there were some herbs that gave off a fresh scent.

Melody grinned. "This is a gorgeous view with the pool and then the ocean." She sat down and adjusted herself with a slight wince.

"Are you okay?"

"I'm fine. My body's just changing every day and it sometimes feels weird."

He sat down next to her and put his arm around her shoulders. She rested her head against his shoulder and twined her fingers with his. "I never gave serious thought to becoming a mom. I had, have, a great mom, so I've got a great example. But I could never see myself having a kid with any of the men I'd been with, or going out and doing it on my own. It wasn't a priority."

He turned his head and rested his chin against the crown of her head. "Even with us getting married..."

She poked him in the ribs. "We still need to talk about that, too."

He grinned since she couldn't see him. "I know. I'm also sorry I didn't bring it up before. I should have."

Melody blew out a long breath. "I should have, too." She cupped her hand over her stomach. "I don't usually run from conversations like that. I like putting all my cards on the table in relationships. That's usually why the more serious ones didn't last all that long. I'm too blunt."

He pressed a kiss against the side of her head. "I like your bluntness."

She chuckled and let it trail off. "I think I didn't want to face the pain again. It hurt so much and was scabbing over."

Tony hugged her closer. "I know I can be overly optimistic. Thinking things will work out. If I can clearly see a problem, I do my best to fix it. Like with Robert. But I was scared, too. I wasn't able to be with you, but you were still communicating with me. I didn't want to give you a reason to cut ties because I wasn't there after I told you I would be." He cleared his throat. "Getting back to the kids question. Even after we got married, you never thought about the possibility of kids with me?"

She was quiet for a few minutes. Recognizing she needed the mental space, he also stayed quiet, slowly rubbing his thumb against her fingers.

Eventually, her words came slowly. "No. I was still struggling with the idea of being married to someone. Until I took the pregnancy test, I truly didn't think about the possibility of kids." She placed her free hand on her stomach. "I'm glad Peanut's here. But it was so far outside my vision of my future."

"And now that Peanut exists?"

She went silent again for a few minutes. "I know you've got this life here, but I want to raise them, and any more kids we decide to bring into the family, in Sunflower Falls."

His dad had been right. He'd been so wrapped up in trying to avoid giving her a reason to cut him out while he was gone that he hadn't been clear in his communications about his vision of their future. He'd just latched on and barreled forward. He paused in rubbing her hand, felt her hand tense, and began rubbing again. Pressed a kiss to her head. "I'm just thinking. That's all."

"I know that's probably not what you wanted to hear."

"Remember, just thinking."

She nodded against his shoulder. He breathed in the scents of rosemary and sage. When he'd first bought this house, his Nonna Schreiber had come over and planted them. Told him how he should always have the scents of the home country near. Even though her own parents had been born and raised in America and he had more than Italian heritage to his name, she was insistent. And then tutted about the plants not being nearer to the kitchen so he could use them like she'd taught him.

But Nonna had been right. Any time he'd need space for thinking, this is where he came.

When he felt like he'd gotten his thoughts in enough order, he turned and tipped up Melody's chin. "Again, I'm sorry for tiptoeing around the hard discussions and making assumptions. I'm not saying I won't move to Sunflower Falls. I want to be very clear that's not what I'm about to say. However, my work is here, at least partially, and even if I move to Sunflower Falls, I'm going to have to be here or on location on a regular basis. I won't be able to be full time in Sunflower Falls."

She blinked, then nodded. "My work's in Sunflower

Falls, and even if Eric and I can land a show deal, that will always be our base of operations. How are we going to make this work?"

He wrapped both arms around her and gave her a hug. "One day at a time. We need to learn to communicate better. I promise you, other than my identity that I had to keep hidden..."

Melody placed a finger against his lips. "I get it. I do. I still don't like it, but I understand why you did it." She let out a quiet laugh that had a bit of a sarcastic edge to it. "Something else for me to go back to therapy for."

He pressed another kiss to her temple. "We should probably look into finding a couples therapist. I don't want that poisoning our future. Or our kids. If we're going to make all this work, we're going to need help."

She snuggled her head back into his shoulder. "A lot of it."

They both fell silent. He didn't know what was running through her mind, but he was trying to figure out the logistics of living in Sunflower Falls on an at least more-than-half-time basis. He could do a lot of meetings from the house, but there were going to be times he'd need to be on set.

His parents had raised him on sets as he grew up, placing him with the on-set tutors for most of his younger schooling years. And since they basically traded project time and minimized overlap, he'd grown up with both his parents around most of the time. But they were in the same industry which made working out that kind of schedule a lot easier.

He and Melody had years before they had to think about things like school for Peanut and any other kids Melody wanted to have, though. The fact she even broached the possibility of more kids blew his mind. However many kids she wanted was fine with him. And if she only wanted Peanut, they could find ways to ensure no more kids and still explore kinkier adult fun times like this morning.

Melody pulled at his left hand, lifting it. "I think you're missing some jewelry."

He leaned back and pulled out the chain he wore beneath his shirt every day. The ring she'd first put on him back in Niagara Falls hung from it. "Whenever you want to put it back on, I'm ready."

She lifted her face and kissed him. "I'll let you know. But first, do you think we can have some more fun before your mom kidnaps me for a shopping expedition?"

He grinned. "To quote the Dread Pirate Roberts, as you wish."

# *twenty*

A COUPLE HOURS LATER, Melody was sitting by the pool, debating if she wanted to change into the swimsuit she'd brought with her at Aspen's insistence or do something else. Damien had arrived not too long ago, and he, Tony, Zach, and Leo had holed up in some room. She knew Vicky was likely expecting them to go shopping, but she wasn't sure if she wanted to go.

Vicky was very kind, but the woman was a bit overwhelming. Probably needed to be to survive in Hollywood for as long as she had.

"There you are. Zach arranged for a car and driver from his company. He'll be here in ten minutes. Put on your walking shoes because we'll be hitting all the stores."

Closing her eyes for a moment, Melody drew in a breath that was scented with chlorine and salt. She sent a smile over her shoulder. "Hi, Vicky. I think I might sit out here for a bit. But thank you."

Vicky sat down next to her. She had dressed in close-fitting white capris and a blue and white striped top. Very relaxed until you saw the jewelry she wore with it. Melody was sure the sapphire or whatever it was hanging from the gold chain was the size of the nuts they used to secure bolts in I-beams.

"Are you not feeling well?"

She shook her head. "Everything's just been a lot. And I've got the meetings tomorrow with Triple H. I may want to go over my notes later."

Vicky tapped her lips with a finger. "How about a deal?"

Realizing where Tony had likely gotten his tendency to bet on things from, Melody remained wary. "What kind of deal?"

"I would very much like to spend time with you to get to know you a bit better, but I'll scale back my plans. Just one area I think you might like. And everything will be my treat. I told Anthony earlier that I'm looking forward to spoiling his child as far as you'll let me."

Melody snorted. "I'm sure Tony had some things to say about that."

"Oh, no. I will spoil his child forever and a day, no matter what he says. But if you say enough, then I'll pull back. He may deserve spoiled children, but he is my child."

She winked, and Melody couldn't help but feel the charismatic spell that had charmed audiences for decades and had people throwing awards at Vicky every chance they got. Aspen had the same charisma. But what made Melody like them was how it had been obvious how they very much liked each other and were interested in other people. There wasn't any cattiness to them.

"Okay. One area. Is it that shopping center you mentioned earlier?"

"Oh, no. After talking with Norma, we realized they didn't have enough variety of baby items. The main place I want to go to is a cute little Main Street-like area with lots of boutiques. Even better, it's not too far from here, so if you want to come back and nap this afternoon, we can. I napped all the time when I was pregnant with Anthony."

Realizing this trip would be an excellent opportunity to get to know Tony better through an outside, though still biased, perspective, Melody got up. "Give me a few minutes to grab my bag and change my shoes. Should I change my clothes?"

"No. You're perfectly fine."

Melody looked down at the carpenter's pants and loose shirt she was wearing. Looked back over at Vicky. "Are you sure?"

"You'll be with me, my dear girl. No one will question you. Because they know if they do, I'll never shop with them again. Whatever you're most comfortable in is perfect."

Taking Vicky at her word, Melody went up to the room she'd slept in and changed her flip-flops for a pair of sneakers. She grabbed the sling bag Ana had given her for her last birthday and slung it over her head.

When she went back downstairs to meet Vicky, Zach was standing at the door. He looked her up and down and nodded. "If the paparazzi follows you, follow Derek's lead. Move quickly and avoid touching them."

Melody blinked. "Paparazzi? Is that an issue for Vicky?"

"Not so much these days, but from what she just told me, you're going to an area that's popular with them to see who's buying baby stuff."

Melody froze. "Is that an issue for Tony? Are people going to care if he's having a kid and that I'm the mother?"

"You're not showing yet, you're not a known name, and Tony's stayed out of the gossip spotlight for the most part. At least for his personal life. You'll blend with the regulars.

Remind Vicky that she shouldn't be telling anyone that what she's purchasing is for you and Tony. She can just say a family member if she feels the absolute need to tell anyone her business."

Vicky's timing was perfect as she appeared behind Zach in the hallway. "I know how to conduct myself in public, Zach Troy, and have been doing so since before you were born."

Zach shook his head. "Be careful. Derek will call me if there are any issues since I'll be the closest backup, but I'd prefer not to leave your son without coverage."

Vicky reached up and kissed his cheek. Melody was surprised to see a blush stain his cheeks. "You're very good at your job, and so are your people, so I'm sure there will be no issues."

He let out a low sound Melody couldn't figure out how to describe, and then opened the door. A tall Black man with close cropped hair stood outside. He nodded at Zach, and then Vicky and Melody. "Ladies."

"Derek. It's so lovely to see you again. How is Keshia doing?" Vicky slipped her hand into the crook of his elbow. Melody wasn't sure which one was leading the other to the car.

She looked up at Zach and raised an eyebrow.

He shook his head and mouthed good luck at her before closing the door.

Derek handed Vicky up into the dark blue SUV parked in Tony's driveway, and then turned to Melody and held out his hand. "Ma'am. Derek Thompson."

She knew he was holding out his hand to help her into the car, but she held her own out for a shake. He didn't hesitate and shook her hand. "Nice to meet you. Melody Keller. Please call me Melody." She looked into the car and

Vicky patted the seat next to her. Shifting her gaze back to Derek. "I can sit in the front."

He gave her a small smile. "Protocol, ma...Melody."

"Fair enough." She climbed into the back seat with Vicky and buckled up.

As they pulled out onto the road, Melody spotted a car pulling out from a parked position down the street, but got caught up in the conversation between Vicky and Derek talking about his children and how they were doing in school.

The area that Vicky wanted to go to ended up being a half-hour ride from Tony's house. As Vicky had promised, there were a lot of boutique stores. It felt like the area only allowed boutique stores. There was not one chain store to be found. Even for coffee. Their first stop in fact was a tea shop which also offered pastries. At Vicky's urging, Melody selected the peanut butter fig breakfast pastry to go with the peppermint tea she'd ordered.

And then she realized that the name of the shop was the same as the brand on the tea bags Tony had arranged to be sent to her house when he'd first found out she was pregnant. She looked around and saw there was a window into a back room. The clerk saw where she was looking. "Our bagging room. We mix and package all our blends here. We ship all over the United States if you'd like to send anything to a friend."

Melody smiled at the clerk. "I think a friend sent some to me last month. It was delicious."

The clerk grinned at her. "Excellent. I'll let our owner know. They love it when people come into the shop after receiving a shipment."

As they exited, Vicky leaned in. "I found out about this

place from Aspen. Did she order something for you from here?"

"No, Tony did. But I think he asked Aspen for advice."

"Let's sit for a moment. Not savoring these pastries would be a crime." They sat down at a shaded table near the front wall of the store. Derek wasn't pleased with sitting outside, but he positioned his chair so that he had a view of both of them and whoever was passing by.

As Melody sipped from her tea, she had an itch in the middle of her back. She looked over her shoulder, through the plate-glass window into the shop, but no one was watching them. Scanning the surrounding area, she didn't see anyone obviously looking at them either.

Derek must have seen what she was doing because his shoulders tensed and his attention arrowed in on her. "Something wrong?"

"I don't think so. Just an itchy feeling in the middle of my back. It's gone away."

He looked around, but must not have seen anything either. "Don't discount your instincts. If you get the feeling again, let me know."

They finished eating—the peanut butter fig pastry had indeed been delicious—and headed to the first stop. It was a housewares shop with an extensive baby section.

Vicky immediately went to the blankets and began petting them. A clerk came over and talked about the fiber content, how each was a natural fiber sourced from only the most ethical vendors. Vicky quizzed them about how easy they were to wash.

Melody grimaced. She'd have to remember to tell Vicky not to get anything that required special care. She didn't have time to do things like handwash in a special soap and hang out to dry on a perfect seventy-five degree day with no humidity.

Out of the corner of her eye, she spotted a gorgeous little decorative statue. Two figures flowed together, the larger one wrapped protectively around the smaller one. Ana and her romance-loving heart would adore it. She picked up the figure to see the price tag, and winced. A bit out of her budget. She took a picture of the figure and the price so that she could think about it.

"Melody, can you come here for a minute?"

She went over to where Vicky and the clerk were standing. The clerk was scrolling through a tablet as they only kept one color of a particular blanket in stock, but their supplier had other offerings and Vicky wanted her input.

Melody hadn't thought about how she intended to decorate the baby's nursery. At this point, she wasn't even sure which house or houses she needed to decorate as she and Tony hadn't gotten around to discussing specifics before Damien had arrived. She pointed out her own favorite color of the ones on offer, a deep rich blue with green undertones. Both the clerk and Vicky grinned, so she guessed she'd chosen correctly.

After making a few more selections and directing the clerk to send them to Tony's house here, Vicky led the way to the next store. At each stop, the head clerk or the store's owner greeted Vicky personally. And at every store, Vicky made some selections. From baby clothes to a bassinet that would live at Vicky and Leo's house if not at Tony and Melody's, Melody got a deeper understanding as to the wealth at hand for the family her baby was being born into.

Vicky was particular about her decisions with regards to how to care for the items and their long-term sturdiness, but she didn't seem to care about the price.

Melody got the impression that if the item was exactly what Vicky wanted, it could have been two dollars at a thrift store and Vicky would happily pay that and then give a donation to the charity running the shop.

Her phone pinged, and Melody looked down to see a text from Ana with more pictures of Button. Vicky looked over her shoulder. "Oh, how gorgeous. What kind of dog is that?"

Shrugging, Melody opened her text app to respond. "We don't know for sure. The vet thinks at least partially lab and husky, but that's more because my brother's girlfriend has Button's mom."

"Button? Such a cute name. Wait, is that your dog?"

"Yep. Libby, my brother's girlfriend, found Mayzie, the mom, on the side of the road. Turned out Mayzie had a litter of puppies with her, and Button was one of them. Libby fostered them all until the puppies could be adopted. Button was always mine, though." She sent kissy face emojis to Ana and saved the photos to her phone.

"She looks like she's a handful."

Melody grinned and put her phone back into her bag. "She is, but I love her." Making the decision on the figurine, she looked over at where Derek was standing. "I want to go back to one of the earlier stores to grab something for my friend who's dog sitting for me. I won't be long."

The owner of this store had gone in back to find something Vicky had asked about. Derek frowned, but looked at Vicky. "I don't like splitting up since you had that feeling earlier."

"I haven't felt it since. Promise. It will only take a few minutes. I know exactly what I want to get, and if it's been sold since we left, I'll come right back here."

Derek's lips thinned, but he nodded. "Fine. What's your

phone number? I'll text you so you can save mine and call me if there are any issues."

As soon as they had that sorted, Melody headed back to the store with the figurine.

It was as she was exiting the store, the figurine expertly boxed up and bagged, that she got the sensation again. But this time, it didn't go away.

She moved to a small alley between stores and looked around. A man slithered out from behind a group of people walking past her on the sidewalk and taking photos, or maybe videos, of themselves.

His features were worn, the edges she remembered softened. It was how Eric would look in about twenty-five years if he didn't give a fuck about himself or anyone else. Anger flashed through her.

"Melody." His voice was grittier than she remembered, even though she'd only seen him a few months ago when he'd tried again to get money out of her mom. He stepped closer, and she stepped back, not wanting him in her personal space. The urge to place her hand over her stomach so that Peanut wouldn't even feel his vibes was strong.

"Dad. Why are you here? How are you here?"

He grinned at her. It was the same grin she remembered as a kid when he said he had a new game to play and needed her "help". "Just getting a taste of my new life."

When he didn't continue, Melody blinked. "Your new life? What the fuck are you talking about?"

He took another step closer, and she stepped back again. The sour scent of worn, unwashed clothes triggered her gag reflex. She swallowed it down as she wasn't about to lose that peanut butter fig pastry. It had been too delicious to waste on her trash father.

"The new life you're going to help me get."

She narrowed her eyes. "Listen old man, I've been done with your shit for decades. Remember when you tried to hit Mom up for money a few months ago? I'll do it. I'll call the cops on your ass."

His lips twisted and the asshole inside of him seeped out for all to see. He crowded up into her space and she moved back again until her back hit a wall. She winced, but didn't want to touch him if she could avoid it. "Do it. I'll go to the news sites. Tell them how you're whoring yourself out to rich people to get that show you want. People like us don't belong here unless we're taking it for ourselves." His face was inches away from her own, and she could see the calculation and the arrogance in his eyes.

Laughter burst from deep in her gut, surprising both herself and, from the look on his face, her DNA donor. "People like us? Jesus. I'm not like you. I will never be like you despite how much I tried to be as a kid. Gods. Why the hell had I ever thought if I tried hard enough, you'd love me? Get the fuck out of here. Don't ever contact me again."

He looked to the side, and a nasty smile bloomed on his face. Melody realized that as they'd been talking, she'd moved further back in the alley and couldn't see who might be coming on the sidewalk. Shit.

She tried to slip out without touching him and head back to the front of the alley, but he grabbed the strap of her bag and pulled her back. He pushed her back up against the wall, her head bouncing a bit against the brick. His hands pushed against her shoulders, pinning her.

Peanut. She had to protect Peanut.

"You stay right where you are and listen to me, you little whore. You owe me. You owe me your life."

"Fuck, no." The training she'd done over the years

flashed through her mind. Triggering muscles with no more than a brief thought. She bent down to one side, breaking his hold, and punched him in the face. Kept punching him.

"Ow."

He crumpled back a bit, and she followed, still trying to punch him. Hurt him. All that training, all the courses had been for this moment. He wasn't ever going to hurt her or her family again.

Strong arms wrapped around her waist and pulled her off him. "No. Let me at him."

"Help. Please help me, she was trying to mug me."

Her mouth dropped even as she was maneuvered behind a large body that she realized a moment later was Derek.

"She was trying to mug you?"

"Yes. Call the cops. I want to press charges."

"You fucking bastard." She tried to get around Derek, but he kept her contained behind him. If he hadn't been preventing her from saving the rest of the planet from the existence of her asshole father, she would have commended him for his bodyguard skills.

Sirens sounded in the distance, and she saw her father shift his eyes. "You watch her, and I'll go sit over there. I don't want to be around her. She'll hurt me again."

"You bet your ass I will."

Derek looked over his shoulder and glared at her. "Ma'am. Please step to the side."

The ma'am broke through the haze of her anger, and she realized that as he'd been giving her that instruction, he'd collared her father. Even thinking of him as such after what he'd just said and done made her nauseous again.

She stepped back. Realized that a crowd had gathered

around them. Some in the crowd had their phones out. Shit. A soft hand lightly touched her upper arm. She jerked, raising her fist before she caught herself. It was a clerk from one of the stores they'd been in earlier. "Come sit down. The cops should be here in a minute."

Melody spotted Vicky at the edge of the crowd, and she also nodded her head toward the store's entrance. Looking back at Derek, she saw he had her father well in hand and off to the edge of the sidewalk near where a cop car was pulling up. She turned back to the clerk. "Thank you."

The clerk's smile was nearly feral. "We got an alert on our security camera feed that there was activity by our alley entrance and saw what happened. He shouldn't have touched you."

As they were about to enter the store, one of the other clerks ran out carrying a tablet and headed toward the cops. The clerk escorting her led her to what was likely the staff room. Vicky was already there. She came over, her hands outstretched. "Thank you so much for your help, Evan."

Evan took her hands and leaned in to kiss Vicky's cheeks as he had when she and Vicky had first visited the store. "For you? Always. I'm sure the cops are going to want to talk with your friend, so just stay here and I'll bring them back. No need for you to do this out in public."

He left them alone. Melody stared at Vicky. When the other woman enfolded her in a hug, she burst out into tears. She couldn't have her own mother at the moment, but Tony's mom was nearly as good.

"Oh, my dear. Who was that man? I'm so sorry we left you on your own."

Melody began crying even harder, unable to answer. Vicky led her over to a small couch, and they sat down.

When the tears finally subsided, she sat there in Vicky's embrace, hollowed out.

"Let me get you some water."

Melody nodded, but regretted it a moment later when Vicky let go of her. It felt like the older woman was the only thing keeping her upright. There was a knock on the door, and Evan stuck his head in. "The officers would like to speak with you."

She swallowed, forcing the word out. "Okay."

Evan looked a little worried, but opened the door further and two uniformed cops came in. Vicky shut the refrigerator door harder than she probably needed to, and both the cops froze as they spotted her. She brought the chilled bottle to Melody and sat back down next to her. Vicky's smile was hard as she addressed the cops. "Officers. Have you arrested the man who assaulted my daughter-in-law?"

The older cop grimaced. "We've detained him, but we need to take a statement. He's claiming she assaulted him." The cop looked at Melody. "Do you know who the man is?"

She nodded. "My father. Rick Keller. You should check for any outstanding warrants."

<h1 style="text-align:center">twenty-one</h1>

TONY RESISTED the urge to roll his eyes or do anything else that would piss off the federal investigators. He and Damien were sitting on this side of the camera for the group meeting that had been set up an hour ago with them and the state prosecutors and investigators, while his father and Zach sat on the other side, out of sight.

The lead federal investigator continued droning on about jurisdiction and precedence and other legal stuff he paid Damien good money to explain in plain English to him after the fact.

Zach pulled out his phone from his pocket, looked at the screen, and frowned. He got up and left the room. Desperately curious about what was going on since this meeting was beyond boring as the various investigators and prosecutors were having a pissing match about who got to prosecute Robert first, Tony moved to follow Zach.

However, Damien still had the quick reflexes that had once made him a star football player, and his attorney gripped his arm until he settled back down.

Eventually, it was agreed that with Robert in federal

custody, and the fact jury selection at the state level hadn't even been scheduled yet, the state charges would be deferred until a later date. Tony and Damien were released from the call as he wouldn't be needed as a witness any time soon.

Tony closed the videoconferencing program and sat back in his seat. Looked at Damien. "We're really all good?"

Damien nodded. "Looks like. Not sure what prompted them to call a meeting on a Sunday since we were due in court tomorrow, but whatever it was, that wrapped up faster than I expected and we don't have to head to the courthouse tomorrow. I'm sure there will still be a couple of court calls while the state takes care of deferring the trial in favor of the feds, but you shouldn't be needed for those. You can get back to your regularly scheduled life."

His regularly scheduled life. He didn't know what that was anymore. A year ago, he'd been happily living the bachelor life here in Los Angeles. Now? He'd found the woman he wanted to spend the rest of his life with and they were expecting a baby, but he still wasn't sure what their life together would look like. They'd agreed they wanted to figure it out, but they hadn't discussed any of the medium-sized details, let alone specifics like where they'd be living.

He looked over at his father who'd stood up to look out the windows of the office. "Dad? Is there anything outstanding I need to do to finalize the close of the production?"

"No. Emerson and I got everything shelved for now. With all the publicity surrounding what happened, and everyone moving on to different projects, we'd probably have to spend another year rescheduling and recasting for anyone who wanted out."

Their head of operations was nothing if not efficient.

"I'll reach out to everyone now and thank them for the work they did."

His father nodded. "None of the other projects are at an urgent stage. In fact, we've got a rare moment of calm."

There was a contemplative tone to his father's words that had Tony looking at him closer. "What's up, Dad?"

"With the baby on the way...you've got an opportunity now that I didn't have when you were first born."

Tony frowned. "I'm not following."

His dad came over and sat back down. "I've been thinking about this since we found out about the baby..."

"Which was only yesterday."

"Anthony Michael."

He held up his hands. "Sorry."

"Thank you. As I was saying, I've been thinking about this and between the current production schedule's point of calm and you being released from this case for the time being, you have an opportunity I didn't. You can be there for your child."

Tony frowned again. "Dad, you were always there for me."

"I don't think this is a conversation I need to be a part of." Damien stood up from his chair.

His dad shook his head. "Sit down. You're Anthony's legal counsel. You need to be a part of this."

Confused, Tony looked over at Damien who shrugged. He looked back to his dad. "I'm not following."

"Wherever you and Melody decide to live, you've got the opportunity to truly be present for your child's early years. If you want to be. I wanted to be around more when you were younger, and I was very blessed that your mother and I were able to trade projects, but more often than not it was one of my projects. I was always working."

"You were there when I needed you, Dad. And I got to spend a lot of time around you when we were on set."

"Around me. Not with me. Frankly, I've always given thanks you turned out as well as you did and that you still like me considering what a workaholic I was. Am."

"Dad, I never got the impression that you didn't want me around. Believe me. I had plenty of friends whose parents obviously couldn't have cared less what my friends were doing. The time that you were present with me, you were present."

His dad let out a long breath. Nodded. "Good. Good." He was silent for a minute, maybe longer. "To cut to the chase, I want to buy you out of the production company."

Blinking, Tony didn't know how to respond. The production company had been something for him and his dad to do together. A shared interest. After this heart-to-heart and to have his dad say that he wanted to buy out Tony?

His dad leaned forward, looked him straight in the eye. "This is not to cut you out. This is to give you the opportunity to truly be with your child with no other responsibilities pulling you away. Be there for every midnight wake up call. See their first tooth come in. Catch them when they take their first stumbling steps. I missed all those. And I regret not being there for every single one of them."

Hearing what his father was truly saying, Tony sat back in his chair. This was something else he and Melody hadn't had a chance yet to discuss. He'd assumed they would get a nanny while they were both working. But if he was the stay-at-home parent?

Before he could respond, though, the door to the office opened and Zach escorted his mother and Melody in. Melody's face was red and a little puffy. He stood up.

Looking closer, her eyes appeared suspiciously pink. Frowning, he looked over at Zach who shook his head.

"Melody? Everything okay?"

She came over and wrapped her arms around him, burying her face in his chest. He realized she'd started crying. Alarmed, he looked at his mother as he hugged Melody to him. "What happened?"

His mother's lips were firm. "Everyone's okay. I think Melody should be the one to tell you."

"She's crying. She isn't okay."

Melody said something, but it was muffled against his chest. Damien, his parents, and Zach all left the room. He maneuvered Melody over to the small couch along one wall. He gave thanks for his decorator who had an unhealthy obsession with couches and loveseats.

When they were seated, he brushed the hair that had fallen out of her top knot from her face. "What was that?"

"I said I'll be okay. Apparently I just need to cry it out today."

Shifting so that they were seated comfortably, but she could still burrow into his embrace if needed, he pressed a kiss to the top of her head. "What do you need to cry out?" A sudden thought hit him, but since his mom said everyone was okay, he didn't say it out loud so he wouldn't worry Melody. But he moved his one hand down so that it pressed against where Peanut was growing.

Melody shuddered against him. "I'd left Vicky and Derek to go get something for Ana. For dog sitting Button. On my way back, my dad approached me."

Confused, he looked down at her. She was tracing designs on his stomach. "Your dad? Isn't he in New York?"

"Nope. Mom called me this morning. I'm not sure how, but he'd found out I'd come to California. I have even less of an idea how he got the money to come out here on short notice, but he found out where you live and parked outside this morning. He followed us when we left, and when I was alone, he came up to me and demanded that I give him money."

"He what?"

"He tried to blackmail me."

"How?"

"I don't know? By trying to make up a story about me seducing you and getting pregnant on purpose to entrap you? Not that it was going to work, but that's how his mind works. How he's actually Stef's brother, I don't understand."

Tony pulled her one hand up to kiss it and realized bruises covered her knuckles. He very lightly rubbed his thumb against the discoloration. "Melody? What happened?"

"He grabbed me and pushed me up against a wall. I wasn't having it, so I punched him. And, damn it, I just realized I lost the present I bought for Ana. I must have dropped it when I punched him."

Holding back the laughter that wanted to escape at the thought of Melody dropping a bag in order to punch her father instead of beating him with the bag, he pressed a kiss to her knuckles. "We'll order a new one for her."

Melody wrinkled her nose. "I don't think they had any left."

He pulled her in even tighter, not wanting her any farther from him than necessary. "We'll find something. I promise." Soft silence enveloped them. In the distance, he could periodically hear his mother's softer tones and his father's harder ones. The closed door helped to muffle whatever was being said, so they remained in their own world. Soaking in the feeling of Melody next to him, safe, he let the conversation with his dad tumble through his mind.

"My dad..."

"My dad..."

They spoke at the same time, and he paused. When her head tilted back, he leaned back enough to meet her gaze and nodded at her. "You first. Your dad?"

She swallowed and burrowed back into him. "My dad got arrested. We were in an alley between a couple stores, and one of them had a security camera set up. It captured everything. They were the ones who called the cops. My dad tried to say that I was the one who attacked him, and I had tried to mug him."

"What?"

She nodded against his chest. "I shouldn't be surprised. I really shouldn't be. I've known what he's like since I was a kid. He only pretends to treat me like a loved child when it's convenient for him. If it wasn't for that video, I think the cops would have arrested me, too, since I was obviously hitting him and he had more damage. And I may have threatened to hit him more in front of witnesses."

Growling, he hugged her again. "I'll hit him more. You have houses to build."

Her laugh was watery, but it was a laugh. "Yeah, I probably should wear gloves or something to the meetings tomorrow. That or blame the bruises on not watching what I was hitting with the hammer."

It was his turn to laugh. "Just say that you were knocking down a wall. With your bare hands. They'll love that. Isn't demolition day a prime feature of any home improvement show?"

"Everyone loves demo day. There's something intensely

satisfying about ripping out avocado green shag carpeting that's older than you are."

"There you go. A sentiment that everyone can understand."

She hummed and resumed tracing patterns on his stomach. Then she poked his belly button. "What were you going to say?"

"When?"

"You said 'my dad', too. What about Leo?"

Taking hold of her hand, he pressed a gentle kiss against her bruised knuckles. "I'm sorry your dad couldn't have been like my dad."

"I had Stef. And you're avoiding my question."

He pressed another kiss to the knuckles and then held her hand to his heart. "No. Just stating that as a preface to what I'm about to tell you."

She shifted to look up at him. Narrowed her eyes. "What's going on?"

"First, they've released me, for now, as a witness in Robert's trial. The state is deferring prosecution as the feds are claiming priority or something."

She blinked, then grinned. "Congratulations. I think? Does this mean you can go back to work?"

"That's what Damien said. But then my dad made an offer."

Her voice softened. "What kind of offer?"

He brushed a lock of hair back behind her ear. "To buy me out of the production company."

Her brow furrowed. "What?"

Wanting her closer, but still in a position so they could look each other in the face, he took hold of her one knee and shifted her until she straddled his lap.

Melody crossed her arms against her chest even as she

settled her ass against him. "You're not planning on trying to distract me, are you?"

Holding her hips in his hands and massaging the muscles there, he shook his head. "This is my favorite position to have you in whether or not we're wearing clothes. I just want a better view of you as we talk about this."

She leaned in and kissed the tip of his nose, making him grin at her. "Sounds serious."

"It is. A good serious, I hope."

"Okay. Why does your dad want to buy you out of the production company?"

"So I can be a full-time parent, at least for a few years. He said that he missed doing things with me as a small kid even though we were always traveling with him when he was on location. And later when Mom began working again and was on location, he was the one who was my primary caregiver."

"Leo doesn't seem like he was a neglectful parent. What I've seen of the two of you? I'd say you actually like him. Because I sure as hell don't like my dad. Not sure if I ever have. I used to love him, but I don't know that I ever liked him."

She looked so contemplative, he hated to interrupt her thought processes. But he wanted to finish this conversation before one of his parents or Damien decided they needed to interrupt for whatever reason. "I've always liked Dad in addition to loving him, and enjoyed working with him. Which is why I was surprised. But the more he talked about missing the small things with me because he was a workaholic, and I can't argue that point, the more I realized I wanted them with you." He moved one of his hands over her stomach. "With Peanut. And whoever else we decide to add to the family."

She moved her hands to cup his over her stomach. "You want to be a stay-at-home parent? Are you sure? We could get a nanny. Or something. You're the rich one. What's the fancy term for nanny?"

He laughed. "Au pair? Yeah, that's what I was thinking, too. But I really like the idea. I think we should try it. If it's not what's right for our family, we look into getting a nanny. Or an au pair. Whatever."

She looked down at their joined hands. Even though she was sitting on his lap, he had to strain to hear her next question. "Where would you be this stay-at-home parent?"

Understanding she needed reassurance, he moved his other hand to cup her neck and bring her face to his so he could kiss her. When the kiss began to blaze, he broke away. "Sunflower Falls. We'll keep this house because I don't want to be crashing at my parents when we come out here for visits or when you have meetings with Triple H. But I like the idea of moving to a small town."

She snorted. "Why?"

He rubbed her jaw. "Where else could I find a Harry? Or a Nancy?" He pressed another kiss to her lips. "Or you. Wherever you want to live is where I want to be. You're my home, Melody Nikki Keller. You have been since the day we met. I'm only sorry I couldn't be that for you, too."

Tears filled her eyes again. She cupped his face and kissed him. "You are. You're my home. I just...couldn't accept it. I never thought anyone could be my home. But you are."

"Even though I lied about my name, and didn't tell you before we got married?"

She found a patch of looser skin on his waist and squeezed. "Yes. Do you want to know why?"

"Please, my oh so glorious wife to whom I will always tell the truth from now on."

She snorted again and shook her head. "That. You're genuinely remorseful. My father has never regretted or been truly remorseful for a thing he's done that's hurt someone in his entire life. That's what I realized today. You hid who you really were for as long as you could. But you hid it for a specific reason, which was in service to finding justice for others. And when you finally told me, you recognized the harm you did."

He cupped her face again. "I'm so sorry, Melody. I hated hiding it from you, but I didn't know what else to do."

"I understand. I do. And we will go to couples therapy to discuss it because I also don't want this poisoning our future. But you've shown me that who you are at your core is not someone who hides and manipulates in order to get your own way. You try to protect and champion others. You'll always be there for me. You're my home. My safe harbor."

"I love you, Melody."

The glow that filled her smile, her eyes, had him imagining every milestone of their life together. To be gifted the honor of being her safe harbor was something he would treasure and nurture for the rest of his life.

She leaned down, but paused with her lips a breath from his. "I love you, Anthony Michael Dewitt aka Tony Caputo."

The feeling of everything inside him locking into place in a way it never had before, had him gripping her close as they kissed. Sealing their commitment. Life with her would be an adventure he couldn't wait to start.

# *epilogue*

## SIX MONTHS LATER

MELODY WALKED AROUND, talking with guests. She and Tony were hosting a housewarming party for the new house. This was a friends and family only event, but at Tony's urging, she and Eric had done a walkthrough earlier in the week with some of the production team they'd be working with at Triple H.

Thankfully, neither Tony's parents or Aspen, Damien, and the kids had arrived until after the Triple H people left. The Triple H production team had briefly floated the idea that they have celebrity guests once they realized who Melody was seeing, but she and Eric had shut that down. They wanted to succeed or fail on their own without stunt casting.

Vicky waved her over to where she sat talking with Melody's mom. Melody bent down and kissed her mom on the cheek. "How are you holding up?" Her mom had fallen while out walking a few weeks ago and had broken her wrist. Thankfully, she'd been able to get into a hand surgeon quickly.

Her mom held up her arm in the black sling her doctor demanded she use, if only to remind her to limit use of the hand. "Listening to the doctor's orders. I want to hold Peanut as soon as she arrives."

Melody rubbed her belly. The pregnancy had gone smoothly mostly, but Peanut kept punching at her organs lately, and sleeping through the night was a thing of the past. "We'll take all the help we can get."

Vicky smiled up at her. "Did you get that delivery I told you about?"

Biting the inside of her cheek, Melody shook her head. "Not yet. It might be held up in customs."

Vicky wrinkled her nose. "I'll have my assistant look into it. The shopkeeper said it needed to be hung up in the baby's room before they come home to help heal any lingering negative energy."

Swallowing the urge to remind Vicky that the house was a brand new build, Melody instead smiled. "I'll tell Tony to keep an eye out for it. In fact, I need to go find him. Have either of you seen him?"

Vicky waved her hand. "I think I saw him talking with that bar owner friend of yours. I heard something about grovels and black moments."

Grinning, Melody kissed each of their cheeks and headed off. Harry shouldn't be hard to spot, but Tony might have taken him into the house. Hannah, Kieran, and Bethie's oldest ran past screaming as they squirted water cannons at each other. That had to have been Bethie's husband's idea. Button and Mayzie chased after them, trying to catch the water squirts in their mouths.

Ana came over, a pinched expression on her face. "Melody, can we talk somewhere private?"

Frowning, Melody nodded. "Sure. What's up?"

Ana looked over her shoulder, which then slumped. "Too late."

Wondering what the hell was going on, Melody followed Ana's gaze and saw Ana's parents. "What are they doing here?"

"I don't know. I got a text from Mom a couple minutes ago that they were on their way, and she wanted to know if her favorite wine was on offer."

Melody looked back at Ana. "Seriously?"

"Seriously. I don't know what's gotten into her. She's never been the greatest, but she's gotten so bad lately."

They watched as Ana's mother, followed by her father, made a beeline for Alex Kavanaugh who was talking with Nancy and Mrs. Smith. She interrupted whatever he was saying to Andy and began fawning over him. Alex had been enjoying some time back with his family during breaks in the season as he planned for his retirement from pro hockey, and everyone in Sunflower Falls had been giving him space. Until now. Even from this distance, they could see Alex's confusion and Melody winced.

"I should probably go save him."

Ana drew in a deep breath. "No. I'll do it."

Neither of them had to as Zach appeared by Alex's side and extracted him from Mrs. Rogers' clutches.

"Whoa." The look on Ana's mom's face would have seriously wounded Zach if they'd been daggers. "What is the deal with your mother?"

Ana sighed. "I wish I knew."

Libby came over. "Sorry to interrupt, but have either of you seen Eric?"

Melody pointed to the grill Tony had bought a couple weeks ago. "I think he got deputized by Harry."

Libby grinned. "Thanks. How are you feeling?"

Melody rubbed her belly. "Fine. I wouldn't mind sitting for a little bit." She held up her red cup. "But first, I need a refill."

"We've got it out here. Go pamper yourself. Take fifteen if you need to."

Melody headed inside. The sound level dropped immediately. She let out a happy sigh at the sign of a well-built house. Tony and Harry weren't to be seen in the open kitchen, but she could hear some sounds coming from the office they'd carved out for Tony from the front entrance area. Ignoring them for the moment, she headed for the fridge. The gallon container with her name prominently marked on it was getting down to empty, so she poured what she could into her cup, and then drank what was left directly from the jug. She tossed it into the recycling bin.

She was poking around in the pantry for a replacement to put in the fridge when she heard the door to Tony's office open.

"And you're good with this?"

"To be part of a grand gesture like this is an honor."

"What are you two talking about?" She found the other jugs of electrolytes on a shelf behind some bags of dried beans. Wondering why those were there, she started moving them to their designated space.

"Are you okay? What are you doing inside?" Tony appeared in the pantry doorway.

She held up a bag of beans. "What are these doing in front of my drink?"

"To hide your drink from the kids in case they get inside and start poking around."

She tossed the beans onto their shelf, and then grabbed a jug and held it up. "You've marked every single one of them with my name."

"So? Kids are going to kid. If they're thirsty, they'll probably open it, take a sip, and then put it back with the lid on if we're lucky."

Laughing, she pushed past him. "Are you okay? You're acting weird."

"I'm fine. Do you need to rest or anything? No one's tiring you out?"

She put the jug in the fridge. "I'm fine. We should probably head back outside, though. Ana's parents arrived."

Tony frowned. "Ana's parents? We didn't invite them. We had a very specific guest list."

Melody picked up her drink and sipped at it. He was definitely being weird. "We did not invite them, but this is Sunflower Falls. Unless you're mortal enemies with war declared, you might find some unexpected guests when you're throwing an outdoor barbecue. While Ana's mother is on my least favorite list, we have not declared open war on each other. Though, if she gets near your mother, that might have to change."

Tony pulled her in as close as he could with Peanut between them. "What about your mother?"

She waved a hand. "Mom can handle herself. She's been dealing with Helen Rogers for decades."

Tony kissed her nose. "Fine. Do you want me to carry a refill for you?"

"Thanks, but I should be good." She backed away and bumped her hip against his. Her hip met something hard. She backed away and saw a square outline in his pocket. "What's that?"

"Uh, nothing. We should get outside."

Narrowing her eyes at him, she set her cup down on the island, and crossed her arms. "No. I heard Harry when I was in the pantry. Where did he go?"

"Back outside. He had to man the grill."

"Eric was doing that."

"You know Harry."

"Tony."

He sighed and wrapped a hand around the back of her neck. Rested his forehead against hers. "Can you give me some space to surprise you?"

"It's not exactly a surprise right now."

"No details have been shared. Please?"

Recognizing this to be one of the moments he needed in their relationship, she tilted her chin up and kissed him. "Fine. Let's go save whoever Mrs. Rogers is antagonizing."

"Can we sic Zach on her?"

"Probably. He saved Alex earlier, and Mrs. Rogers does not appear to be a fan of Zach. It was a classic 'if looks could kill' moment."

After a brief detour to the bathroom, they headed back into the yard hand in hand. But once outside, instead of letting her go, Tony led her to a table he'd set up close to their small strip of beach earlier in the day. He'd covered it with a silky dark green cloth overlaid with an airy white lace thing. A heavy candle in the center and two tapers on either side held it all down.

When she'd asked him about it, he just said that he wanted something that they could sit at together later.

He'd even ensured that no one put anything down on it by putting a big sign that read "Reserved for Melody and Tony" on it, anchored by the central candle.

"Attention." He held up his hands and waved. Everyone quieted and turned their attention to him. "Melody and I want to thank you today for coming to help us celebrate our new home and the start of our lives together as a family."

She looked around and saw various people tear up as tissues were pulled from purses and pockets. She lifted her cup in the air. "Thank you."

Tony took her free hand and lifted it to his mouth, kissing her knuckles. "In fact," he dropped to a knee and gasps filled the air. "Melody Keller, would you do me the greatest honor of becoming my wife? Again? Today? In front of all our friends and family? For almost an entire year now, you've been the bright light of my day, and you bring me joy every time you smile. When you're sad, I want to be there for you in whatever way you need me to be. Being the best partner I can be to you is my biggest mission in life, and I can't wait to go on the new adventure with you of becoming parents to this little one." He placed his hand on her belly, and she began tearing up herself.

She tugged on his hand to pull him up and kiss him. "Tony."

He winked at her. "Just a moment. One more thing." Still holding her hand, he reached into his pocket and pulled out the box she'd felt earlier. He popped it open single-handed, and she gasped. The ring was a deep green oval, surrounded by brilliant white stones. "Tony…"

"Will you marry me, Melody?"

She tugged hard on his hand until he stood up. Pulling his face down to hers with both hands, she kissed him. "You always have to make a big production out of things, don't you?"

He kissed her again. And his reply was barely above a whisper. "As much as you'll let me. Marry me?"

She looked into his eyes and saw the love shining there. This man would always be there for her, supporting her, finding ways to show he loved her. Her reply was equally soft. "Yes."

He grinned and picked her up, swinging her around even with an eight-months-pregnant belly.

Everyone cheered.

He put on the ring and held up their hands to show the crowd. "We're getting married!" He looked over to one side of the crowd and waved. "Harry."

Harry came over with a suit jacket over his graphic t-shirt from an event the bar had held a few years ago. He carried a sheet of paper in one hand and a bouquet of flowers in the other.

Confused, Melody looked up at Tony. "What?"

He bent down close to her ear. "Remember when we redid the marriage license?"

She nodded as they had decided to go to the courthouse before Peanut got here to make sure everything truly was legal. "Yeah?"

He kissed her cheek. "I figured you deserved to have everyone you liked here for this wedding. Surprised?"

Laughing, she kissed him again. "Yeah. I love it."

Being the producer he was, Tony soon got everyone organized. All the kids walked down the hastily assembled aisle because none of them wanted to be left out of the proceedings. Tony had magically produced floofy green dog dresses for both Button and Mayzie, and Libby walked them down the aisle.

Ana had also gotten a bouquet as her maid of honor, and her best friend gave her a huge hug before she walked toward where Tony was standing with Harry and Zach as his best man.

Finally, it was time for Eric and her mom to escort her. She'd never thought she'd be getting married, again, like this. She'd been more dressed up for her first wedding, but this was who she and Tony were. Comfortable with each other and valuing the presence of family and friends over pomp and fancy decorations.

Someone thought to start playing some instrumental music on their phone. Halfway down the aisle, she doubled over as much as she could with her pregnancy belly, laughing. It was an instrumental version of a popular song featuring a portion of the alphabet that was most assuredly not one would expect to play as a bride walked down the aisle to her groom.

But it was right for her, and it was right for them. They'd had a rocky start, but now they had this beautiful transition to the next phase of their lives together. She pulled herself together and continued walking.

First Eric kissed her cheek, and then her mom. They sat next to Libby and the dogs, and Harry began his welcome.

"We are gathered here, a bit unexpectedly, to celebrate the joining of Melody Keller and Anthony, Tony to most of us here in the Falls, Dewitt in loving marriage. I got my certificate to do this kind of thing online a few years ago after reading one of my wife's romance novels. And you know how much I've come to love them, too. Being asked to be a part of this is truly an honor. Watching these two get together, break up, and then work out their differences in order to build a life together, and to welcome a little one into their love is a blessing in which we all share. So, thank you, Melody and Tony. Now, let me tell you about the books I told Tony to read when he fucked shit up."

Everyone laughed, and they were soon married. At the end of the ceremony, Tony planted his feet alongside her, wrapped his arms around her back, and tilted her back to kiss her. She grinned up at him and did her best to wrap her one leg around his hip while she hung on tight to his neck with one arm.

"I love you, Melody Keller."

"Love you, too, Tony Caputo."

"That's Tony Dewitt."

She winked at him, even as his lips met hers.

After, they were wandering around talking with their guests. At one point, she was showing the ring to Ana who squealed over the design.

"That's so gorgeous. You'll have to be careful when you're working on site, though."

Tony hooked an arm around Melody's shoulders. "I've got silicone bands for her when she's working. No need to accidentally injure herself just to wear this."

Melody kissed Tony's jaw and was about to say something to Ana when a harsh voice interrupted them.

"Admire that ring as much as you want, but you're never going to get a man to give one like that to you."

Melody watched as Ana's face first flushed with what looked to be embarrassment, and then complete and total fury.

Ana squared her shoulders and turned to where her mother was standing a few feet away from them.

Melody felt Tony stiffen next to her, but she squeezed his waist as she knew Ana had to have her say to that pile of bullshit.

"The thing is, Mother, I don't want a ring like that, and my fiance knows that."

Fighting to not let shock show through on her face, Melody kept her gaze on Ana, refusing to look at Mrs. Rogers.

"Fiance? You haven't been dating. There is no fiance."

None of them saw Zach approach until he wrapped an

arm around Ana's waist and pulled her in tight against his chest. Melody looked up at him and saw him staring dead into Mrs. Rogers' eyes. "I'm her fiance."

---

Curious about what life with Peanut is like?
Sign up for my newsletter to get Melody & Tony's bonus epilogue!

You'll also be among the first to know about what the deal is with Zach claiming to be Ana's fiance 👀

Use your phone's camera to scan this QR code to sign up for Katie's newsletter:

If you don't use a smartphone, you can type this address into the browser on your computer:
https://geni.us/HTW-BE-Print

# acknowledgments

The hugest of thanks go to the my compatriots in the Write All the Things Slack group. If it weren't for all of you, I would not have, as an author, personally gotten to the point I needed to be in order to write this book in the first place, but also get the book to the place it needed to be after I had finally fucking drafted it.

Special thanks to Adriana who helped me figure out where the real start of the book was, Jayne for asking me the hard question during retreat and everyone else who was there for the follow up discussion (I'm afraid to list you because I know I'm going to forget someone), and Sophie for doing the manuscript critique that I bought in an charity auction because I still have a hard time asking for major level help like this despite therapy.

More huge thanks to my therapist and coaches for the personal stuff!

# about the author

Katie Lillig is the author of light-hearted, funny, small town romance. This is her second book set in the world of Sunflower Falls. She has an unhealthy obsession with pens, planners, and office supplies, and is constantly planning vacations she may or may not take in the future.

You can follow her on the following sites:

- instagram.com/katielillig
- facebook.com/authorkatielillig
- amazon.com/stores/Katie-Lillig/author/B0C5GVN3QJ

www.ingramcontent.com/pod-product-compliance
Lightning Source LLC
Chambersburg PA
CBHW011129190726
48289CB00012B/2970